DAUGHTER OF THE
BAMBOO FOREST

D0066914

DAUGHTER OF THE BAMBOO FOREST

SHENG-SHIH LIN

TWIN FOREST BOOKS

Copyright © 2012 Sheng-Shih Liu-lin
Cover design © 2012 Julia Lin

The moral right of the author has been asserted.

All rights reserved.
No part of this publication may be reproduced, stored in a retrieval system, or
transmitted, in any form or by any means, without the prior permission in writing of
the publisher, nor be otherwise circulated in any form of binding or cover other than
that in which it is published and without a similar condition including this condition
being imposed on the subsequent purchaser.

This is a work of fiction. Names, characters, places, and incidents either are the
product of author's imagination or are used fictitiously, and any resemblance to actual
persons, living or dead, events, or locales is entirely coincidental.

Typesetting services by BOOKOW.COM

For my mother and father

ACKNOWLEDGEMENTS

Book cover: Julia Lin

Book design: Kathryn Lin

Author photograph: Russell Grant

Historical Background:

In 1932, northeastern China fell under Japan's influence when the Imperial Japanese Army turned Manchuria into the puppet government of Manchukuo. Because Japan was using Manchukuo as a base to invade the rest of China, the Japanese occupation provided relative stability and peace in the region. For a short while, Japan was eager to show the League of Nations that Manchukuo was a peaceful and happy place. This ended when Japan withdrew from the League in 1933.

Four years later, in 1937, Japan took over Peking, Shanghai, and later Nanking. On December 7, 1941, the Japanese Navy attacked Pearl Harbor in Hawaii. As the Japanese army invaded deeper and deeper into China's heartland, there were not enough Japanese troops to occupy the vastness of northern China. The ensuing power vacuum was filled by local strongmen and bandits, and life in the countryside of northern China was on the cusp of revolutionary change.

But in the summer of 1941, life ebbed and flowed and remained, for just a bit longer, as it had always been.

CHAPTER 1:
LITTLE JADE

Time: Summer 1941

Place: The countryside of northern China

There is a place where time stops and eternity survives under a shade of green. Even shadows come with a green tinge. In the deep of the bamboo forest, the land is damp and dark. A velvety layer of moss covers the earth. No sunlight or moonlight penetrates the thick layers of bamboo leaves, and the wind vibrates to the secret rhythms of the forest. When the wind touches the leaves they whisper to one another, and the entire forest sighs and sighs with the soothing gentleness of a lullaby.

Little Jade was the only red spot in the soft green of the forest. Her grandmother liked to dress her in bright colors for summer: a red silk top and pants embroidered with children playing and rowing a dragon boat. The silk was soft to the touch, and felt cool and slippery against her skin. She also wore red shoes embroidered with a lotus flower and a golden frog. Most children her age wore blue, the peasant color, and their clothes were made of rough cotton which had to be worn for months before it became soft against their tender skin. Red was a color worn only during holidays or on festive occasions like weddings, and sometimes, at funerals. For If someone died at an old age, or of natural causes, a funeral was a time of celebration rather than mourning. If the family was rich enough, the celebration could continue for weeks.

Little Jade had been to a funeral and a wedding within the past few months. Each occasion was as elaborate as the celebration of the New Year which was another reason that she was still being dressed in red instead of peach blossom pink or duckling yellow, her usual summer colors.

Little Jade knew all the corners of the forest. She looked up at the bamboo stalks overhead as each reached straight for the sky above. The tallest stems could almost touch the lowest hanging stars at night. She picked up a bamboo stick, and drew a circle on the damp ground. Then she drew bigger and bigger circles, each of which overlapping the last one. She loved to play in the forest. She was not afraid of the green bamboo snakes, which her grandmother warned were among the most poisonous of all snakes. Once, she saw a snake as green as new bamboo leaves hanging from a branch. It opened a mouth of bloody red, but it did not scare her. This forest was hers. It belonged to her family along with probably the rest of the world.

"Little Jade! Little Jade!" Her grandmother called, standing at the very edge of the forest where the family's vegetable garden ended. It was a long walk for her.

"I'm coming, grandma!" She called as loudly as she could, and she began running toward the house. She did not know what time it was. She could never keep track of time in the forest.

"Little Jade! Little Jade!"

"I'm coming! I'm coming!" Hurrying along, Little Jade almost tripped over a bamboo shoot. She could see her grandmother standing behind the vegetable garden fence.

"I knew you were playing in the bamboo forest again. Little Jade, you never listen to me. How many times have I told you not to play there?"

"Yes, grandma." Little Jade tried to catch her breath.

"Your father wants to see you," the grandmother said with a worried glance at her granddaughter.

"Why?" she asked, sensing that something bad was about to happen.

"He wants to talk to you before he leaves," the grandmother sighed.

"Is he leaving again? When?"

"In two weeks. Just after he visits the temple."

"But he just got back!" cried Little Jade. "He just got married."

"Your father and your new mother are leaving for their honeymoon," the grandmother said quietly.

Little Jade followed her grandmother through the vegetable garden. It was late afternoon, almost evening. The sunlight was warm on her face. She rubbed her dusty hands against the sides of her pants, thinking about what she might say to her father.

"Why are you so quiet, Little Jade? Look at you, your lips stick out so much that I could hang an oil bottle on them. Are you angry with your father? Well, you know how it is. Young couples these days go on honeymoons. I don't want to see your father leaving so soon either. He is my only son. I haven't seen him for so long..." The grandmother's voice grew weak and faded away. The only sounds that reached Little Jade were the cries of the ravens from far away.

"Oh, grandma, I'm not angry with father."

"Then what is it? You're such a little girl, just six years old."

"No, I'm not. I am seven..." Little Jade's voice was small.

"I am getting old. You have to forgive your grandma for not remembering your age. Why, you're only a baby to me. Seven years old! You are too small for a seven-year old."

Little Jade did not respond because if she did, there would be no way to hold back the tears. Slowly, they walked underneath a lattice arbor laden with ripe squash, which led to the back door of the house. The grandmother pushed aside the falling vines, and they entered through the heavy wooden kitchen door. Two slave girls worked busily in the kitchen. White steam from a large pot of soup filled the room. Little Jade's old nanny sat in front of the stove, stoking the fire with a bamboo fan. They all greeted Little Jade and her grandmother cheerfully: "Good evening, Old Mistress and Little Lady."

"Good evening," the grandmother replied.

"What's for dinner tonight, grandma?"

"We are having fish and duck."

Orchid, the slave girl with two pigtails said, "It's your favorite, Little Jade."

"I don't feel like eating," Little Jade said. She left the kitchen, went to her room, and crawled into bed. She felt a piercing sensation inside her chest as she buried her head under the cool green quilt to block out the world. Teardrops rolled down her cheeks and sank into the pillow. To silence her weeping, she bit a corner of the quilt. She did not want to think of her father and his new wife. Instead, she thought of her grandmother.

Suddenly, Little Jade knew her grandmother was nearby. She could smell the faint scent of sandalwood incense burning in front of the white porcelain statue of Kwan Yin, the Buddhist Goddess of Mercy. Under the soft, newly lit candlelight of early evening, the grandmother knelt and chanted mantras in a quiet voice, gently flowing like the steady currents of a river on a calm day. Her eyes were downcast and her lips barely moved as she recited mantras from memory. Kwan Yin wore a flowing white robe tied with a trailing blue sash, her face held a tolerant smile. The smoke from the incense coiled into continuous circles in the room as it wafted into the mosquito nettings. Sometimes Little Jade imitated her grandmother and knelt and chanted, but she could never last more than the time it took to burn half an incense stick.

Little Jade shared a room and a bed with her grandmother. She had been sleeping next to her grandmother for as long as she could remember. It was a large room with a high ceiling. The walls were whitewashed and the wooden window frames were painted dark red—the color of congealed blood caught in a bowl from the neck of a chicken. The screens were bright green, the color of bamboo. There was a rectangular window through which Little Jade could see the west courtyard where a maple tree stood in the middle. There was also a round window, so high up that it could not be reached. The room was filled with the grandmother's dowry furniture. The heavy teak bed had a frame for hanging the mosquito nets. The white nets were soft and fun to play with. Little Jade always imagined that Kwan Yin's cloud-like long skirt and sleeves were made of mosquito netting. Sometimes she wrapped the netting around her body, pretending that she was a goddess who rode the smoke of sandalwood incense all the way to heaven.

✳ ✳ ✳

"Little Jade! Little Jade! Where are you?" She could hear her grandmother's voice getting nearer and nearer. She closed her eyes and pretended to sleep.

"She is sleeping," a man's voice answered. It was Little Jade's father.

"She can't be asleep. She just returned from playing in the bamboo forest." Her grandmother and her father were approaching the bed. They looked down at Little Jade.

"She has been crying," said the father. "Her cheeks are wet." The father's low voice trailed off as the girl squeezed her eyes shut.

"I don't think she likes you leaving so soon," said the grandmother.

"Yes, Mother."

"I don't want to say too much. It's just that you've been busy ever since you came back to get married. You've hardly spent any time with her. She had waited a long time for your return."

"Yes, Mother."

Little Jade held her breath, careful not to make a sound, while squeezing her eyes shut. She thought of her father. She had never really talked to him. She had not met him until two months ago. He was a tall man, taller than anyone in the village. He had a handsome face with a square jaw, thick dark hair, arching eyebrows, and deep-set eyes. He was probably looking at the floor now. He was not supposed to talk back to his mother.

Little Jade had been very young when her father left, and she had no memory of him. Over the years, she had sketched pictures of him in her mind. He looked happy in the photograph hanging on the wall in the family hall. He was smiling, unlike most people in their portraits. In the background was a Japanese building. He was wearing a dark western-style suit, a white shirt, and a tie. He had studied in Japan for three years.

Little Jade thought her father looked just like his photograph, even though he didn't smile much around her. She remembered the day he returned. He had walked into the front gate carrying a leather suitcase. She had been looking out the window, and she knew immediately that he was her father. He had cut a striking figure as he strode toward the inner courtyard. There was something magnetic about him.

Upon seeing her father, Little Jade went running through the house calling excitedly for her grandmother. She met her father later that day after he had washed and changed into a blue silk gown. The grandmother led her down the sun-lit hall to his room. The grandmother's hand squeezed Little Jade's hand tightly as the two of them walked toward the door. Finally, they were in the room, and the grandmother pushed Little Jade in front of her. "Son," she said, "come and meet your daughter."

Sitting on the chair next to the window, he rose and walked toward her. As he drew near, it seemed that his blue gown grew large, as if it were going to swallow her. She stood silently and looked at her shoes as he knelt down to see her. She shot one look at her father and couldn't take her eyes off him. He looked tired, but he was smiling. His face leaned toward her. His shiny black hair was still wet from washing and combed back smoothly. He carried a faint smell of soap.

She smiled back, but then his face changed. He muttered, "Little Jade looks like her mother."

The grandmother did not respond. The father stared at his daughter's face as if searching for something familiar. Little Jade stood frozen and confused. He noticed his daughter's discomfort and smiled again at her, reluctantly. He handed her a blue velvet box the size of a teapot. "This is for you," he said, "It's a special toy. I hope you like it." Little Jade reached over and held the box with both hands. She stared expectedly at her father.

"Don't be afraid of me, Little Jade. I haven't seen you since you were a baby. I just want to take a good look at you." Slowly, he stood up. His eyes pierced the child. His blue gown moved like a curtain rising on the girl's face. Gently, he touched the top of her head before he walked back to the bed and sat down. Looking at his daughter, he said, "You have your mother's eyes."

He turned to his mother. "You can take Little Jade away now," he said, "I'm sorry to have troubled you with her all these years."

The grandmother answered gently, "Nonsense! She is my only grand-child, and you are my only son. She is the root of my life."

Quiet engulfed the room as he looked at the floor. She continued, "We will leave you now. You need your rest."

As Little Jade and her grandmother left the room, she held on tight to her grandmother's hand. Thinking, as she walked, of how her father had touched the top of her head with his long fingers.

Days passed and Little Jade couldn't decide how she felt about her father. She wished that she could run to him and swing her arms around his neck the way she always did with her grandmother. But, deep down, something told her that she couldn't. The father hadn't talked to her since he met her in his room. Little Jade would run into him in the big house, and she would pass him in the hallway. In the evening, they would eat at the same dinner table. She found her-self looking for him around the family compound, and she became familiar with the sight of her father, but she never heard his voice.

Sometimes, when she played in the courtyard alone, she stopped sud-denly—sensing that someone was watching. Turning around, she would often see the back of her father's blue gown growing smaller as he passed through the ranks of moon gates.

Now her father must be watching from the doorway. Thoughts of him were racing through her head, and there was a heavy weight on her chest. She felt cold and hot at once. She was scared. She could no longer pretend that she did not care to know about her father, or her mother. Where was her mother? What had happened to her?

When her father had remarried, she had been given a new mother, but where was her mother, the real one? She had been thinking hard about this. All the other children had a mother and a father. But she knew only her grandmother. No one mentioned Little Jade's mother. It was a forbidden subject. When she asked her grandmother about her mother, she always looked sad and shook her head and Little Jade dared not ask again. Once she asked the old nanny whether her mother was dead. The wizened old woman would only say she did not think she was dead and nothing more. Where was she? No one knew. Or, if they knew, they were not about to tell her. Where did they hide her? What had happed to her? Little Jade had gone through all the family photographs, all the portraits of her ancestors, but she could not find her mother. The last two months since her father's return had been terrible for her. She wanted to ask her father where her mother was, but he continued to avoid her. She was hoping that maybe after another month or so, when everything settled down, she could just go over to him and ask, "Father, where is my mother?" It was such a simple question. She had been reciting it over and over in her head, and the voice inside her was growing louder and louder making her head hurt. She could hear a thundering voice shouting: "Father, where is my mother?"

Little Jade heard her own voice sounding weak and timid. Sobbing, she uttered the question she longed to have answered. She could not see clearly because of her watery eyes, but she could picture her father's face turning pale. Nobody answered. Suddenly, she felt her grandmother's skinny hand on her forehead. Her hand was cold and soothing as she touched Little Jade's face.

"Little Jade has a fever. She is burning up." She heard her grand-mother, but that was not what she wanted to hear.

"Where is my mother?" Little Jade screamed as loudly as she could, but her voice barely came out. All the sounds she wished to utter seemed enclosed in her head.

"Poor child, she is sick. An Ling, go fetch a doctor," the grandmother ordered. "And get Orchid to bring me some cold towels. She is hot."

The father did not say a word. He walked away. Little Jade could hear the quickening pace of his footsteps against the tiled floor.

Little Jade clutched her grandmother's skinny hands. She felt too hot to shed tears, as if all the tears were steamed out of her eyes. "Grandma," she whimpered.

"Don't be afraid. Grandma is right here. Kwan Yin will take care of you."

A cold towel was placed on her forehead. Slowly, she started to drifted off.

As she slept, she dreamed that she was flying with wings made of mosquito netting. She was riding the smoke wafting from a sandal-wood incense stick. She flew out the round window, heaven-bound, leaving her grandmother and father behind. She reached the clouds at the gate of heaven, but she was still looking back for her house, for her father. She shouted, "Father, where is my mother?" But he just stared back at her with glassy eyes. His eyes grew bigger and sadder and, like magnets, pulled her down. Her wings could no longer carry her, and she was slipping away and falling from the sky. She could not resist the pull of her father's eyes, and she continued to fall, lightly and gently. As her body fell onto the soft quilt and pillow of her bed, Little Jade opened her eyes. Her father's eyes met hers. She was not surprised or scared. She smiled at her father. He smiled back. He looked tired.

Little Jade tried to sit up as she looked around. Just as if he was read-ing her mind, her father said, "Your grandmother is in the kitchen brewing a tonic for you." Hearing this, Little Jade smiled shyly, and looked up at her father's face. She felt her father's hand reach over and hold her's gently–a moment that seemed to be suspended in time as the white porcelain Kwan Yin witnessed from a distance. Little Jade watched as her father reached into his pocket and produced a small padded red silk pouch. He loosened the string and pulled out a necklace. "Look," he said as he laid the necklace across the quilt over her lap. It was a necklace with a disk of translucent green jade with a square cut out in the middle which was threaded through with a red string. The string was tied in an elaborate knot and, above it, the string threaded through a beautiful single, pink pearl, and another knot secured it on top of the disk of jade. Little Jade sat still as her father put the necklace over her head and tightened it by adjusting the looped silk cord. "Look, one side of the jade is carved with your name, and the other side is carved two words "Wei" and "An." This piece of jade was made when you were born. The jeweler carved one side of the jade with your name "Ming Yu" and the other side with a combination of your mother's name, the "Wei" from her name Wei Jen, and the "An"from my name An Ling. The word "Wei" means "to keep", the word "An" means "safety." The four words together mean "To keep the bright jade safe. "

Little Jade listened intently as her father continued to speak. His words were measured as he halted between sentences as if needing to take a breath. He said, "After I married your mother, Chang Wei Jen, we went to study at the Peking University as we had always planned. Wei Jen was very studious and was a favorite among the professors. She couldn't finish the first year because she became pregnant with you. We determined that it would be best for us to go home until she gave birth. After your birth, Wei Jen was eager to return to the University, but the in-laws were against it. She fought hard and finally returned to Peking. Afraid that she might get pregnant again, she encouraged me to study in Japan while she stayed behind at Peking University. I visited her only once during the summer. This turned out to be a mistake. A young couple should never be parted during a chaotic time. When the war with Japan broke in 1937, I lost touch with her. When I went back to Peking to look for her, she had left the university. I was able to get in touch with an old classmate and was told that Wei Jen was pregnant and gave birth to another daughter while in Peking, but she disappeared after giving birth in the local hospital. I searched all over the city and could not find her."

"I am sorry I cannot tell you more," her father said. "You have a younger sister. Maybe we can see her one day." He looked up wistfully, "This necklace was made for you. I added the pearl when I was in Japan. I am glad that you are finally wearing it."

CHAPTER 2:
SILVER PEARL

Silver Pearl sat before the mirror, watching the maid brushing her hair. She had just learned that dinner would be delayed because Little Jade had a fever. Silver Pearl frowned, and asked: "Where is the Master?"

"The Master is getting the doctor and the Old Mistress is in her room looking after Little Lady," the maid answered, counting the brush strokes silently.

The rich are certainly different, Silver Pearl thought. *The entire family fusses over an illness that is no bigger than a garlic skin.*

In Silver Pearl's silence, the maid said, "Young Mistress, you hair is so thick and shiny. Look, it falls like a black waterfall, and it is as smooth as a mirror." She lifted the hair and let it fall over Silver Pearl's back.

Silver Pearl turned sideways to look at her hair and said, "It's getting too long. I want to cut it."

"Don't cut it, Young Mistress. It is beautiful. Beautiful hair is a woman's most precious possession. Beautiful hair is her crown."

Silver Pearl laughed, "Stupid girl, don't you argue with me."

"I wouldn't dare, Young Mistress. Do you want some scented oil in your hair?"

Silver Pearl nodded and let the maid rub jasmine oil into her hair. The room was suddenly filled with the fragrance of a garden on a summer evening. Silver Pearl absent-mindedly opened the jewelry box on top of the vanity table and fingered its contents: two heavy yellow gold bracelets, a jade pendant with matching earrings, and several diamond and pearl-encrusted hair pins. She took out a black and white photograph from the bottom of the box and stared at it. The young woman in the picture looked back at her with startled eyes. Silver Pearl remembered the day she had that picture taken, just five months earlier.

* * *

It had been a chilly spring morning. The frost on the rooftops was beginning to melt as strands of cooking smoke drifted out of the chimneys. In the kitchen, Silver Pearl had sipped from a bowl of steaming porridge and scalded her tongue. Embarrassed, she did not make a sound. She opened her mouth a little, sucking in cold air to ease the pain, and poured the rest of her porridge back into the pot. Her mother was not looking.

Silver Pearl's mother stood over the stove making breakfast for her husband. She threw a handful of peanuts into the wok, roasting them with a pinch of salt. The aroma of the roasted peanuts filled the kitchen, and oily smoke rose from the wok and tearing up her eyes. The mother turned her face to wipe her eyes with the back of her left hand. She saw her daughter through her tears and sighed. Silver Pearl was squatting next to a basin of cold water, washing the dishes. She patiently rubbed a piece of rag against the smooth surface of each ceramic bowl, but she could not remove the greasy film that covered them. Silver Pearl felt as if her very soul was filmed over with a layer of poverty, greasy and stubborn. She had a sudden urge to smash the chipped bowl against the floor. Instead, she pressed her lips together as a tide of pink flush rose across her face. Finally, she gave up and stacked the bowls together and put them on the shelf which was dripping with water.

Her mother poured the peanuts into a deep dish and took some for herself. She chewed with small cracking sounds. She gave a few to Silver Pearl and said, "Have a taste." Silver Pearl took the peanuts but did not eat them. She held them loosely in her fist and shook them gently to cool them. They felt hot and greasy against her palm. They were still roasting in their own oil, like secret wishes smoldering in her dreams. She kept shaking her hand, feeling the peanuts cool as she bounced against her cold fingers. Silver Pearl followed her mother into the main room. She put the peanuts in her mouth, pushing them to one side of her mouth with her tongue. She smiled with her lips pressed together.

Her mother said, "Let's get ready to go." They were going to journey many miles to the next town where Silver Pearl would have her picture taken.

It was her mother's idea. Her friend, the matchmaker, had told her that the young master of the Su family was looking for a second wife. This was the opportunity the mother had been waiting for. She knew that a rich and prominent family like the Su's would not care about the size of the bride's dowry. Moreover, taking a second wife was not like taking a first wife. Family background was not as important. The Su family was simply looking for a suitable young woman to carry on the family line. According to the matchmaker, the young woman herself would be the most important element in deciding the match. The mother knew that Silver Pearl, the daughter of a man who owned a tofu shop, would never have a chance to be chosen as the first wife of young master Su, but for a second wife she would do fine. The matchmaker also said that the young master's first wife gave birth to a daughter who was six now. The young wife went away to a university and was lost in the Sino-Japanese war. The Su family was anxious to have the young master marry again so that he could produce sons. Silver Pearl had many child-bearing years before her. She was only fifteen. The second wife would be regarded as a proper wife, not a concubine. Her sons would be heirs to the Su fortune.

The mother knew that many families with grown daughters were sending cards with young women's birthdays on them to the Su family. A fortuneteller would match the young master's birthday against that of each young woman and decide on the best match. But Silver Pearl's mother wanted to send something more than just a card with words and numbers. She heard that the young master Su was a man of modern mind. He had gone to Peking to attend university and then to Japan. She decided that in the red envelope containing Silver Pearl's name and birthday there would also be a photograph.

"What a pretty girl," the women of the Su family would say as they passed the photograph around the family hall. The young Su's mother would nod and think: "Let him marry a pretty one. Maybe she will keep him at home." The fortuneteller would be able to judge Silver Pearl's future both by her birthday and her photograph. The mother was confident that the fortuneteller would predict sons and good fortune for Silver Pearl, and even better if the young master ever stole a glimpse of Silver Pearl's photograph. How could he resist choosing her? The other young women could only rely on the matchmakers to describe them. No one ever believed the lavish words of the matchmakers anyway.

There was just a hint of fog in the air as the mother and daughter set out. They walked down the street with their arms linked. The mother glanced at her daughter's profile and saw how thoughtful she looked. Her eyes were downcast, half-veiled by thick, long lashes above her smoothly curving cheeks. Her pink lips were pressed together. What was the girl thinking? The mother muttered a prayer to Buddha when she thought of how soon her daughter would become a rich man's wife, that is if her plan worked. Silver Pearl was holding her tongue still and crunching the peanuts slowly, savoring the flavor. She felt her mother squeezing her arm, but ignored her. Silver Pearl was thinking of what her mother said to her several days ago.

The conversation had happened after dinner. Silver Pearl had cleared the table and was wiping the table top with a damp cloth. The last of the evening light was leaving the room and Silver Pearl moved hurriedly. Next to the table, her father sat crouching forward in a stiff-backed chair, fumbling to light his pipe. As Silver Pearl walked away, she saw a flame blossom near her father's lips. The fire trembled briefly in the darkening room before it was blown out into white smoke that dissolved into the air in front of him. Reluctantly, Silver Pearl walked into the brightly lit kitchen carrying a stack of dirty dishes. Her mother had lit a new red candle which was usually saved for holidays. Silver Pearl thought it was odd and wasteful, but said nothing as she put the dishes in a basin of soapy water.

The mother had been waiting for her daughter. She watched Silver Pearl's slender figure bending over the dirty dishes and said, "Don't bother with the dishes. I want to talk to you." She took her daughter's hands, which were cold and greasy, and led her to two squeaking wicker chairs.

They sat facing each other, knees touching, holding hands. Warmth flowed from the mother's thick, coarse palms to the daughter's slim fingers. She held up Silver Pearl's hands, looking at them lovingly. She said, "If things go as I plan, your hands will never wash another dirty dish again." Silver Pearl studied her mother's face. It was flushed. The mother's eyes sparkled like glazed porcelain reflecting the candlelight. She wet her lips and began to reminisce.

Silver Pearl had heard it all before. Her mother had been a maid in a rich man's house. She had often told Silver Pearl about life inside a rich household and about the extraordinary food: the fin of sharks, the paws of bears, the cucumbers picked from ocean floor, the black glistening eggs of a giant fish from the deep northern river. Her mother also told her about the fine clothes that the wealthy wore: chiffon and silk during the summer, sable-lined brocade in winter. Instead of working, the rich thought up ways to pass the time. They played chess, watched operas in their private courtyards and planned lavish dinner parties. The young mistresses would spend the entire spring chasing butterflies with silk fans in gardens where a hundred different flowers bloomed. Anticipating the same story, Silver Pearl tried to hold back her irritation. Her mother's dreamy description of the past only made the present and future bleaker, but her mother said something different this time.

"Silver Pearl," the mother whispered conspiratorially, "I have a plan to marry you to the young master of the Su family."

"But I thought he was already married," Silver Pearl said in surprise.

No one in the county was likely to forget the Su wedding, even though it had taken place seven years ago. The young Su master had married a girl from the neighboring county. On the wedding day, the procession climbed over hills and crossed rivers, traveling miles to reach the groom's house. The villagers who witnessed the wedding procession claimed later that it had stretched as far as the eyes could see. There had been hundreds of coolies carrying boxes and crates with yokes and pulling donkey carts full of dowry furniture. A group of musicians wearing red cloth bands across their foreheads led the procession, playing a wedding tune over and over again.

It was a hot July afternoon without a trace of wind. The sunlight beat the earth relentlessly. In the trees the cicadas sang, holding a note infinitely in the stagnant heat. The streets were empty. Behind the counter in the tofu shop, Silver Pearl had been sitting on a short stool, watching her baby brother sleeping in a wicker crib. The boy had had the measles. His body was covered with tiny pink dots. That afternoon he had been sleeping, his mouth dripping with saliva and his nostrils flaring rhythmically. Silver Pearl could smell the mixed scents of sour milk and sweat as she rested her chin on her knees. Her hands massaged her bare calves, and she felt the bumps of new mosquito bites from the night before.

Suddenly, Silver Pearl heard music approaching from far away accented with cymbals and gongs that reverberated in the still air. She ran out of the store and saw dust rising at one end of the main street. The wedding procession emerged from behind the dust. People came out of their houses and lined the street, chatting loudly as they fanned themselves. Among them, Silver Pearl stood in her straw sandals in front of the tofu shop where she watched the coolies and donkey carts passing by, and she waved at them. People talked and looked on with envy as they watched the handsome dowry parading by. Children chanted, "Where is the bride? Where is the bride?"

At last the bride's red sedan chair appeared, but Silver Pearl was disappointed. A red curtain shielded the bride from the villagers' view. The crowd dispersed after the procession passed, but Silver Pearl ran after the red sedan chair along with a few shouting children. They ran and ran, and then they stopped at the edge of the village. The sun was losing its strength as she walked back to the tofu shop. She was filled with resentment and emptiness and thought how unfair fate had been to her.

Back in the tofu store, she found her baby brother crying loudly and incessantly. His face and body were bright red and bloated. Silver Pearl went running to the backroom calling for her mother. But to be poor was to be short on effective remedies. The infant died two weeks later.

✳ ✳ ✳

The sun was high in the sky when the mother and daughter reached the center of the small town. The streets were bustling with people exchanging greetings. Silver Pearl felt anxious. She had only been to town a few times before, and today the streets seemed even busier than she had remembered. Her eyes darted about, and her attention was distracted by the noises and the heat of the crowd. Then she saw an elegant woman sitting primly on a sedan chair being carried down the street. She was wearing a yellow silk gown with glittering gold earrings to match a gold flower in her smooth, black, hair bun. Silver Pearl's eyes followed the sedan chair until her mother took her hand, and led her around a corner. They wove through the crowded street and ended up in front of a shop with glass windowpanes.

A small boy was splashing water from a bucket to wet the dust in front of the store. In the window, displayed against faded blue velvet drapes, enlarged photographs of smiling women and children were framed. As they opened the door and walked inside, two copper bells tied to the door handle jingled. A plump woman greeted them and directed them to two cushioned chairs. She poured them cups of tea before disappearing behind a curtained screen. Her face was one of those displayed in the window.

Silver Pearl picked up the teacup and held it close to her chin. She enjoyed the feeling of the steam warming her nose and cheeks. The room was dim. Rays of sunlight shone through the gaps at the edges of the heavy drapes. Silver Pearl noticed a layer of dust on the folds of the curtained screen. She was thinking about the photographs of the couples displayed in the window. She could imagine her own face smiling from behind the glass, wearing jade and gold on her earlobes and at the throat of her mandarin gown. The only thing missing was the face of a man, her husband, smiling beside her.

The plump woman beckoned to them and they followed her into a spacious room lit by bright kerosene lamps shining on a single spot. A chair was positioned directly in the light. Behind it hung a large canvas painted with trees and flowers, a garden scene. The woman led them to the chair and said, "Why don't you take a few minutes to get ready? You can stand over there when you are done." She pointed to the other side of the room.

The mother said nervously, "I'll just take a little time to fix her hair."

Silver Pearl stood next to the chair stiffly, blinded by the lamplight. Her mother pressed her to sit and began to comb her hair. Silver Pearl shaded her eyes with her hands and tried to see beyond the light. She could see a man's figure moving in and out of a black cloth that covered a black box that held a wide, round lens. Whenever he turned to look in her direction, Silver Pearl saw two dots of light reflecting from his face. He was wearing glasses.

The mother spat into her palms and smoothed Silver Pearl's hair. She braided the young woman's hair into a thick braid and set it over her chest. When she was done, she looked at her daughter and broke into a frowning half smile. Silver Pearl watched her mother turn and walk into the darkness. She could see shadowy figures as her mother whispered to the plump woman, but she could not make out what they were saying.

From behind the camera, the photographer shouted orders across the room: "Look at the lens!" "Lower your chin!" "Now just hold still!"

He thrust his arms out of the black cloth to emphasize his commands.

Stiffly, Silver Pearl adjusted herself while she watched the camera with awe. The machine stood there with arms and many legs–a one-eyed monster staring back at her. What was the big, unblinking eye seeing? The white kerosene light surrounding Silver Pearl was like the light that lit up an opera stage. Opera was the only form of entertainment in the countryside where it was played on an open air stage and performed by traveling singers and a few musicians, one of whom clapped together two pieces of wood to mark the singer's movements. But here, there was no music, no steady beats of clapping wood to guide her steps. It was a slowed-down, muted opera, something she had seen at the edge of her dreams. Silver Pearl could only sit still, looking into the camera with a locked-in smile that was getting harder and harder to maintain.

The photographer shouted dramatically, "Ready: one, two, three!"

A brilliant light exploded and faded into green glowing dots that danced in Silver Pearl's eyes. Slowly, she was able to see again, though the green dots persisted. The stench of burnt metal filled the air.

CHAPTER 3:
THE NEW COUPLE

Sunshine and the smell of soap filled the back yard. Newly washed clothes belonging to Silver Pearl and An Ling hung from bamboo poles that stretched across the yard—one end on a low brick wall, the other end resting on the squash stand. The bright clothes rippled in the wind, casting dancing shadows on the ground. The sleeves of shirts and jackets hit each other like quarreling lovers refusing to hold hands. The legs of trousers swung back and forth like a child's legs dangling from a high chair. From time to time, the wind blew the clothes against each other with a whipping sound. After the wind died, the clothes separated and hung suspended in the air, like ghosts waiting to be reincarnated.

Orchid, the slave girl, sat before a large pile of dirty clothes. Her sleeves were rolled above her elbows as she scrubbed a white undershirt on the washboard which leaned inside a basin filled with soapy water. Her face was flushed, and beads of sweat dotted her hairline as her bare arms moved briskly up and down the washboard. Little Jade sat down on the wooden bench across from Orchid. Orchid looked up and said, "Are you feeling better, Little Jade?"

Little Jade pressed her hands between her thighs for warmth, "I'm much better," she said, "It's stuffy inside."

A strand of hair fell over Orchid's face, and she curled it back behind her ear with a dripping hand. A cluster of bubbles stuck to the hair by her ear.

Orchid kept working as she talked to Little Jade. She nodded at the heap of dirty clothes in front of her and said, "These are from the Master. Young Mistress just cleared out all the clothes that need washing." Orchid was sorting the clothes into smaller piles: a pile of trousers, a pile of shirts, a pile of underwear and socks. Little Jade asked, "Doesn't she have anything to be washed?"

"Young Mistress has a lot of dirty clothes," said Orchid, "Look, all those are hers." She gestured with her chin to the clothes drying on the bamboo poles. "I spent the entire morning washing her clothes."

She picked out a few pink underpants and a pair of silk stockings from the heap of men's clothes. The soft colors stung Little Jade's eyes, and she forced a cough. "These are hers too," Orchid said, and put them aside in a ball. "Your new mother is pretty!" The slave girl said cheerfully as she started on the shirts.

"She is not my mother," Little jade said stiffly, looking at the pink ball of clothing next to father's white underpants.

"Sh-h-h-h-h, not so loud. Someone will hear you," Orchid whispered in alarm, her wet finger dripping next to her lips.

They listened for a moment, but no one was nearby. "Little Jade, you better be careful from now on," warned Orchid, "Things are different now. Master wouldn't like it if he heard what you just said."

"I'm not afraid," Little Jade said in a lowered voice, looking at a blue striped shirt. Little Jade recognized that shirt. Her father was wearing it the day he returned home. Little Jade thought: *Things have changed a lot if even Orchid knows it. Everyone in the house is getting used to the changes, except for me. The servants call her Young Mistress this, Young Mistress that, all the time. And she acts as if she owns the house, ordering the servants around and disciplining them whenever they do something wrong. She hasn't started with me yet, but I know that she is waiting to get me back for the embarrassment I caused her on her wedding day.*

* * *

Little Jade remembered that day clearly for it was just three months ago. The family hall had been noisy with people and firecrackers. Operas were playing in the main courtyard. The entire house was decorated in red. Golden foil cutouts of the lucky character for "double happiness" were displayed on every door. Little Jade was wearing red and hiding in the crowd. The band was playing wedding music. The flutes and gongs were loud, endlessly repeating a melody.

"Here comes the new couple!" someone shouted. And Little Jade saw her father walk into the hall, wearing a special blue silk gown embellished with a thick red ribbon that ran across his chest and a large red satin flower on his left shoulder. His bride was next to him in a red and gold embroidered gown, her face covered with a red silk scarf.

Firecracker smoke burned Little Jade's eyes. She wanted to go back to her room and close the door. But someone took her hand and said, "Come meet your new mother." And there she was, her painted face smiling at Little Jade, offering her a cup of sweet tea. Little Jade knocked the teacup over. It shattered into pieces all over the floor. The lotus seeds tea spilled a brown stain on Silver Pearl's red satin skirt.

The bride looked away. The guests whispered to each other. Little Jade knew it was bad luck to break things on a wedding day. She wanted to upset the fortune of her stepmother. She wanted her to have a bad start.

Someone muttered, "Each year a peaceful year." It was said whenever something was broken; the sounds of the words "each year" were the same as "broken."

***

The clothes sailed in the wind against the shining blue sky. Silver Pearl's silk clothes, her apricot camisole, lime green bathrobe, cherry red blouse—all were rising above the bamboo poles wavering in the air. Behind them, strands of white clouds drifted by. Something in Little Jade's chest was winding tighter, tighter, about to snap.

"She can't touch me," Little Jade said bitterly.

"She is still a bride. But she is sharp with the servants," Orchid sighed. "Do you know what she did to the kitchen maid? The maid broke a bowl when she was washing dishes and she made her pay for it, deducting money from her pay. But Old Mistress secretly gave the maid some money. Old Mistress is a living Buddha!"

"Did grandma say anything to her?" Little Jade asked.

"No, probably because she is still new. Old Mistress said to the maid that maybe given time, Young Mistress's edges would soften."

"Grandma will never say anything harsh to anyone," Little Jade said wistfully.

"Little Jade, listen to me," said Orchid. "Don't be too stubborn. If you clash with her, you will suffer." Orchid's voice was barely audible.

"Grandma won't allow it," Little Jade said uncertainly.

"Remember, she's the one who shares a pillow with the Master. Little Jade, you can't rely on your grandmother forever. What if she isn't around? Then what will you do?"

"I'll be with grandma wherever she goes," Little Jade said stubbornly.

Orchid shook her head. "You aren't listening to me. Forget it. Pretend I never said these words. If Young Mistress ever finds out, she'll slap my face. Why don't you go inside? The wind is getting strong. I don't want you to catch another cold. The Master will blame it on me if you do."

"I'm sorry, Orchid," Little Jade said. She paused and asked, "Orchid, did you know my mother?"

The slave girl shook her head. "No, she left before I came. Old Nanny said that she was good to the servants—not like this one."

"What else did she say?" Little Jade asked hopefully. She had asked Old Nanny about her mother many times, but the nanny would never say a thing. "Oh, nothing much, just that your mother was quiet and always smiled at everyone. She didn't look like someone who would run away." Orchid stopped and glanced at Little Jade apologetically and went back to rubbing a blue shirt on the washboard.

The sun was getting hotter and Little Jade could see rainbow colors gliding on the surfaces of the soap bubbles. Only minutes ago she had felt like crying, but now she calmed down. She felt the cool surface of her jade necklace next to her heart. She loved the fact that the letters on the jade spelled "Wei", the name of her mother, and if she pressed hard enough, she could literally imprint her mother's name into her skin. The jade was meant to guard against unknown evil. Little Jade had heard that a piece of jade protects its owner so that no harm could be done to the one who wears it.

Orchid threw the pink ball of underwear and stockings into the soapy water and rubbed them together carefully. When she finished, she put them in a bucket of clean water to soak. She lifted her head and smiled at Little Jade. Little Jade winced at the sight of Silver Pearl's pink, triangle shaped, silk underwear. Averting her eyes from pale legs of stockings floating in the clear water, she hurriedly got on her feet. She wanted to get away.

She walked back to her room. The sun was bright and the trees were sprouting new leaves in the courtyard, but none of this had anything to do with her. She walked down the corridor, stepping over the shadows of columns that cut across the winding passageway ahead of her. She imagined she was climbing a ladder that would lead her to a place where she could hide. She closed the door behind her. The room was quiet and the windows were shut. The shaded air was cool and still around her, like water from a well. She opened the bureau drawer and took out a package wrapped in a piece of blue velvet. She opened the cloth and looked at the glass box inside. It was a gift from her father. In the box, a pretty lady with golden hair and a short gauze skirt was standing on one leg on a mirrored floor, her other leg lifted high behind her head.

Little Jade wound up the key on the side of the box. The lady started to turn, unhurriedly, her arms stretching over her head, her red lips smiling just a little. A stream of music flew out of the box. "*Ding ding ding dong, ding dong dong dong...*" She held the box close to her face so closely that her breath fogged the glass.

The door opened suddenly, startling Little Jade. Silver Pearl walked into the room, a shower of sunshine splashing behind her. She left the door open and came toward Little Jade. The smell of her jasmine hair oil reeked in the air. Little Jade sneezed and looked up at her. She was wearing a golden yellow gown, and she smiled brightly at Little Jade. She bent over and looked at the box and said in a lilting voice, "What is this clever thing?"

"It's a music box," Little Jade said, watching as Silver Pearl picked up the glass box and looked at it closely. "*Ding ding ding dong, ding ding ding dong...*"

"Look at it. The girl is dancing on her toes." She held the glass box next to her ear.

"Be careful," Little Jade mumbled.

Her hand was holding the box casually and her lips were parted slightly as she listened. "Don't worry. I won't break it." She flashed another smile at Little Jade and said, "Watch!" She tossed the box into the air.

It gleamed briefly, catching the sunlight, and fell back into her hands. She put it gently on the bed and walked out the door. Her slender figure merged into the golden afternoon sunlight outside. As she walked away, she picked up the melody where the music box left off and sang, "*Ding ding ding dong, ding ding dong dong...*"

✳ ✳ ✳

It was breakfast time, but Little Jade's father and stepmother were still sleeping. The heavy brocade curtains were drawn. Orchid said that she could not hear anything from outside their bedroom door. No one dared to wake them. The roosters were no longer crowing and the sun was high. The servants shuffled quietly about the house. Little Jade and her grandmother looked at each other across the dining table and began to eat their breakfast. Two extra sets of chopsticks and bowls were on the table, waiting for the new couple.

They were having porridge cooked with sweet lotus seeds and dates, Little Jade's favorite. There were also cold dishes of shredded pig's ears, salted fish, pickled vegetables, and poached eggs. The room was quiet. The sunlight cut across the table to shine on Little Jade, warming up her neck and cheeks, and drawing up her blood. The grandmother sat across from Little Jade on the shadowy side of the table. Her head was lowered and her hand slowly stirred a spoon in her bowl. Little Jade couldn't see her grandmother's face clearly. The sun was in her eyes. The grandmother put some pig's ears into her mouth. Little Jade listened to the light crunching of the soft bone as she chewed, like indecipherable murmurs from far away. Little Jade sucked at the soft yolk of the poached egg. It tasted bitter.

The grandmother put down her chopsticks and shook her head. Little Jade looked up at her, swallowing slowly, waiting.

"When I was a daughter-in-law, I had to get up before daylight to make breakfast for the entire family," the grandmother said. She stopped and looked into the bowl, still shaking her head. The room darkened as a cloud drifted over the sun, and then lit up again. Little Jade blinked, feeling drowsy in the bright and quiet room. She picked up some pig's ears with her chopsticks, eating them loudly, filling the silence of the room.

Orchid walked over to the grandmother and said carefully, "Old Mistress, Master and Young Mistress are up. They want to eat breakfast in their room."

The grandmother nodded solemnly and said, "Go ahead and tell the kitchen maid to warm up the breakfast, and take away these chopsticks and bowls." She pointed at the table.

Orchid paused and continued: "Master and Young Mistress want to go out to the market place after they eat."

"What are you waiting for? Go tell the driver to get the wagon ready." The grandmother was frowning.

The slave girl answered, "Yes, yes," and quickly walked away. Little Jade listened to her calling the kitchen maid, the driver. The house was suddenly humming with the noises of servants talking and moving furniture. Her father was coughing loudly in his room, clearing his throat and spitting into the chamber pot. Her stepmother was ordering the maid, "Put it here. Don't drop it!"

After breakfast, Little Jade followed her grandmother back to their room. She always chanted two hours of mantras after breakfast as part of her daily prayers to Kwan Yin. She sat on the bed, absently fingering the heavy prayer beads. Her eyes moved slowly. Little Jade sat next to her, leaning her shoulder and elbow against her grandmother's arm, but she ignored her.

Outside the window, the horses were neighing. The father and his new wife were getting ready to leave for the market. They barely touched breakfast. Little Jade wished her father would take her to the market place. She hardly ever went anywhere. Her grandmother never allowed her to go shopping with the maids who went all the time. Orchid always came back with candies and trinkets: a rag doll, a wind-propelled paper wheel, candied apples, a dragonfly kite.

When Orchid returned from the market place, she told Little Jade what she saw there: the monkey that pushed a wheelbarrow and then went around the crowd asking for money with a tin can; the "wild opera," where singers sang in a roped-in-stage, reenacting a recent murder trial that had shocked the entire province; the dwarf who challenged anyone to a game of chess for money; and the centipede kite and dragon kite she did not buy. Orchid knew everything.

The grandmother put one arm around Little Jade. "Look at you, hanging around me like a little monkey. You are growing up and should learn to behave like a lady." The grandmother laughed, pushing her away.

"I don't want to grow up, grandma," Little Jade said. She hooked her arms around her grandmother's neck.

"Nonsense, you will grow up to be a pretty girl and get married to a good husband someday." She patted Little Jade's head.

"I don't want to get married!" Little Jade exclaimed. "Never, never, never!"

She hid her face in her grandmother's neck.

"What are you going to do if you don't get married? You want to be a Buddhist nun? You'll have to shave your head," the grandmother teased, rocking her back and forth.

CHAPTER 4:
THE GRANDMOTHER, 1941

It was raining outside. Little Jade pressed her nose against the window. The rain fell quietly upon the earth, washing the maple tree in the courtyard. The maple leaves trembled gently in the wind. The gray sky hovered above.

The rain was light. It brushed against the newly pasted window paper, making a scratching noise. Little Jade could hear the sounds of people in the hall: footsteps, talking, shouts for servants. Soon the grandmother would lead the family to the temple. Little Jade had accompanied her grandmother there many times before. She was always awed by the great hall with the painted Buddha statues that reached to the ceiling. The monks at the temple had received scheduled donations and deliveries of grain and oil from the Su family for generations. The Su's had their private prayer hall behind the main temple.

Ever since Little Jade's great-grandfather died while he was sunning in the courtyard, the family had not been the same. For all of the great-grandfather's life, he had been rich. He boasted that he had never been anywhere without owning some part of it. He owned countless acres of farmlands and orchards, blocks of streets in different cities throughout the province, and land in several mountains to the west. It was difficult to keep track of the properties and income from the tenant farmers. He had a network of accountants to estimate rents to collect and taxes to be paid to the local magistrate. But starting with the demise of the Qing Dynasty in 1911, vast ownership of land became less and less profitable and meaningful.

After the great-grandfather's death, his property was split up into lots. Each of his four sons and his one grandson, Little Jade's father, got a share. After the family estate was divided, the four great-uncles moved out of the big house with their wives and daughters, leaving Little Jade and her grandmother to look after the old house along with a dozen servants. Much of the old housing compound was no longer occupied.

The grandmother wanted to visit the temple to pray for her son and daughter-in-law's safe journey during their honeymoon. An Ling wanted to survey his share of the family properties in nearby towns and counties. Silver Pearl wanted to go along, but the roads were no longer peaceful. An Ling said that with the war raging between the invading Japanese Army and both factions of Nationalist and Communist Armies of China, there were no functioning governing bodies in the surrounding counties, leaving the bandits to the roam the countryside. He insisted that they be accompanied by two guards and a maid to look after Silver Pearl.

"Little Jade," the grandmother's voice came from behind the young child. She placed her hands on the girl's shoulders.

"Are we leaving soon?" Little Jade turned and saw her grandmother smiling at her.

"I have decided that you are not going to the temple with us. It's raining and it's chilly outside, and you're still weak. I don't want you to get another wind-chill," the grandmother said.

"But I don't want to be in the house alone."

The grandmother smiled, stretching the web of fine wrinkles across her face. She hugged her granddaughter and said, "Orchid will be home to keep you company. I'll be back as soon as I can. Stay home and rest. Don't go out in the rain."

She patted Little Jade's head and walked away. Little Jade noticed her grandmother's back hunched over slightly and that there was more white in her hair. She could hear her grandmother and her father talking and getting ready to leave in the family hall. The noises moved farther and farther away.

The house grew quiet. Little Jade wanted to go out. She was tired of staring out the window. She put on a quilted jacket and red rubber boots. Outside, Orchid was feeding the pigs. Little Jade took an oilpaper umbrella and stole out of the kitchen door. The big door closed behind her with a squeak, and a cool breeze swept across her face as she hurried down to the vegetable garden. The rain fell like soft cow's hair on Little Jade's face and clothes leaving traces of dampness on her skin. Her heart leapt. The squash vines scratched the top of her umbrella. She walked carefully and kicked the growing stems of the vegetables out of her way, trying not to splash mud on her boots. Beyond the vegetable garden, the bamboo forest hung like mist. In the other direction, wheat field stretched endlessly under the gray sky.

Little Jade heard someone singing. In a distance, she saw the figure of a boy slowly riding an ox along the side of a wheat field. He wore a broad brim hat made of bamboo leaves and a cape of matted reeds. He played a bamboo flute, and Little Jade stood and listened to the stream of clear notes. It was an ancient song about the spirits, about how cold and lonely it is beneath the earth.

"Today you cry over my tomb,

and make an offer of grain and wine to my soul.

But in this world of chaos,

who knows what will happen tomorrow?

The soldiers will march over the graveyard,

disturbing the dead.

And you won't be here

to clear the weeds off my tombstone

next year."

Little Jade listened to the song, watching the boy and the ox moving away, disappearing into the mist. She felt an unnamed sadness. She wished that she were in the family temple, kneeling and praying next to her grandmother among the ancestral tablets and statues of the Buddha, listening to the temple bell, and inhaling the smoke of the incense.

✷ ✷ ✷

Little Jade's father and stepmother left for their honeymoon in the city the next morning. Little Jade stood next to her grandmother in the front yard, watching the servants load the luggage into two waiting wagons. The stepmother tried not to look happy, but she could not conceal a trace of a smile. The father smoked a cigarette as he waited for the wagon to be loaded, standing next to his mother, their arms touching. The sun was shining behind a thin layer of cloud. The sky was the color of tin. The wagons were finally ready. And the grandmother said over and over, "Take care of yourselves. Come home soon."

Little Jade's father came over to her. She looked up at him as he touched her cheeks. "I'll be back soon, Little Jade," he said.

Then he turned and stepped into the wagon as he was smiling and waving at his mother and daughter. Silver Pearl waved a pink hand-kerchief as the wagon pulled away.

✷ ✷ ✷

The grandmother sat in front of the vanity table and combed her long graying hair under the light of a single candle. The hair fell loosely on her shoulders. She moved slowly and silently, gazing into the mirror. Is that really she looking back at her from inside the mirror? She wore pale blue pajamas and her thin body cast a large shadow on the wall. The flame of the lamp flickered, changing the shape of the shadow.

Holding a pillow in her arms, Little Jade curled up in the bed, watching her grandmother. She looked frail next to the looming shadow on the wall. She made Little Jade feel sad and comforted at the same time. The grandmother put the comb on the vanity table and started to rub oil from a small jar into her hands.

She said, "Little Jade, grandma is getting old. I didn't do much today and my back is aching. Come over and pound my back for me."

"Yes, grandma."

The grandmother walked over and sat on the edge of the bed. Little Jade crawled over and drummed on her shoulders.

"Is it too hard, grandma?"

"No, it's just fine, Little Jade. You are a good girl." She sighed and said, "My bones are getting too old. Every time the weather changes, my back and shoulders become sore and painful."

"Grandma," Little Jade interrupted.

"Yes?"

"When is father coming back?"

"I don't know. I hope he will return in time for the Autumn Moon Festival."

Little Jade stopped pounding and asked, "Grandma, did you go on a honeymoon when you got married?"

"No, of course not. Honeymoons are for the young generation. When I got married, I stayed home to take care of the family."

"How did you get married?"

"I was from the neighboring village. The matchmaker arranged everything. I didn't see my husband until I married him. I only saw his braid of hair, his queue." The grandmother's face softened as she remembered. "It's an old family tale by now. One day I was sitting alone in my room, and my mother came in and threw a thick braid of hair on my bed. She told me that it was my future husband's queue. He had cut his hair and sent it to his parents to show his rebellion against the Qing court. He was a revolutionary."

Little Jade started pounding her grandmother's back again, waiting for her to continue the story. But she sighed and said nothing, staring into the mirror.

"Is grandpa dead?" Little Jade asked, assuming that since she had never seen him, he must have passed away.

"I don't know," the grandmother said weakly, but then she quickly straightened her back and added, "You have too many questions for a little girl."

Little Jade's hands were getting sore. "Does your back feel better now?"

"Yes, Little Jade. I never thought that you'd end up taking care of me."

Little Jade hugged her grandmother from behind. The old woman held on to her granddaughter's hands and squeezed them tight.

* * *

Listening to her granddaughter breathing evenly beside her, the grandmother could not sleep. Scenes from the past appeared in her mind like silent, stage operas. She remembered how everyone congratulated her when the news spread that she was marrying into the Su family. She was going to marry the youngest son and would be the youngest daughter-in-law. Nobody suspected that the rich Su family would need a daughter-in-law to do the housework. There would be plenty of servants in the family so that she could surely lead a comfortable life. But the old poem was right.

"The third day after the wedding,

the new bride washes her hands in the kitchen.

She is ready to cook

for all of her in-laws."

Her father-in-law was a traditional gentleman who believed in putting women in their proper place. He demanded that the youngest daughter-in-law wait on him. So she did for twenty-five years.

She spent her life taking care of the father-in-law, the son, and her granddaughter. She knew her duties, and she fulfilled them without a word of complaint. She had been the ideal woman who obeyed the traditional "Three-to-follow Rule": "A woman should follow her father's wishes before she is married; after she is married, she follows her husband's wishes; after her husband dies, she follows the wishes of her son."

It might have hurt less if her husband had not deserted her and run away from the family for the sake of that demon woman. She should have known that there was another woman on her husband's mind, even on her wedding night. The groom looked so cheerless through-out the wedding ceremony that it set the relatives talking. She re-membered waiting for him in her red wedding gown, sitting on the bed by the red candles that were burning high. Her cheeks were hot from the heat and from shyness. She could hear him far away in the family hall, laughing after he had too much to drink. He was so drunk when he finally came to the bedchamber that he could barely walk. He threw himself on the bed, slouching over her red pleated skirt that spread over the pink satin quilt. She remembered that her mother had told her: "Don't let him sit on your skirt. If you do, you will have to lower yourself to him the rest of your life." But it was already too late. She had not been careful and she was doomed.

Her husband was not aware of what was on her mind. He started to sing in a foreign tongue that she didn't understand and suddenly broke down in tears. She felt bad for him but didn't know how to comfort him. She leaned over to him and tried to help him out of his stained clothes. That was when he tried to kiss her and tore at the buttons of her red gown. She could still remember his drunken breath.

They slept with their backs to each other for many nights before she was awakened one night. His hands caressed her under the slippery quilt, enclosing her thin waist. She lay still, feeling his touch, her eyes closed. The two of them would struggle, intertwined into a tangled knot. She felt the heat in his blood as sweat broke out of his skin and the bed was permeated with the scent of his perspiration. His breath was hot against her neck, until he collapsed upon her. Feeling the weight of his body on top of her, she felt a stifling excitement, even in her exhaustion. But he soon pulled away, turned over and fell into a deep sleep.

She stayed awake watching him sleep. Sometimes he turned in his sleep and threw one arm over his head, his armpit lush with black curly hair. His skin looked pale green under the moonlight, and his bare chest heaved evenly. Carefully, she moved closer to him, inhaling his scent. How she wanted to touch his skin, which looked cool and smooth under the still moonlight—like a stone under a lake. His hair was like waterweed that grew beside the stone. She traced the outline of his profile with her fingers, almost touching him.

During the day he avoided her. Every day she sat across from him during meals, but he never looked at her directly. He would stare into his bowl as if it were the only thing that concerned him. He always glanced past her as if he were in a hurry. She suspected that he had never taken a good look at her. She felt like the woman in the ghost story who erased her eyes, nose, and mouth with one wipe of a hand and left her face as blank and bald as an egg. Nevertheless she loved him, in a confused, inevitable way. She loved the man who slept beside her at night, whose thick eyelashes fluttered when he dreamt, whose lips were relaxed and sensual. Perhaps love was just an instinct that depended on smell and taste, and whenever she collected sheets and pillowcases from their bed to be washed, she would bury her face in the armful of laundry and become intoxicated in his smell. She felt like an animal, identifying her mate by scent.

Her husband had been a pilot. He had been sent over to Europe by the Chinese government to learn to fly an airplane. When she first heard that he flew, she didn't believe it. "He knows how to work a machine with wings," the matchmaker had said, "and by doing that he can fly in the sky, like a bird."

She once asked him about the airplane. "Do the wings of the flying machines flap like a bird's wings?" Her husband broke into a laughing roar and didn't stop for a while. She was embarrassed by her stupidity.

"You ignorant country woman!" he exclaimed.

"Can you explain to me what makes those machines fly?" She asked.

"What's the use?" he answered. "You'll never understand."

The demon woman must have known how a plane worked. He probably took her flying with him all over the foreign landscape with buildings as tall as mountains and streets as wide as rivers. She saw a photograph of that woman once. She found it in a cardboard box underneath the clothing in her husband's drawer. The foreign girl smiled next to her husband without shame, her light-colored hair flying in the wind. Her husband was also smiling. They were standing in front of an airplane.

He rarely talked to her during the two years they were together. She often found him sitting along on the marble bench in the courtyard, staring into the sky. She had hoped that the birth of their son would change his feelings toward her. But her husband deserted her and their son when the boy was a year old. The infant was just learning to talk, to say "Baba." But "Baba" did not want his son, his wife or his family. "Baba" abandoned them all for a demon woman with pale hair and pale eyes.

The family disowned her husband. Perhaps he felt that he had fulfilled his share of filial duty for his family. He had planted the seeds and had a son, and now the family line could continue without him. After he left, she slept in the bed alone and tried to recapture the violent memories of his touches. Over the years, his scent had faded and his ghost had dissipated.

How well she remembered the knives and swords of the sneers her sisters-in-law used to assault her. She had brought to the family bad luck and shame. She was a woman who broke the family, rather than held it together. If not for her son, her life would not have been worth enduring. Giving birth to a son had secured her a solid place in the family. Nobody could chase her out because she had extended the family line. None of the other daughters-in-law gave birth to sons. No matter how many more concubines her brothers-in-law took, it only meant more girls. Girls were running wild in the house.

She watched her son mature with a perplexed mixture of loving pride and secret resentment. How strange and fascinating it was to see the soft flesh and bones of an infant turn into a man with long legs, a deep voice, and a shade of green on his chin and upper lip. How suddenly he had grown out of her reach. Silently, he turned away from her, just as his father once did. She became frantic on the day that she caught her son sitting on the marble bench in the courtyard holding his knees together while staring into the sky. "Just like his father! Just like his father!" She screamed inside herself. She felt such faintness that she had to support herself against a wall.

She knew that her son was no longer hers. He had grown into a man and she resented it. She had been afraid of his maturity and her fear was confirmed. She resented him for being so big, so full of masculine energy, and so confident about it. He was so different from her and so much like his father. She had filled his growing years with warnings, all of which had the same theme: "Don't be like your father."

"When you grow up and get married," she would tell him, "be good to your wife. "If you want a woman besides your wife, take a second wife or even a third one. Don't be like your father. He deserted his parents, son and wife for a demon woman. He turned me into a living widow when I was nineteen.

"When you have children, you should take good care of them, so they will grow up properly. Don't be like your father. He did not stay around to watch you grow up."

She had succeeded in educating her son. Her son was not like his father. He did not desert his wife. His wife deserted him.

It was a cruel joke. Sometime she wondered if the gods had purposely arranged all this to punish her. She had wanted to find her son a wife who could read the classical texts and therefore understand the proper roles of different people. Who would have suspected that the "woman scholar" would turn out wanting to be like a man, wanting more than a woman could ever ask? Her dream of having a daughter-in-law to share her burden was gone. Instead of enjoying her old age, cared for by her daughter-in-law, she ended up taking care of her granddaughter alone in this big house. *It's all fate. Everything is like clouds and smoke that pass before the eyes,* the grandmother thought. *What do I have left now? No husband, son, daughter-in-law. There is only Little Jade to keep me company.*

She smiled, turning her head to see Little Jade. The girl was sleeping soundly, her face calm and without a care. She saw the red string with the jade next to the Little Jade's face on the pillow. It was better that the necklace was made of string and not gold. She was too young to bear the weight of both gold and jade, not to mention the pearl, a memento from the island nation of Japan. It would only invite envy and trouble. *May Kwan Yin look after Little Jade, my son and his young wife.* She prayed silently. *When did the rain stop,* she wondered, *and the moon grow so bright that it lit up the window?*

Chapter 5:
The Great Grandfather

Little Jade surveyed the land in front of her from the hillside of the Su family cemetery. The countryside extended from the foot of the mountain that was shaped like a sitting ox. She could see the bamboo forest that was swathed in a deeper shade of green than the wheat fields surrounding it. The wheat was tall and swayed in the fields in rhythm with the sweeping of the wind. In the fields, she could see farmers hunching over weeding in the field. She could see a gathering of oxen grazing at the edge of the pond. The oxen splashed water on their backs with their tails, chasing away flies. She could see the gray-tiled roofs and earth-colored wall of her house and other houses in the village. She imagined Orchid feeding the animals in the barn, the pigs' snouts trashing in the feeding tray, flocks of chickens and ducks following her about, their wings flapping. She imagined her great-grandfather pointing and telling her, "Look, all this land belongs to our family." Little Jade imagined turning to see him leaning against a tombstone, smiling at her, fingering his long white beard. But Little Jade's great-grandfather was dead, buried next to his own father beneath this wet earth.

Little Jade's great-grandfather had liked to tell her stories. She was his only great-grandchild. There were no boys to steal his affection from her. He was lonely in his old age. His concubines preferred playing Mahjong together and his sons were afraid of him. By the time Little Jade was five years old, he took long walks with her, and he told her stories endlessly. Little Jade remembered the stories as his voice slowly flew into her memory. "Our ancestors were poor peasants from the north. Driven by famine and drought, they put their only son in a basket and carried him on one end of a yoke. On the other end, they carried a sack of grain.

"It was a chaotic time. There were bandits on the road and many travelers were killed. There were girls sitting by the roadside with long grass tied across their foreheads. They were for sale. Their families watched from behind, inspecting the passersby for prospective buyers.

"The girls would look down at the ground, listening to their fates being bargained. Some would be sold to brothels and some would be slaves for wealthy families. The lucky ones were bought by men looking for wives to carry on their lines.

"The land was dry and would grow only dry yellow weeds and no grains. People were reduced to eating roots, mice, and insects from the fields. The only fat ones were ravens, which fed on the carcasses of animals and people. Your ancestors had to harden themselves with hearts of stone and guts of iron. If they shared their food, there would not be enough left to feed themselves.

"After they finally reached Kai Yuan county, they bought a small plot of land at the foot of a mountain that was shaped like a sitting ox. They worked hard on the land and built up their household gradually. They painted the front door red to welcome good fortune and keep evil away. It was the beginning of the Su village.

"The Su's were peasants, Little Jade. Your ancestors established the family on a sack of grain and hard work. You must remember this and never take this land for granted. Maybe you are too young to understand, but someone has to teach you this. Just remember what I say and someday you'll understand.

"The world is strange to me now. I can no longer understand how things work and this new idea of a Republic is confusing. There has always been chaos before a great turn in history. I'm old, and I won't live to see what will come out of all the changes. Without an emperor, everything will be different.

"Little Jade, when I die, tell them to bury me deep down next to my father. In a famine, the wild dogs dig into the earth to find food. I want to sleep without being disturbed."

Little Jade did not respond. She did not want her great-grandfather to die. She grasped his bony hand in hers, and held it tightly.

* * *

The wind blew the wheat field into waves of a green sea. Little Jade remembered visiting the family cemetery with her great-grandfather last year and the year before. This year she was paying a visit to him, seeing his name carved in stone among the other names of her ancestors.

The grandmother was calling. Little Jade turned around and walked between the two stone lions that guarded the cemetery gate. The grandmother had already lit the incense, and the smoke blew quickly away in the wind as if the dead were anxious for a visit from the living.

The grandmother instructed Little Jade to kneel in front of the new tomb covered with yellow earth. A thin layer of grass was already growing on its surface. Soon the grass would cover the great-grandfather's grave, and it would be as green as the rest of the mountain.

Little Jade kowtowed three times and mumbled what she could remember the Buddhist chant her grandmother had taught her. Silently, the grandmother burned gold foil and silver foil, folded in shape of ingots. The stone lions looked on fiercely, their teeth showing. But without pupils in their eyes, they were blind.

* * *

Why doesn't grandma sleep anymore? Why does she keep the windows open at night when the air is cold? Little Jade thought to herself as she watched her grandmother from the bed. It was no longer summer and the autumn moonlight flowed through the windows and poured onto the floor like white frost. Lately, the grandmother would stand in front of the window every night before Little Jade fell asleep and every morning before she awoke. It was getting harder and harder for Little Jade to sleep, knowing that her grandmother didn't sleep anymore.

Little Jade used to hold her grandmother's hand as she fell asleep. She knew every rough spot along her grandmother's fingers and every line on her palms. She remembered how her grandmother once read her palm. She showed her the lifeline, the marriage line, and where the wealth line met the marriage line and where the travel line crossed the lifeline. But when she asked what they meant, the grandmother told her that she was too young to know her fate, and wouldn't tell her any more. Little Jade used to open up her grandmother's hand, comparing it with her own. The old woman's palm was a deep cut of branches under a web of fine lines—like the veins of an autumn maple leaf, dry to the touch and fragile, as if it could be broken with a grasp.

Little Jade missed the touch of her grandmother's hands and the smell of her hair mixed with the fragrance of her favorite cream. When her grandmother lay next to her, Little Jade felt safe as she listened to the night wind shook the flaming maple tree in the courtyard. But for days the grandmother kept the windows open, allowing the evil spirits of the night to enter the room. Little Jade hugged the quilt closely and tightly closed her eyes. She was chilled by the night wind blowing through her ears—knowing her grandmother was standing in front of the open window, her long, loose hair flying like a gray cloud in the wind.

✳ ✳ ✳

The grandmother was time traveling, and her life came floating by. *Don't cry, my son. Your little face turned red like beets when you screamed, using the energy with which you sucked on my breasts. Don't wave your fists in the air. And don't come pulling on my breasts, my hands, my hair.*

It was hard to raise you, my son. You were always sick, needy, demanding. There were times I felt that I had stolen you from the Buddha and was not allowed to keep you for too long. But now you are as tall as your father and far away from me.

Where are you, my son? Do you travel by airplanes or do you ride the train? Maybe you would pass by your father on the street in a big city and not recognize him. Maybe he had already forgotten you. Your father, he used to fly an airplane, but he never took me anywhere. You are your father's son, the flying kind. But I am tired of waiting. I have been trying to fly for years. I had been gathering feathers, but they fell off my body like leaves in autumn. Nobody can stop me now that the old are buried, and the young too restless to care. I have been waiting for years. And my husband, why is your ghost standing outside my window, blocking my view of the sky?

I remember how, long ago, I slept next to you and knew that I could never have you. And you knew that I wanted you, as you watched me falter with your cold eyes. But this heart is like a spider's web. In every knot is tangled a look, a silence, a sigh. Full of dust, your heart is a harp I never learned to play. But I never ceased loving you.

✳ ✳ ✳

Little Jade's body trembled as she woke up. Her soul was scattered about in the house, in the courtyard, in the garden. She closed her eyes, closed her fingers into fists, and clenched her toes. She opened her eyes and things fell into place in the room. The mosquito netting clouded her vision like the morning fog. The windows were wide open. Little Jade looked at the light outside the windows, guessing the time of the day. She could see the white porcelain Kwan Yin statue in the shadowy side of the room. "Grandma," she whispered, feeling her grandmother next to her, and waited for a response.

Little Jade turned to see her grandmother. Her lips were closed in a tight thin line. Her brows were thickly knotted. Her hair was spread on the pillow. She looked disturbed, as though she was having a bad dream. Little Jade pulled on her grandmother's sleeve and called again, "Grandma! Grandma!"

She did not answer.

The mosquito netting flapped in the morning breeze. The first crows of a rooster from the other side of the courtyard tore open the quiet of the morning. It was getting brighter in the room. Little Jade knelt beside her grandmother. She pulled and tugged at her arms, but could not wake her. She had drifted away in a bad dream to an unknown place, from where she could not find her way back to the Su village. Maybe her soul was flying over the continent, lost between the mountains in a province thousands of miles from home. She would ask for directions from the local spirits, but would not understand their dialect. She has never traveled outside her village, and without a guide, she is forever lost.

Enclosed in the mosquito netting, Little Jade tried to wake her grandmother. The bed was an island; the mosquito netting was the smoke and mist of the early morning. A day was ahead and much needed to be done. The porcelain Kwan Yin smiled in the shadow as if she knew a secret that no one else had yet discovered. Yesterday's sandalwood incense ash lay in the green copper pot. The smell of sandalwood hung faintly in the air–a memory of what was no longer there.

CHAPTER 6:
AN LING

The servants carried Little Jade from her bedroom. She did not struggle, and she did not say a word. She could hear the old nanny crying and talking to herself as she washed the grandmother's body in the bedroom. The curtains were drawn , and the door was closed. She could hear Orchid's footsteps running back and forth, carrying water for the wash. Why? They told Little Jade that her grandmother had gone to the Western Heaven to be with Buddha. Little Jade wanted to stay with her in the bedroom, but they sent her to the library. *How could she be dead?* Little Jade thought. *She was just sleeping. The bed is still warm.*

The maids spent the day decorating the house with white cloth. Yards of white fabric draped around the ancestor altar in the family hall. A newly carved wooden tablet with Little Jade's grandmother's name was added to the altar. A pair of tall white pillar candles burned on either side of the altar. Long strips of white hemp hung from the ceiling beams of the family hall. A pair of paper dolls stood on either side of the family altar—the grandmother's servants in the underworld. The maids were making mourning robes out of white hemp for everyone. All the servants tied a white sash around their heads and waists to show respect for the dead.

The old nanny had asked the letter-writer to inform all the relatives. Little Jade wondered if her father would come back. Maybe her father didn't want to come back.

In the evening, the grandmother was placed in the family hall in a coffin. She was wearing her best silk gown, a shimmering royal blue fabric trimmed with gold with matching slippers. Death did not remove the furrow between her brows. It was as if she was still enduring painful thoughts. The rich gown covered her slight body. Her thin fingers folded across her chest. Her face was the color of incense ash, and her hair was neatly oiled and combed smoothly. Two monks in yellow robes chanted in unison beside her. Without a family member present to make decisions, the accountant allocated minimum funds for a bare-bones funeral for the matriarch of the house. She would be there for seven days and nights. A full funeral would have taken forty-nine days, as was the funeral for Little Jade's great-grandfather.

Relatives sent condolences, but no one came to pay respects because they did not want to travel when the roads were not safe. Many were planning to move south to escape the chaos of the war, and some had left already. The household was in flux, and news from the outside world was not peaceful.

Little Jade was no longer allowed to sleep in the grandmother's bedroom. The servants moved her belongings to a guest room.

Little Jade was awakened by noise outside the windows early in the morning. She opened the windows, and looked out eagerly, thinking that perhaps her father had returned. The morning air was chilly. Little Jade could see Orchid in the near distance, helping the gardener drain water from the goldfish pond. The gardener used a large net to scoop up the fish. Orchid separated the goldfish and put them into terra cotta urns. Little Jade watched Orchid put her hands in the water to play with the goldfish, laughing. Her hands were red from the cold, but she didn't seem to mind. As Little Jade looked on through the open window, her breath turned into white fog. Her father was still not home.

Little Jade put on her padded jacket and pants. She had wanted to join Orchid and play with the fish, but she changed her mind. The house was quiet. She tiptoed to the kitchen. On the stove, a pot of porridge was warming over the dying ashes of the coals. Little Jade knew the porridge was for breakfast. She opened the screened food closet, took out a piece of sweet red bean cake and bit into it. The oily sweet cake was chewy and stuck to her teeth.

The back door opened silently at the touch of her fingertips. Outside, she almost stepped on a chicken. The chickens must have been hungry because they thought someone had come to feed them and were making grumbled noises of approval. Little Jade went over to the barn and took out a basket full of dried corn, scattering kernels over the ground. She watched the chickens busily pecking at the yellow dirt as she finished the last bite of her red beab cake. She rubbed her oily hands on the sides of her pants and squatted down to play with the small yellow chicks, letting them peck at her hands, even though their beaks were sharp. She picked up a yellow chick with black dots on its head and felt the small body. The chick was soft in her palm. She stuck her fingers under the tiny wings for warmth. The downy chick trembled as her cold fingers slid beneath its tender feathers.

Little Jade felt something tugging at her pants. She turned around and was face-to-face with an old hen. It had pecked through the outer layer of her padded cotton pants. It looked angrily at her with bits of white cotton fiber hanging from its beaks. Little Jade put down the chick, got up and kicked at the flock of chickens, sending them away, flying and screeching.

She walked into the vegetable garden and looked around. The dried squash vines hung from the arbor. She pulled down a strand of dried leaves and crushed them into small pieces that slipped through her fingers. A few large squashes had rotted through, leaving behind brown fiber in the shapes of the original fruits. The wheat field next to the vegetable garden was naked, no longer green. The farmers had harvested the crop weeks ago. Bundles of hay were piled up in the middle of the wheat field. Stubbles of wheat plants dotted the yellow earth.

She looked straight ahead and saw the bamboo forest green against the pale purple sky. She walked through the vegetable garden. Crowds of brown sparrows pecked at the overgrown vegetation. The pea pods had popped open, and the seeds had been eaten by birds or carried away by ants. The leaves of the cabbages were blue with dark purple veins and thick like giant seashells. They opened to let out tall stems full of small yellow flowers, rising high from the hearts, luring the last white butterflies of the season.

Little Jade stopped at the edge of the bamboo forest, standing under the shadow where the dark green moss grew. She could hear the forest—the rustle of bamboo leaves sighing and sighing at the urging of the autumn wind. She remembered her grandmother sighing whenever she stopped in the middle of her needlework. She would look up at her grandmother, questioning her with her eyes.

She would sigh again, and say, "You don't understand. In this life, seeds are seeds and fruits are fruits. Little Jade, remember: Plant good seeds in this life and you will harvest good fruits in your next life. Whatever happened to me in my life was already decided before I was born. I must have taken more than I gave in my previous life, and I have tasted bitter fruits this time around."

Little Jade stood there thinking hard. *What was the seed and what was the fruit? What seeds were planted by my mother, by father? Does my mother ever think about me?* Little Jade reached for her necklace, touching the pendant with the tips of her fingers. *My mother wanted to protect me and watch me grow up. Father said so. She is out there, somewhere far away, with my younger sister. Even if I someday see my mother, will I be able to recognize her? Will she recognize me? Where is father? What if he doesn't come back?* Her thoughts stopped as she faced the bamboo forest in front of her.

For the very first time, Little Jade was afraid to enter the bamboo forest. She knew that she would get lost among the bamboo shoots that had grown into slender trees since she was last there. There must be many more green bamboo snakes in the forest. Each bamboo branch would be occupied by a snake of matching color, waiting in the dark, its tongue darting like the thin red light at the tip of a burning incense stick. In the piles of rotted leaves, brown frogs with yellow stripes sang in one great throaty voice, while the black, shiny ear-shaped fungi listened. She was certain that if she went into the forest she would trip on the new shoots and lose her shoes. Her hair would become tangled in the poisonous spider's web, and her cries would be drowned in the wind as the snakes ate her alive. Only the black ear fungus would hear her, but there was no one it could tell. There was no one to tell if she died. No one would ever find out. Little Jade was all by herself. The bamboo leaves were shrilling in the wind. There was no one to listen to her, to hold her hands. There was no one to comfort her, to braid her hair or to wipe clean her eyes and nose and the corners of her mouth.

Little Jade didn't know how long she had been standing there, but she finally stopped crying. She wiped her face with both sleeves. She rubbed her eyes with fingers still oily from the sweet red bean cake. She dug the tips of her shoes into the mossy ground, smearing the smooth green surface into dark shiny mud. She turned around and saw that the sun was high. The bright rays jabbed her eyes like needles. Her nose was stuffy and her face felt hot. Little Jade wanted to go back to her bed. She ran through the vegetable garden.

As soon as Little Jade opened the back door, she heard unfamiliar voices in the family hall. Her heart leapt into her mouth as she walked toward the voices. Little Jade saw her father. He was kneeling next to the coffin, his face buried in his arms. He was crying. His new wife knelt next to him, talking to him in a low voice. She was wearing a turquoise gown. She offered the father her pink handkerchief. Her fingernails were narrow and long. They were painted dark red, the color of the strings of the dried red pepper hung by the kitchen door.

No one noticed Little Jade, except the old nanny who went over to her and squatted down, facing her. She carefully picked off strands of hair that stuck to Little Jade's cheeks and smoothed them behind her ears. Little Jade stood still, letting the old nanny fuss over her. She stared at her father who stood at the other side of the room. He was looking at her and so was his wife. Little Jade tried to smile at him. But he did not respond. The old nanny said, "Young Master and Mistress, why don't you two go to your room and rest a while? You must be tired from the journey. I'll take Little Jade to wash up." The old nanny stood up, took Little Jade's hand and walked out of the family hall. Little Jade turned around to get one last glimpse of her father, but he wasn't looking at her any more.

* * *

The honeymooners retired to their quarters. The servants took their luggage and placed it against the wall. An Ling and Silver Pearl occupied the West wing of the family compound. It was a connected suite of rooms along a sheltered corridor that faced the courtyard. An Ling took off his jacket and asked the maid to run a bath for him. Silver Pearl also demanded warm water to wash her face. It had been a long and dusty journey.

Silver Pearl went into the bedroom and lay on the bed, facing the ceiling. She kicked off her shoes and let her toes stretch inside her silk stockings. She covered her face with her right hand. Five long red nails rested on her left cheek like bloody scratch marks. She closed her eyes, breathing in her own perfume. Tired, she lay perfectly still, nearly drifting off to sleep. The maid came in to inform her that the water was ready. She entered the bathroom, stood over the basin of steaming water, and splashed it on her face. She straightened up in front of the mirror, looking at her reflected image. Her skin was sallow and her lips were dry. She opened a jar of cream and spread it thickly over her face.

Holding a hairbrush in her hand, Silver Pearl returned to the bedroom and saw her husband smoking a cigarette. He was listening to music from a hand-cranked phonograph machine, another purchase from the city.

A single lamp illuminated half the bedroom. Dim yellow light caressed the bed, a watercolor landscape scroll hung on the wall, an ashtray on the night table. A pair of man's leather slippers was placed beside the bed. An Ling sunk into the sofa, arms folded across his chest, his eyes half closed, listening to a woman's low and throaty crooning:

"Cannot forget, cannot forget you

Cannot forget your mistakes

Cannot forget the things you did

Cannot forget the walks in the rain

Cannot forget the embraces in the wind…"

His eyelashes fluttered briefly and his brows knitted more tightly, but otherwise he sat motionless. The smoke of the cigarette was rising and rising, curling upward to heaven, but there were no prayers—there was nothing to tell.

"Forgotten, forgotten

the wind chime is telling me

to forget, forget…you…"

Who was he thinking of, Silver Pearl wondered as she watched the red spark fall from the tip of his cigarette, turned to gray ash.

"An Ling."

Silver Pearl looked at her husband and called his name. He did not move. She let out a deep and lingering sigh. She was annoyed, but tried to suppress her irritation.

"Why don't you answer me?" she asked. "You've been lying there like a piece of wood. Why don't you take a bath to wash off the dust? You will feel better." She softened her voice. "An Ling, don't be so quiet. You can tell me what's on your mind. Are you thinking about your mother? You mustn't. What happened, happened. You can't change anything. An Ling, we must go on with our…"

"Will you stop?"

"Have I said something wrong? You shouldn't keep things inside. Why don't you talk to me?" An Ling opened his eyes. His brows were still knitted together. Even under the bright kerosene lamp, his face was dark—as if it was burning with a black fire from within. Silver Pearl fell silent immediately and sat in front of the vanity table. She massaged her cold-cream covered face with the tips of her fingers—something she had learned from a beauty salon in the city. When she was done, she wiped her fingers clean, picked up a pack of cigarettes, and lit one with a slim silver lighter.

"An Ling, do you want another cigarette?"

An Ling turned toward his wife and saw the reflection of her face in the mirror. It was covered in grease. He hesitated, and then said, "I'll get my own." He took a pipe and a silver box from a drawer, and scooped up some black paste into his pipe with a small silver spoon. Silver Pearl smiled and put her cigarette into the ashtray. She helped him to shape the black opium paste into small lumps, getting the opium lamp ready for him. The air soon became potent with the mixed scents of opium and cigarette smoke. This was the only time she could be helpful to him. He handed her his pipe and nodded, and she took in the sweet smelling smoke. It felt better than the smoke of a cigarette.

In the haze of the opium smoke, images appeared to An Ling and disappeared in the air, distorted, changing. There was vast sunshine from another time. Someone was weeping under a quilt. And Mother, Mother's hand approaching. In this vision, her face was sad, and her hair had the scent and warmth of his favorite pillow. As An Ling reached out to the image of his mother, her face changed, then disappeared, and the season changed. He murmured something to himself, and his arms encircled Silver Pearl's waist pulling her closer to him.

The man and the woman entangled in separate dreams. The night before his mother's burial, the son wrestled with his past and future. The heaving of bodies could be heard from the family hall. The dead woman lay undisturbed in the coffin. Beside her, two monks chanted in unison, like a river flowing, never-ending and unhurried. Night grew deeper and the chanting went on, oblivious to the stifled groans from the bedroom.

* * *

Funeral music came out of woodwind instruments. It sounded like the high-pitched wailing of a woman. Every now and then the gong rang solemnly, reaching the outer corners of the house, and startling the animals in the barn. The sun was bright. Little Jade could see a small band of musicians, dressed in white, performing in the front yard.

Everyone was wearing a hooded mourning robe of white hemp. They stood in the family hall watching two men lower the lid onto the coffin and sealing it with long shining nails. The room was embarrassingly quiet. There were dark circles under Little Jade's father's eyes. He had not talked to his daughter, and he still avoided looking at her.

"Gong! Gong! Gong!" The loud music and sound of hammering frightened Little Jade. Panicked, she began to cry. Everyone in the room turned to look at her. The old nanny took out her handkerchief and wiped Little Jade's eyes. She too sobbed uncontrollably, her thin white hair loosened from her bun. She said, "Cry, Little Jade. Your grandmother is dead. Your poor grandmother, not even her own son sheds a tear for her." She turned to An Ling and addressed him in a hoarse cry. "Where is your heart? You can't even cry for your mother? Aren't you ashamed? I should have hired mourners to cry at your mother's funeral."

Soon the family hall was filled with the sound of An Ling's weeping. It was a cleansing sound. The spirit of the dead rose from the coffin and drifted out of the house of Su, satisfied. She was heading toward the glorious west, riding on the incense smoke toward the bright light of heaven. There, she would be rewarded for all her chanting and suffering of her life past. The grandmother was buried on a sunny hillside. That night the sky was full of bright autumn stars.

CHAPTER 7:
SILVER PEARL'S HOMECOMING
1942

An Ling suggested that she take Little Jade to stay with her parents while he went to collect rent money from the tenant farmers. Silver Pearl jumped at the chance to go home. *Returning to her childhood home would be glorious*, Silver Pearl thought. *She would go back to her village as a rich man's wife, a lady from the big house.*

Silver Pearl was carrying An Ling's baby. It was too dangerous for a young pregnant woman and a child to stay in a big house without men, An Ling said—especially since bandits roamed all over the countryside these days. They would take just a bodyguard and a maid with them this time. The rest of the servants could choose to stay at the big house until their return or go back to their own homes.

An Ling was thinking that this would be the first time he had looked after his inheritance since the death of his grandfather. He had finally picked up the burden of providing for his family.

Silver Pearl was thinking about wearing her patent leather high-heeled shoes in her village. They would make her waist sway like a willow branch when she walked, as if she had bound feet. She would wear her leopard fur coat, a luscious golden fur with thick black dots. She could still fit into one of the gowns despite her larger waistline, thanks to an alteration that was made hastily by a tailor in the city.

People would gather to watch as she disembarked from the horse-drawn wagon in front of her parents' modest house. They would whisper to each other, "Who is this elegant city lady? What is she doing in our humble village?" They would not be able to recognize her with her new hair and her new clothes.

She was returning home to her parents and to her father's tofu shop where Silver Pearl grew up eating soft tofu and drinking soymilk. Her mother's breasts had been dry after she gave birth. Silver Pearl's father fed her by dipping a corner of a clean cotton handkerchief in soymilk for her to suck on. Her father said that Silver Pearl's fine skin came from being a tofu man's daughter. Silver Pearl thought that she had inherited her lovely skin from her mother.

She had grown up in the tofu shop, helping out in the dark back room with the familiar smell of soybeans, seeing her father smiling and bowing to the customers, wearing cotton and never silk. Her younger brother was always tied to her back so her parents could work. It had never occurred to Silver Pearl that there was a way to live other than being the daughter of her parents in a tofu shop.

Each day her mother had worked the counter while her father made deliveries. In the evenings, both parents worked in the backroom to make new batches of tofu for the next day. The shop sold a variety of tofu: dried brown squares for stir-frying; tofu skins the size of a a chopping board for making vegetarian rolls for Buddhists, and left over pieces that they shredded into tofu strings to be sold cheaply and by the handful next to the counter. Squares of tofu of different degrees of firmness were covered with cheesecloth and stacked high on wooden trays. A big bucket of steaming tofu pudding was scooped with a shallow ladle into customers' bowls and topped off with ginger-flavored syrup and a sprinkle of crushed peanuts.

Every night, Silver Pearl had fallen asleep with the smell of fermented soybean that soured the air. People called her father the Tofu Man. He was always happy and her mother never complained. But her mother's once-beautiful hands became rough, and the skin on her fingertips split open into many small red slits in the wintertime. Silver Pearl remembered one day when her mother had finished working, and she was soaking her hands in a bucket of hot water. She had closed her eyes with such satisfaction that the corners of her mouth and eyes relaxed. Afterwards, she carefully wiped off the water with her blue apron and rubbed soybean oil on her hands. It was then that her mother told Silver Pearl that her father was not really her father, and about how she had met and married him.

She had been a maid in a rich man's house. She used to buy tofu when Silver Pearl's father wheeled his cart by the back door of the mansion. When the young master made her pregnant, the mistress of the house gave her some money and sent her away. She ran into the tofu man in the market place, where she was wandering around with nowhere to go. He took her home and made her his wife, and Silver Pearl was born seven months later. She had had another child with the tofu man. The son had died in infancy. With the money she was given by the mistress of the big house, she helped the tofu man set up a shop in the center of the village. He no longer had to push the wheelbarrow cart.

Silver Pearl remembered her mother telling her, "You are not a tofu man's daughter. In your blood there is the fragrance of books and the nobility of a learned man. There is another life: a rich man's life. I have lived inside such a man's house. A house filled with mahogany furniture inlaid with mother-of-pearl. There were winding roads that weaved through many gardens, a garden for each court, and a carving of eight gods on a boat made of an entire tusk of ivory. There was a board game made of black and white jade pieces, a porcelain tea set trimmed with gold, and the library filled with different musical instruments. Out of the ancient harps flew winding melody. The master, your real father, used to teach me to sing poems. I used to sing this song for him:

"When the moon lit up the empty sea,

Mermaids' tears turned into pearls.

When the sun warmed the Blue Acre Mountain,

> Smoke steamed from the rocks of jade.
>
> Such feelings should be remembered for the days to come,
>
> Yet even then it was already in vain."

Silver Pearl remembered that her mother sang in a sweet low voice, and her face flushed with memories. Silver Pearl knew the reason she had been given her name: to signify that she is a pearl of a girl and her mother's only precious jewel.

Listening to her mother, Silver Pearl closed her eyes, imagining herself a real princess lost in the chaos of changing dynasties. She imagined that in her veins flowed imperial royal blood from the previous dynasty. She smiled when imagining a shining pearl covered with dust in the back room of the tofu shop. Silver Pearl was unwilling to be poor all her life. She did not want to live the fate of a tofu man's daughter.

When Silver Pearl was ten, her mother took her to a fortune-teller in the market place. Silver Pearl held her baby brother while her mother haggled with the farmers over the prices of vegetables. Then her mother noticed a small banner of yellow fabric with three large black characters written on it: "Iron-Mouth Wu." An old man in a dirty, faded blue gown, with a waxy yellow face and the beard of a mountain goat, was sitting on a bench, reading a book with a torn cover. Silver Pearl's mother went over and bowed, and said, "Mr. Fortune teller, Sir, please tell me my daughter's fortune."

The fortune-teller lifted his head slowly. "A girl? You want to know your daughter's fortune? How about the fortune of your son?" Silver Pearl remembered traces of red in his turgid eyes.

Her mother put her basket of food on the ground, and picked up her son from Silver Pearl's arms, patting his back. "No, Sir, I want to know my daughter's fortune."

"Very well. Little girl, come closer so I can look at you carefully."

Silver Pearl peered at the fortuneteller distrustfully. Her mother freed one of her hands and pushed her toward the fortuneteller, saying, "Don't be shy. Let Mr. Fortuneteller take a good look at you."

"Her eyebrows are like willow leaves, her forehead open and high. Her eyes move fast like poured mercury. Her nose is straight and her nostrils hidden. Her lips open a gap, not too bad. Her ears are close to her head, a sign of modesty. She doesn't look like she's from a poor family."

"How about her future?" the mother interrupted. "We are not here to hear about the past. The past is easy."

The fortuneteller cleared his throat and spat into the dust next to his feet. "Madam, you are right. The past is easy. It is the future that is hard. Big changes are coming soon. People are spilling grains on the ground, letting animals eat full-grain. This is a bad omen. The people will be punished for wasting food."

"Sir, I'm a humble woman. What is going on in the world does not concern me. The dynasty changes and the emperor changes, but whatever happens, people still live the way they always have. In this village, heaven is high and the emperor is far away. I want to know my daughter's fortune, and that is all."

"Madam, you're wrong this time. The changes that are coming are different from any dynasty changes in the history of China. I don't know whether it is a blessing or a calamity, but we will be witnessing changes that are unlike anything that had ever happened before. The emperor will not be far away any more. What's the use of knowing one person's fortune? Nothing can alter the forces that spring from the changes of the stars, the earth, the sun, and the moon."

"Mr. Fortuneteller, please don't waste your breath telling me what's going to happen to the emperor. I won't pay you for it. All I want to know is my daughter's fortune."

"Yes, Madam. This little girl will be able to see more than you and I can ever see. She will travel to far places. She will marry a rich husband and she will have a son."

"Thank you, Mr. Fortuneteller." The mother bowed and bowed, and could not help smiling to herself as she counted three copper coins and placed them in the fortuneteller's palm. She walked away holding her daughter's hand, thinking that she knew it all along. Her daughter would not spend the rest of her life having children and growing old in a poor man's home. She would wear jewelry, and she would have servants. A rich husband meant that she would be taken care of all the days of her life. A son meant that she would not lose her husband to another woman. What more could any woman want? Good fortune!

***

Because of the fortune-teller, Silver Pearl knew, by the time she reached the marriageable age of fifteen, that her husband would be a learned gentleman from a rich family. She knew this on that sunny day when a young carpenter came into the tofu shop to buy a few pieces of dry tofu. He saw that Silver Pearl was pretty and started to tease her, saying that he bet she would taste just like the tender flesh of the softest tofu. Silver Pearl blushed and looked at him from the corners of her eyes, and she knew that he would never enter her life. She ignored his words and his broad shoulders under his work shirt, which was stained yellow with sweat. Her heart was jumping like a young deer, hitting her rib cage. The smell of fresh wood shavings and sweat, and the way he looked at her, was exciting. He was not handsome. He had heavy lips and thin mischievous eyes. But what she remembered most were his hands—thick and rough, large-knuckled, and covered with calluses.

Silver Pearl had noticed his hands when he gave her a red silk handkerchief. She did not want to accept his gift. But when the carpenter dropped a square silk handkerchief—light like air and slippery like water—into her hands, she held onto the redness with both hands as if she was holding a pool of blood from her own heart while his hands cupped around hers. Silver Pearl knew it wasn't proper and she was ashamed as she tried hard to stop herself from trembling. She felt the wet palms of his hands and the warmth of his fingers. She felt his gaze burning on her face, and she was afraid to look up and see him. She just kept looking at his hands.

Silver Pearl did not tell her mother about the silk handkerchief. She tied the red silk around her wrist when she went to sleep at night, and if she had dreams that night, she had forgotten them. She only knew that she wanted more, and she must have more. She wanted to be wrapped by the finest satin from head to toe every season of the year. And her husband's hands would be soft and white with a green jade ring on the index finger of his left hand. His long fingers would leisurely flip the pages of a book of poems from Tang Dynasty. He would never have to sweat to earn his livelihood.

The night before Silver Pearl's wedding, her mother talked throughout most of the night. She said, "My daughter, after tomorrow, you will belong to your husband's family. They say that a married daughter is like spilled water, never to be recovered. But when you become the young mistress of the Su family, don't forget your parents. Your father and I have worked hard all our lives, and we are no longer young. Parents raise sons to prevent hardship in their old age. Since your poor little brother died, you are all we have." The mother's voice broke. She wiped her eyes with her sleeve and continued. "I have prayed for this happy occasion ever since you were born. Your destiny is about to be realized. From now on, your life will be different. Always remember that even though you are An Ling's second wife, you are his proper wife—not a concubine. If the first wife ever comes back, she will be the concubine. The little girl of the first wife will have to call you 'Mother'. You will be married into the family with the full ceremony of a wife, nothing less. Treat the girl kindly, but you don't need to bribe her with candy or new clothes. Only concubines wanting to win the master's favor would do that. Don't heed the girl. She will soon become some other family's daughter-in-law.

"Don't mention the first wife. Think of her as dead. You are the wife now. Take care of your husband and bear him sons. Please your husband and fulfill his wishes so he won't go to other women."

* * *

On her wedding night, Silver Pearl sat on the slippery satin bed-spread, exhausted and confused. A bridesmaid was wiping away at tea stains on Silver Pearl's skirt. The room was crowded with bawdy wedding guests. It was the custom to have the guests carouse and make fun of the new couple in their wedding chamber. An Ling stood near the window, smoking a cigarette while he looked on as if he were a bystander. The wedding guests were drunk and laughing, their faces red and shiny. A distant cousin of An Ling's was particularly rowdy. He was a short heavy-set man. He shouted in a loud voice that resembled a broken gong, "We want the bride to sing a song!"

"Or dance for us!" someone echoed.

"If you don't agree, you will have to kiss the groom," the cousin declared. He smacked his lips loudly and the crowd roared.

"When is the bride going to have sons?" a woman chuckled.

"The sooner the better. The groom cannot wait!" Everyone laughed and applauded.

"Why doesn't the bride smile? Is she afraid of her wedding night?"

The cousin went over to An Ling and dragged him toward the bed and chanted, "The groom kisses the bride. The groom kisses the bride."

An Ling jerked his hand away from his cousin's grasp. The room quieted down for a moment. The bridesmaid quickly said: "The bride is shy and very tired. Why don't we ask the new couple to hold hands?"

The crowd applauded, covering their collective embarrassment. The groom was cheerless and in poor spirit. The bridesmaid pulled An Ling's hands and Silver Pearl's hands together. The guests were finally satisfied and left the room.

An Ling's hand was soft and white, just as Silver Pearl expected. Silver Pearl realized that she was still holding his hand after he has already let go of hers. She withdrew her fingers and lowered her head as far down as she could. She could feel her heart beating wildly, and her hands were shaking. She glanced at her skirt and saw the tea stain. A wave of blood rushed to her face as she recalled how the first wife's daughter broke the teacup earlier, splattering hot tea all over her red wedding skirt. When Silver Pearl looked up in a panic, she had been chilled by the sight of the little girl's stony face. She could tell, unmistakably, that Little Jade disliked her. Silver Pearl shot another glance at Little Jade and saw that she would not look at her. *It was intentional*, thought Silver Pearl.

An Ling blew out the double red candles. He said, "It's getting late. Go to sleep."

Moonlight filled the room with blue light and shadows. Silver Pearl stood up and started to undress. Her legs were numb. She struggled out of her wedding gown and crawled into bed in her long underwear. There was only one pillow and one quilt on the large spring mattress bed. It was the first time Silver Pearl had slept on a spring mattress. She sank into the soft bed, using a corner of the pillow and quilt, facing the wall. She could sense An Ling getting into the bed, his long, heavy body lying next to her. He did not use the pillow, but merely pulled half of the quilt over himself and slept.

It was not until the next morning that Silver Pearl got a good look at her husband. Looking at the face she had waited for all her life, she felt that she had known him all along, as if she had seen his face many times before, but she never felt a part of him belonged to her—not even now, when she was pregnant with his child.

An Ling was an impenetrable wall. Silver Pearl could not begin to guess his changing moods. She thought about that carpenter. She had known what he wanted. She knew that he was looking for her to smile. When she pretended to be angry and called him a dead man, how his heart must have ached! When he ate that soft tofu, she knew he thought of her. *Oh, it was easy*, Silver Pearl thought indulgently.

With An Ling, everything was difficult. She was clumsy in front of him. He did not pay attention to her. He thought nothing of her hair, clothes, and expensive, imported perfumes. He smiled blankly as she demanded his attention, complimenting her lightly. She could not create a chain to weigh him down. She knew An Ling took care of her only because she belonged to him. Silver Pearl still kept that silk handkerchief at the bottom of her trunk. She wondered whether she would encounter the carpenter when she returned to her parents' house. She wondered what he would think of her. The more she thought about it, the more she wanted to see him again—or rather, she wanted him to see her. Somehow, they would meet on the street, and with a look of recognition, they would greet each other casually, awkwardly. The village was small. The chance would come.

Chapter 8:
Step-grandparents' House

Inside the wagon, Little Jade pretended to sleep under a red coyote fur. Her father and stepmother were smoking cigarettes, narrowing their eyes as they blew out white curls of smoke. They were on their way to Little Jade's step-grandparents' house. Little Jade had said goodbye to Orchid two days ago when An Ling let the servants go. Orchid was to return to her family in the next village. Everybody scattered after the grandmother's death.

The driver whipped the horses as the wagon rolled down the bumpy hillside road. In the midst of the pounding of the horses' hooves, the driver sang against the fierce north wind. The wind tore words away from his lips as quickly as he uttered them and threw them into the mountains behind. He fought the wind and sang to warm his blood and to strengthen his nerves. The countryside was desolate and deadly quiet—except for the shrieks of ravens on the high branches of the pine trees and the howls of wolves from the mountains. The road ahead was deserted. The driver could not see any cooking smoke rising from the nearby villages. It was day, but the sky was dark and low. A storm was coming.

The driver clenched his teeth and whipped the horses harshly, calling: "Go faster!" The horses' neighing ripped open the boundless silence on these dangerous, abandoned roads, and made the travelers' hearts tremble with fear. The driver felt the hard iron of his handgun against his waist. Little Jade heard broken phrases of the driver's singing.

"The heaven is cruel... the heaven is blind... punishes the good, rewards the evil ... People are like pigs and dogs ... pieces of meat on a chopping board ... pieces of meat on a chopping board ..."

She hid her face under the longhaired fur rug, smelling the scent of dead animal skin and thick cigarette smoke. Little Jade listened to the pounding of the hooves.

Little Jade had heard many stories about the bandits. Orchid had told her that when the dark force of the earth and bright force of the heavens were not in harmony, there were bound to be catastrophes. Little Jade had asked why. Orchid said that she didn't know why and that she was only repeating what her grandfather had told her.

Orchid's grandfather was a cripple. His left leg was gone. He limped around with a walking stick. One leg of his trousers hung loosely. He had a hard brown face and a broad grin, and most of his teeth were missing. He was the leader of a gang of beggars that went from village to village asking for money and food. They knocked on the front and back doors of each house, chanting, "Masters and Mistresses, have a good heart, live a long life, give me some money, give me some food. Gold and silver roll into your house, have ten sons and ten daughters-in-law, good luck go to you, bad luck come to me, have a good heart, live a long life."

Little Jade's grandmother had had a good heart. Orchid had been sick when the old Mistress took her in from the beggar. The old beggar would come to visit Orchid several times a year. Whenever he saw Little Jade, he always politely called her "Little Lady." Grandmother would never let Little Jade stay in the kitchen to listen to the stories he told Orchid. Little Jade had to leave the kitchen until he left. Then she would beg Orchid to repeat his stories.

"The bandits have no families and no children," Orchid started one of her stories. "They smell like wild animals because they eat raw meat dripping with blood. During the famine, when all the animals are eaten, the bandits kill people and make steamed buns, using their meat for fillings. They tie the victim to a tree and cut off his legs and arms, piece by piece, while he's still alive. This way the meat stays fresh." Orchid told stories in a hushed voice, drawing Little Jade forward to listen.

"The bandits are a mean lot," Orchid continued. "When they run out of silver, they kidnap the sons of the rich and demand ransoms. But once someone is kidnapped, it's usually hopeless. If he doesn't die, he loses half his life anyway. The bandits cut off his tongue so he can't speak, pierce his eyes with a needle so he can't see, and fill his ears with hot candle wax so he can't hear. It would be worse to live than to die. The bandits are sent down by the heavenly emperor to purge the earth, to show that the gods are all-powerful and to test the wills of men, and to find out whether they curse or pray to heaven."

Maybe Orchid's grandfather used to be a bandit. He probably lost his leg in a battle. Afterwards, he couldn't ride a horse and couldn't be a bandit any more. Or maybe he was a victim, cursing the gods under his breath as he watched a bandit swing an ax at his leg, and fainted in his own blood. Or maybe he really was just a beggar, old and crippled, living in abandoned temples and eating wild dogs.

✳ ✳ ✳

An Ling left Little Jade at her step-grandparents' house and left. Accompanied by a bodyguard, he went to settle business affairs with a family member in the port city of Tianjin. He promised Little Jade that he would come back as soon as he could, so the family could spend the New Year together. Little Jade did not like it there. But she had no choice. It was too dangerous to live in the empty old house, the father said, for now the country was falling into what he called "large chaos." "During small chaos," he explained, "it is better to go into the city. During large chaos, it is better to hide in the country."

Each morning, the step-grandfather went off to work in his shop. The step-grandmother stayed home to look after her daughter and Little Jade. Silver Pearl had also brought a maid from the estate to help out around the small house. Silver Pearl's pregnancy was beginning to show. She spent most of the day with her mother. When Silver Pearl and her mother wanted to talk, one of them would give Little Jade a handful of candies and say, "Little Jade, why don't you go somewhere to play?"

The house was small, with only three rooms. There were no wings, no courtyards, and no front yard. A small kitchen in the back was dark and full of the smells of oil and smoke. It connected to a narrow strip of back yard where a few old hens and their chicks walked to and fro. The ground was littered with chicken droppings. The main room also doubled as a dining room with the ancestral altar on the wall. The altar displayed bright pink paper flowers in a porcelain vase, two red candle stubs in yellow brass holders, a pewter urn without incense, ancestral spirit tablets, and small statues of different gods: a fat Buddha smiling and holding his belly, which spilled out of the opening of his robe, and a white-robed Kwan Yin standing on a lotus blossom, her bare feet visible beneath her flowing skirt. She was holding a bottle in her left hand and a branch of willow in her right hand. She smiled at Little Jade with recognition. Little Jade was drawn to the statue. She went up close and reached over to touch the edge of her robe. Dust came off the statue and onto her fingers.

Looking at the statue of Kwan Yin, Little Jade felt somehow comforted. She knelt down and closed her eyes and prayed, "Kwan Yin Pusa, please help me, help me." She lowered her eyes and recited the lotus sutra from memory. The sutra is long and reassuring and tells how Kwan Yin will help anyone in any danger, should it be fire, flood, attack by fierce animals or bandits, just pray to Kwan Yin and everything will be fine. She forgot certain lines but repeated the lines she remembered over and over. It made her feel as if her grandmother was next to her, right then and there.

Little Jade stood up and looked around the room. She saw the round dining table in the middle of the room. Six chairs surrounded it, all painted a dark red. The walls were decorated with square pictures drawn on red paper. One depicted a naked fat boy sitting on a lily pad, playing with two jumping carps—a lucky symbol for sons, and another one was of the God of Longevity who was pictured as a laughing old man with a long white beard and a walking stick. There was a picture of the God of Good Fortune who had a square face and fat ears. His earlobes drooped down to his shoulders. A bowl of fresh fruit sat on the table. She took an orange and returned to her room.

Her room was partitioned off from the main room. It had no windows. In the narrow space, there was a small hard bed and a small square wooden table. On top of the table, there was a red candle in a white china dish, a jade-colored cup with leftover sweet tea inside, and some red strings for tying braids. A red blanket was thrown over the bed. Her shoes and a chamber pot were under the bed. The room was cold despite the small coal stove burning in the corner.

She climbed onto the bed and pulled the blanket over her lap. She started to peel the orange, but the juice from the skin got into her eyes and stung. She tossed the orange onto the floor and watched it roll toward the corner of the room stopping next to the stove. She pulled the blanket over her head. She wanted to block off the light of the day and the loneliness inside her, but she did not know how. Closing her eyes, she continued to pray, her hands pressing against each other next to her forehead. How she missed her grandmother, and how she wished that her father was around. She did not belong here, or anywhere else. Silver Pearl is going to be having a baby, a baby that will also be her father's– a baby that will have both a mother and a father. Little Jade's thought slowed as she squeezed her eyes shut, and squeezed herself smaller, smaller, into the shape of a baby, an infant. She was trying to remember her mother. She thought of how her mother had carried her inside her belly, and of how she must have held her after she was born. She pictured herself in the arms of her mother. She could imagine her mother looking at her, cooing at her. Little Jade drifted off to sleep thinking of how safe she would have been and felt in her mother's arms.

✳ ✳ ✳

"The window will bring light into the house," said Silver Pearl. She leaned against the wall, her arms folded over her barely protruding belly. She watched the carpenter squatting on the floor, taking out his tools from a wooden box. After finding out that the carpenter had opened his own shop, Silver Pearl had asked her father to hire him to build a glass window in her parents' house.

The carpenter looked up at her and smiled. "Yes, Mistress, there will be plenty of light. This is the best quality glass. Look—clear and smooth like still water." He picked up a small piece of glass and held it in front of his face.

Silver Pearl glanced at the carpenter's face through the glass pane. His smile was distorted by the glass. She said, "They say that glass is made of sand. I can't believe it. Wouldn't you say that modern science is like magic?"

"Yes, Mistress, maybe one day they can make a house out of only glass," the carpenter said, and stood up. He was a full head taller than Silver Pearl.

Feeling uncomfortable, Silver Pearl turned and walked away, saying: "Nonsense, who would want to live in a glass house? You may as well not have a house at all."

Silver Pearl smiled to herself, musing over the idea of a glass house. Then she felt a stark coldness as she imagined her life being played out like an opera for everyone to see. The carpenter was hammering to break open a hole in the wall. Silver Pearl imagined his muscled arm tensing and relaxing as each stroke of the hammer fell. Dong! Dong! Dong! Dong! The sound of the hammer echoed in the quiet house.

✳ ✳ ✳

Clank! Crash!

"Aiya, I broke one." The carpenter shook his head nervously.

"It's only a small piece, not worth much," Silver Pearl said lightly, lifting one eyebrow. She glanced sideways at the carpenter.

"Only you can say that, Mistress. This small piece of pane is worth enough to feed my wife and children for days." The carpenter wiped his forehead with the back of his hand.

"Don't worry. I'll pay for this one too. How many children do you have?" Silver Pearl sat down on a chair and crossed her legs.

"Thank you, Mistress. I have two sons and my wife is pregnant with another one. Looks like you are expecting one yourself. I hope it's going to be a fat son." Bowing, the carpenter smiled warmly, the veins on his forehead bulging.

"Why don't you clean up this mess?" Silver Pearl's right foot dangled in the air, and she glanced at the embroidered flowers on her red silk shoe.

"Yes, yes, I'll get a broom. Be careful not to touch them. They cut like knives."

"How long will it take you to finish this?" Silver Pearl asked as she looked up.

"I'll try to finish it today. You can't leave a hole in the wall overnight. The weather's too cold."

The carpenter was cleaning up the broken glass pieces. Suddenly, Silver Pearl was tired of the carpenter. His breath reeked of garlic and his bald head was tinged green, like a duck's egg. His eyes were downcast when he talked to her, and he smiled and bowed, constantly showing his yellow teeth.

She had wanted to see him, but he was no longer that tall man with sweaty arms and earnest eyes who had held her hands across the counter and wouldn't let go. Now she didn't know why she ever insisted on having a glass window installed in this house. Her father said that the window would look odd in such a modest house. She argued that the house was too dark for her parents' eyes. But Silver Pearl knew that her parents would have preferred to have the money instead— to worry about eyesight is frivolous in a poor family. She looked at the big hole in the wall. It looked like a punishment for Silver Pearl's headlong pursuit of her own wishes.

Cold wind poured into the house, slapping her face until her cheeks burned. Through the hole she could see the villagers gathering to gawk. She turned around, knowing that they were pointing at the window—some smiling and some frowning to themselves and to each other, all talking and joking about her. The window seemed enormous. The carpenter used up all the glass panes in his shop to build it. During the day, the window was filled with the villagers' watchful eyes, and there were always a few neighborhood children knocking on it, pressing their faces against the glass panes. Day and night, chilling wind leaked through the gaps between the window and the wall, rushing into the house. Silver Pearl's mother put a red cloth over the window as a makeshift curtain. No one ever opened it, not even to let light in during the day. The curtain was like a cover over the cage of a wild animal. There was an animal breathing and walking restlessly behind the curtain, waiting to emerge.

The sunlight entered the house through the curtained window and imbued the room with a shimmering red glow, casting waves of light on the walls and ceiling. The waves rose and fell like tides as the wind blew the rippling curtain.

From inside the house, the world beyond the curtain appeared as a shadow theater. Behind the curtain, Little Jade could see silhouettes of neighborhood children waving their arms, fighting with each other to enter into the house. She could hear their chattering voices as they elbowed one another. Someone in the back was crying: "I want to see! I want to see!"

It was a pointed, dry, insistent voice rising above all other noises, pushing into the room by the gushing frigid wind. It was a small girl shorter than Little Jade, with two stiff braids sticking out from behind her neck, her nose running, her fingers balled into fists, looking hot-eyed at the backs of the tall boys pushing each other beside the window. "I want to see," she cried again, "I want to see!"

Her voice drove Little Jade toward the window. She lifted the curtain. Abruptly, Little Jade stood face to face with five boys. There was a moment of silence as their breath and her breath clouded the glass pane between them. The boys' startled faces yielded to uncertain smiles, eyes squinting and mouths hanging open, as if they could not decide whether to stay or to run away. Maybe it was the troubling red light that compelled Little Jade to pound on the window, twisting her face at the boys, as she shouted, "Go away, go away, go away!"

The faces behind the glass started to twist, mimicking her. The older boys began to pound on the window from the outside, and the small ones followed. The window became cloudy as Little Jade breathed harder and faster, pounding and pounding. The window was shaking under her fists. Scared, Little Jade stopped pounding, and she backed away from the window, but it continued to vibrate on its own. Pieces of glass broke off, making shattering sounds. As each piece fell off, it caught the sunlight and shone brilliantly for an instant until it crashed to the ground, raising a splash of light dust that slowly dispersed.

CHAPTER 9:
STEP-GRANDFATHER

The carpenter came back and mended the window. Little Jade's fingers had been cut by small pieces of glass caught in the cuffs of her pants that she had tried to pick out, one by one. The shining grains of glass got stuck under her fingernails; blood oozed from the tips of her fingers.

Nothing seemed to go right in the step-grandparents house. One night, Silver Pearl woke up in the middle of the night, hungry. She went to the kitchen to look for something to eat and tripped over a small wooden stool by the kitchen door. Little Jade had left the stool there, after using it earlier in the day when she sat on it as she helped her step-grandmother shell peas.

Awakened by noises, Little Jade climbed out of her bed and watched Silver Pearl from behind the shadows of the people huddling around her outside the kitchen—the neighbor women, the maid, the herbal doctor, and the step-grandmother. The quivering flame in the oil lamp lit up Silver Pearl's face. It was white as a sheet of blank paper. The expression on her face was like meaningless words scratched by a desperate illiterate. The bloodstain beneath her was growing.

A neighborhood woman told her to go back to sleep. Little Jade went back to her room and climbed into the bed. But for a long time, she could not sleep. Every time she closed her eyes, the same image appeared—a circle of whispering shadows surrounding a fire, and next to the fire a bleeding woman, eyes closed, moaning weakly in her own darkness. It was a primitive ritual that could only happen in ghost stories during long dark nights.

Fearing a miscarriage, Silver Pearl left her parent's house before daybreak, accompanied by the maid and her mother. They traveled on a hired wagon, and then they boarded a train for the hospital in the city of Tianjin where An Ling had gone weeks earlier.

✳ ✳ ✳

The next morning, Little Jade found her step-grandfather hunched next to the dining table, smoking his pipe. On the table, there was an extra set of chopsticks, an empty bowl, a dish of pickled vegetables, a dish of salted fish, and crumbled peanut shells. He had eaten already. Little Jade went to the kitchen and got some water to wet her face and rinse her mouth. A pot of porridge was warming on top of the stove. She opened the lid and white steam rose from the pot to warm her face.

✳ ✳ ✳

Little Jade walked out the front door, into the sunshine and down the street with a bottle in her hand. She was going to the liquor shop to get her grandfather something to soothe his stomach. A wind of dust hit the her face and filled her mouth. She rubbed her eyes until tears came out. Her mouth tasted of mud. The street was empty. Houses and trees lined the street like shadows from another time. The sunlight beat over her head. The weather was summer-like in the middle of winter. It had been sunny for days. The first few days, people had come out to sit under the sun. They spread their clothes and quilts under the sun to rid them of dampness. They hung their straw mats under the sun to kill the eggs of bugs that nestled in the straw.

The harvest was over, people had nothing to do, and they were grateful for the abnormally warm weather. They gathered in the open space in front of the temple to tell stories and improvise operas. They sat on the wooden benches that they had carried on their backs. Old men played games of chess under the sun.

When the evening came, people brought out tables and benches so they could eat outside, fanning themselves all the while. The sky was clear enough to count the stars. They slept on sun-soaked straw mats. Life went on this way for a while, but then the weather had become hotter and hotter, as if the sun were coming closer and closer to the earth. When people greeted each other on the street, they mumbled, "What a good sun!"

* * *

Then the winds had come, lifting the dust off the streets and settling it on the rooftops, and blowing into the eyes of people and animals. Almost overnight, the flies came too—green-headed and red-winged, large and humming like bees. They were everywhere, in every kitchen, and every backyard. A big swarm of them over the garbage heaps. There was another swarm over the night soil pond. People stayed inside and slept beneath mosquito netting and covered their food with screens.

In the empty street there was only Little Jade and a yellow dog. The dog sniffed along the base of the walls and then went from one tree to another, leaving its marks. Its tail wagged lazily. Little Jade was sweating under her quilted jacket. Another wind swept up the dust, forcing her eyes to close. When she opened her eyes again, the dog was gone. She saw thousands of shining dust motes spinning in the air, finer than snow, heavier than fog, falling and falling, settling in her hair, on her skin.

It was getting hotter. Little Jade put the bottle on the ground and took off her jacket, feeling her clothes sticking to her back. She shook the jacket, placed it under her arm, and kept on walking. The liquor shop was near.

An old woman came out to fill the bottle with yellow liquor. Her red eyes looked to Little Jade like the eyes of a dead fish. Little Jade paid her, and the woman gave back a few coins of change. "Little girl," she said, "you shouldn't be playing outside. Go home now."

Little Jade muttered that she was not playing. She was getting things for her grandfather.

The old woman said urgently, "Go home! Go home! There's a plague!" Only then did Little Jade notice that the woman was wearing a small flower made of white strings which marked a death in the family. The shop owner, the man with a garlic-shaped nose, was dead. She must be his widow. Little Jade did not know what a plague was, but she felt the weight of the old woman's words, uttered from her thin lips with a tremor.

Little Jade turned and headed back home, walking faster and faster, almost running, holding the bottle with both hands. The sunlight was grazing the back of her neck, as if gnawing with small, sharp teeth, slowly and persistent. It inflicted traces of pain on her skin, seeping into her blood, making her feverish.

✻ ✻ ✻

Her step-grandfather was in the main room. He was sitting on a short stool, bending over, weaving a basket with stalks of bamboo skin. His knees secured the sides of the basket while his hands flipped swiftly in and out. Pale green bamboo stalks scattered around his feet. He put the basket on the ground, stretched his back, and looked up to smile at Little Jade.

"Here's the bottle." Little Jade put it on top of the dining table.

He looked down again. His hands went through the stalks on the ground and decided on one. He held a stem in front of his face, trimming it a little here and there with a small knife. Little Jade squatted down to look at the unfinished basket. Thin unwoven stalk ends thrust out along the edge of the basket, arching gracefully.

Little Jade ran her fingers over the surface of the basket, the criss-crossing green bamboo skin felt smooth and familiar. She thought of the bamboo forest back at home and closed her eyes. Waves of green shadows rose and fell in her mind and she felt a coolness climbing up her spine.

"Isn't bamboo useful?" her step-grandfather said, trimming a stalk. "You can weave it into baskets and curtains, and make it into houses and fans. We eat with bamboo chopsticks and sit on bamboo stools. It's strong yet flexible. It bends, but does not break. And bamboo shoots are delicious."

"Just like a gentleman," Little Jade interrupted, feeling unsettled. She had heard these words before.

"Yes, like a gentleman. Perhaps Confucius said that." The step-grandfather wove a new stalk into the basket. "But I think bamboo is better than a gentleman," he said, "Every part of a bamboo tree is useful. A gentleman is worthless, in a time like this."

His words reminded Little Jade of the old woman at the liquor store. "Grandpa," she started reluctantly, feeling the words choking at her throat.

"Yes, Little Jade."

"Old Wong is dead. His widow sold me the liquor. And here's the change." Little Jade took the coins from her pocket, squeezing them with her fingers. "She told me there is a plague."

"There *is* a plague," the step-grandfather said. Little Jade stood up, watching him from above, feeling tall. She waited for the old man to say more. But he just kept on nodding, sitting there. She looked around the room. The faces of different gods stared down at her. Their faces were faded in the sunlight. They were powerless, just like her. Kwan Yin smiled down at her blandly from the altar. Little Jade fingered her jade disk, "*keep me safe*" she prayed silently, "*keep grandpa safe!*" The old man stood up slowly, holding the edge of the dining table. Small pieces of bamboo fell off his pants. He said: "Little Jade, let's go out and gather some firewood."

They walked against the wind, toward the small forest behind the house. The old man carried a yoke with ropes dangling from both ends and held an ax in one hand. Little Jade followed him closely, stepping on his shadow. They crossed a shallow stream and saw a forlorn man filling buckets with water. The step-grandfather called out to him, but he merely waved back.

She followed her step-grandfather into the forest. She worked side by side with him, picking up small branches for kindling and piling them under a tree. The old man used the ax to chop the larger branches. They worked silently until dusk. The old man tied the firewood into two large bundles and carried them with the yoke. The sky had turned red, a tide of blood rising from the far horizon. The setting sun was like an incubated yolk, throbbing with vessels and veins.

The chicken cackled as they walked into the back yard. Little Jade went into the kitchen to wash her hands while her step-grandfather put away the firewood and chased the chickens into their cages. Pressing her wet hands over her cheeks, She leaned against the doorway, watching the old man chase the chickens with a tree branch, clucking at them. She laughed, clapping her hands. The old man picked up a tree branch and poked a ball of feathers in a corner of the yard, disrupting the swarm of flies circling the body of a dead chick. He shooed all the other chickens into the bamboo cage. Then he opened the lid of the cage and took the chickens out one by one, examining them closely under the fading daylight, and then he returned them to the cage.

Little Jade heard him sigh. Then, as if he had made a decision, he straightened up silently, and began to build a fire just outside the back yard. The wind swept the flames from side to side and black smoke rose up to heaven, blending into the darkening sky. The old man rolled up his sleeves and took the chickens out again, one by one, to wrench their necks. Little Jade watched him through the flames. She covered her face, overwhelmed by a disturbing mixture of terror and fascination. His features blurred as he grasped a panicking, fighting bird. The wings flapped, the feathers flew. The chicken argued loudly and hopelessly until its broken neck was folded under its wing.

The sky had gone dark. The moon, large as a silver pan, rose from behind the mountains and stared down at them. Dogs were barking from the other end of the village. The bodies of the dead birds were piling up at the old man's feet. Feathers stuck to his bare arms. Sweat glistened all over his face and drenched his shirt. He carried the dead birds to the fire four at a time and threw them into the flames. The flames died down for a moment and then shot up fiercely. The air smelled of burnt feathers and roasted meat. The dogs were howling again. They had picked up the scent and were coming in packs, running noiselessly like shadows, tongues hanging and dripping with saliva, eyes burning red.

Little Jade looked up at the moon and remembered the story of the moon goddess her grandma had told her so long ago.

One night, the roosters crowed at midnight. When people came out of their huts, they saw a sky brighter than ever before. There were ten suns in the sky. The fierce light and heat humbled the people, and they dropped to their knees. After that, the night never returned. People toiled under the evil sky to tend their crops. Their sweat dropped like rain on the ground and was absorbed by the cracking earth. The suns kept on blazing. The rivers were drying, and the trees were dying. Lizards and snakes were trapped in the hardened mud. Birds' wings were burnt, and they dropped from the sky to rot on the parched earth. The only living beings that roamed freely were the green-headed flies with red wings that stung people and animals. People retreated back into their huts and waited for the next sign from heaven.

The emperor selected the fattest animals from the royal stable and sacrificed them to beg heaven for help. Heaven was closer to the earth then, and the Heavenly Emperor sent the god Yi to help the people. Yi descended to earth with his wife Chang Er. He asked the ten suns to take turns and come out to light up the world, one at a time. But the suns refused. They were brothers. They wanted to frolic together. In anger, Yi pulled out his black bow and white arrows and shot down nine suns one by one, leaving only one to fulfill the duty of brightening the days. The heat subsided and people sang and praised Yi, but the Heavenly Emperor was enraged. The suns were his sons. Nine of them had perished under Yi's powerful arrows. He banished Yi to earth to age and die like other mortals.

The moon was glowing quietly, a giant silver pan silently turning in mid-sky as Little Jade thought about the legend of god Yi and his wife Chang Er. Banished to earth, Yi tried to win back the favor of the Heavenly Emperor by helping people to kill off monsters. He sacrificed giant snakes, wild boars, and elephants to heaven, but the Heavenly Emperor ignored him.

Grandma had said that Chang Er did not want to stay on earth to farm and weave like other mortal women. Most of all, she was afraid to grow old and die. Yi went to a Taoist monk to ask for help. The monk gave him a magical pill. If half of the pill was taken, one could live forever young. If the entire pill was taken, one could fly to heaven. Yi took the pill home and showed it to his wife. He wanted to share the pill with Chang Er on a chosen day. But the next day, when Yi was out hunting, Chang Er swallowed the entire pill and flew to heaven alone. The guards at the gate of heaven pushed her away because she had betrayed her husband. Having no other place to go, she went to live on the moon, a cold and lonely place. Yi, also lonely, died on earth.

When grandma told this story she did not say that it was sad for Yi to die alone on earth or that Chang Er had been a bad wife for betraying and leaving her husband. From her sad expression, Little Jade guessed that it must have been what she was thinking. Little Jade had kept quiet back then. She remembered sitting on her grandma's lap. She remembered the feel of having one of her grandmother's arms encircle her while the other arm pointed to the moon as she told the story. Her grandma had been like all other grandmothers telling their grandchildren the same story and looking at the same moon.

Little Jade watched the hunched over silhouette of her step-grandfather against the roaring flames behind her. The tributes to the cruel heaven were a pile of the dead birds with twisted necks. The Jade Emperor would not be pleased.

∗ ∗ ∗

Little Jade and the step-grandfather were eating dinner of tofu cooked with soy sauce and scallion. Little Jade was hungry for roast chicken, but step-grandfather said that the chicken was sick and could not be eaten. The fat of the chicken skin boosted the fire and gave out a mouth-watering aroma that lingered in the air.

Someone knocked urgently. The old man got up to open the door, letting in a neighbor who lived three doors down. The neighbor announced that young Chen who lived in the house at the back of the village with his elderly parents was dead. The step-grandfather said, "I saw him by the river on my way to collect firewood just this afternoon," he said, "We greeted each other. I guess it was the last time we spoke."

Little Jade almost interrupted the old man. *No, he did not speak to you, he only waved*, she thought. But she kept quiet, listening to the neighbor describe how Chen carried the water back to his house, but before he could cross the threshold, he fell face down and died.

The neighbor conversed with the step-grandfather loudly. He wore a cotton shirt, opened in the front, showing a strip of yellow skin underneath. His neck was marked with reddish purple lines where he had used a coin to scrape up and down all around his neck to let out the fire inside his body. The horizontal creases under his chin were black with mud and formed a crisscross pattern with the scrape marks on his neck. He talked cheerfully, his spit flying. He said, "This weather, you know. It's the imbalance between fire and water. Too much fire inside people can burn us to death."

The step-grandfather made an approving sound. The neighbor continued, "We have to let the fire out by drinking grass root soup. I drink a whole lot of grass root soup these days. Say, why did you kill and burn those chickens? The entire village smells of roast chicken. Are you making sacrifices to heaven in your own back yard?" He laughed, masking uneasiness, and looked over the dinner table to see what were in the dishes.

The step-grandfather frowned and said gravely, "The chickens were sick and I had to kill and burn them to stop the disease from spreading. I would not sacrifice sick chicken to heaven." The neighbor nodded knowingly, blinking his eyes as if to remember every word in order to later repeat them to others.

✳ ✳ ✳

The step-grandfather left the next morning to pay condolences to the family of the dead. He told Little Jade to stay home and not to go outside to play. She spent the morning looking at the red dots that blossomed all over her legs. Little Jade scratched them as hard as she could and squeezed them one by one with her fingernails. But only a sticky transparent liquid came out. She put her fingers under her nose and smelled a faint odor like the fish stench in the market place.

Little Jade was feeling nauseous, and didn't want to stay inside anymore. She stepped out of the house and sat underneath a big tree. It was a pine tree, the only kind that hadn't lost its leaves at this time of year. The sunlight fought to penetrate its needles, tossing light dots into the shadow under the tree. Little Jade sat on the thick twisted roots of the pine, feeling a flow of sweat traveling down her back. She looked out in front of her. Sunshine, a dusty yellow color, filmed over the sky—like an oil stain over a deep blue porcelain bowl.

CHAPTER 10:
A NEW BEGINNING, TIANJIN
1943

Silver Pearl felt suspended by the line that connected her and the unborn child. With her lower body elevated and the inside of her legs feeling sticky, blood dried slowly and caked on her skin. She could feel her own heartbeats so well, drumming in the same rhythm with another vibration, weaker but distinct, and in her nauseous helplessness, Silver Pearl felt her belly jumping. The child's fists were pushing from inside her. He could not wait to separate himself, but it was too early. He would not survive if he came out. Silver Pearl would not let go of him. The child had turned into an enemy. They wrestled their bodies and their wills against each other, pushing and pulling throughout the long journey to the city hospital.

When the wagon approached the hospital, the child finally quieted down. Silver Pearl felt calm as she was carried into the hospital ward and lowered in the disinfected air. Her sweating hands rested on the cool iron bed railings.

While Silver Pearl settled into the hospital, her mother went to the grand hotels in the city and looked for An Ling. It was fortunate that An Ling had just returned from a rent collection expedition. It was strange to see An Ling in the hospital setting. Silver Pearl woke one afternoon to find him sitting beside her bed, his hands holding his head. Silver Pearl felt as if they were seeing each other in a different lifetime. She knew she did not look so well. She had her feet elevated and was told to stay in bed as much as possible for fear of losing the baby. An Ling tried to cheer her with a box of chocolate candies and a bundle of red roses. It was comforting for Silver Pearl to see An Ling. For the first time, she felt that he cared for her. When her mother went looking for a glass vase for the roses, An Ling sat next to the hospital bed, holding Silver Pearl's hand and asking her how she was feeling. He opened the box of chocolate and took out a piece to place it in her mouth. Silver Pearl let the richly sweet candy melt in her mouth slowly, savoring the luxury of An Ling's attention. She asked An Ling about the rents collection, but he just shook his head and waved off her questions. He told her just focus on resting and taking care of herself and the baby inside her. Nothing else mattered. He also told her that he would find a place to settle everyone as soon as the baby was born. An Ling told Silver Pearl not to worry about a thing.

After visiting Silver Pearl at the hospital, An Ling quickly rented a house so that Silver Pearl's mother could set up care for her. Each day, Silver Pearl's mother cooked her daughter rich soup made of fatty pork's knuckles and peanuts. In a matter of weeks, Silver Pearl was gaining weight and had better color. An Ling was furnishing a nursery in the rented house. Silver Pearl's mother was asking around for a wet nurse in anticipation of the birth of her grandson in another month or so.

But all were deceived. The newborn pushed his way into the world one night at the hospital when Silver Pearl was too tired and her guard was down—when she thought he had given in and would bide his time until he was ready. Feeling him slipping loose from her, Silver Pearl cried out with fear. His blood-marred body was pulled out of her under harsh hospital light. He was alive, crying loudly for such a small baby.

And there was her son, clutching at her breasts, his mouth fitted tightly around her nipple while she rested in that very bed. She was happy those first few days after she left the hospital with her son. He was a feisty bundle of red, almost translucent, flesh and skin. Silver Pearl looked at him, at his lash less eyes shut close as his tiny fingers held firmly onto her breasts and his mouth suckled greedily. A tingling sensation traveled from Silver Pearl's nipples down to between her thighs as she nursed.

Silver Pearl's mother came into the bedroom and covered the dressing mirror hastily with a red cloth, to prevent the child's spirit from escaping into the world that the mirror duplicated so well. Often, An Ling came to look at his son peering at him gently and smiling at his wife. An Ling had yet to consult the ancestral book of names which is why the child had not yet been given a proper name.

As things turned out, the infant left the world before the goldsmith could forge an elaborate gold locket with the inscription "longevity to one hundred years." The locket would have been worn around his neck to bind him to this world.

One morning Silver Pearl woke before dawn from a terrifying dream in which she had watched herself explode open like a balloon. Pieces of her shot across the room, sticking to the walls and scattering on the floor. Silver Pearl woke with a start, frightened, and feeling her breasts hurting from too much milk. The infant was quiet. Not wanting to wake him and unable to sleep, she sat in bed, squeezing her nipples in the dark. Fine sprays of milk sprouted out of her breasts, wetting her hands. She sniffed and licked her palms. The milk was faintly sweet. Silver Pearl wanted her son to wake with his hunger and cry for her, so she could hug him close and let him drink away the abundance within her. She leaned over to examine his still, tiny figure under the blanket—and let out the scream she had been unable to utter in her nightmare. Her son's body was already cold.

✳ ✳ ✳

An Ling watched the hired hand dig deeply into the earth under a sky heavy with dark clouds. The man shoveled swiftly. The air was cold, and his quickened breath merged with the fog. The dry top layer of earth had been removed, and the man's shovel was reaching for darker, softer soil beneath. This was a corner of the local cemetery. An Ling gave the gatekeeper some money for this plot of land where he would bury his infant son. An Ling watched as snow fell gently over the land before him, vast and open, naked after the harvest. The snow was a promise of water for spring farming in the coming year. He looked for the gray outline of the distant mountains. Every winter, the snow gathered on the mountaintop and melted into a stream when spring came—a delicate balance that the people living in this valley relied on for their livelihood. The snow was coming down thickly. An Ling could not see the mountains anymore. A few flakes of snow fell on his lashes and melted from the warmth of his skin. When the pit was large enough, the hired hand threw the shovel away and climbed out as snow accumulated on the ground.

An Ling walked slowly to a black lacquered box, the size of a tool chest, that lay on the ground a few steps away and knelt down next to it. He cleared away the layer of snow that covered this tiny coffin containing the body of his infant son. As soon as he wiped away the snow, another thin dust settled again. An Ling got up and carried the coffin to the pit. With the help of the hired hand, he laid the tiny coffin gently at the bottom. An Ling inhaled deeply, taking in the scent of mist and earth. Finally, An Ling climbed out of the pit. He shoveled snow and earth back into it, burying his son, whose eyes had hardly opened to see the world and who spent his brief life crying with his toothless mouth wide open, protesting against the pain that pushed him in and then out of life.

An Ling had not given his son a name. Being far from home, he could not bury the infant in the family cemetery. He thought of the two stone lions that guarded the cemetery gate, and he remembered the day his mother was buried. Four coolies had carried the heavy marble headstone carved with her name to be erected in front of her grave. An Ling remembered how the white marble reflected the bright sunlight of the day. Now, he patted the earth firm with the shovel and used a rock the size of a human head to mark the grave. He would send for a stone tablet tomorrow.

With snow dusting his shoulders, he climbed into the waiting wagon and sank back into the seat. The driver let out a shout and the wagon began to move. An Ling pulled up a sheepskin blanket to cover his legs. Silence settled in as the wagon rolled quietly in the soft snow.

The wagon stopped abruptly. An Ling climbed down. The driver, dressed in a dog skin coat, grinned at him and drove away. An Ling parted the pink satin and walked through the doorway of the House of Spring Flowers. A middle-aged woman with a red silk peony in her hair came forward and took his hands, gesturing to him to come inside. She led him through a long, dimly lit hallway to a bright noisy room, where men and women mingled and caroused. A maid greeted An Ling with a goblet full of densely sweet liquor. He drank the entire goblet and felt a slow burning sensation from his throat to his groin. An Ling's head was dizzy and he closed his eyes, letting himself be carried to a bed covered with slippery silk. Soft, nearly boneless hands undressed him. A warm, naked body slid next to him. An Ling could hear her uneven breathing. The air was saturated with perfume and An Ling wondered whether he was drugged. But his thoughts stopped as her lips pressed on his mouth and sucked eagerly. Sweet-tasting saliva sprung from under his tongue and flew from his mouth to hers.

He struggled to move, but her body was firmly on top of him, chest to chest, belly to belly, thighs to thighs. He wanted to speak and he wriggled his tongue and touched the edge of her teeth. He ran his tongue between her lips and teeth. He could feel her long-nailed fingers behind his ears scratching his scalp. Her breathing became heavy and short. His palms were sweating as he thrust his tongue into her mouth to explore her throat. But she had no tongue. And in a flash, her teeth closed in on his tongue and chopped it off like a guillotine slicing off a waiting head...

An Ling woke up as the carriage stopped. His head was pounding. He frowned as the silence around him was pierced by the voice of his mother-in-law. There was a cool wetness in his pants and his face was hot against the cold wind as he dismounted from the wagon. He had not been looking forward to returning to his wife and this rented house.

An Ling wanted to rid himself of the shadows from the past. He thought that after the disintegration of his family and the death of his mother, he could finally be free to live a simple and uncomplicated life within the small unit of himself, a wife and a son. He wanted to start something new, all by himself. He would leave Little Jade with his in-laws. It would have been a good arrangement.

An Ling entered the small house. His mother-in-law fussed around him, scurrying to prepare hot water for his bath. Silver Pearl called out for him from the inner room where she had been bedridden for months since the premature childbirth. An Ling ignored her calls and slumped in a large chair. Much as he yearned to move into the future, he shaded his eyes with one hand and remembered that night at the hospital...

***

The waiting room had been lit by glaring fluorescent lights. His mother-in-law had risen from a wooden bench to greet him. A boy, she said, grinning at him earnestly. The bright light cut harsh lines on her face. An Ling felt his own face smiling as he asked to see his son. He was told to wait, for now the newborn was sleeping. He thought how pleased his mother would have been, and his grandfather as well. An Ling was suddenly optimistic. He would start a new life, just as his ancestors had done generations ago.

***

For the past weeks, An Ling had been reading in the newspaper about the plague. The article was contained in a small square at the corner of the paper, almost unnoticeable. Now, the Japanese controlled most of the Chinese language newspapers and filled them with shocking headlines, "The glorious Japan Empire is victorious!" one headline declared, its propaganda presented in giant red block characters.

The map of China, in the shape of a maple leaf, was steadily being diminished by areas marked: "Japanese Empire" shaded in red, the color of the rising sun of Japan. An Ling grew numb and fearful, hoarding food and coal in the back room of his rented house, and making plans to leave for the south as soon as Silver Pearl was well enough to travel. He knew that all modes of transportation to the countryside had been cut off. Refugees from the north flooded the city, bringing with them unspeakable tales. People were starving in the countryside. Hungry people were digging up new graves to eat the dead.

An Ling was afraid to think of Little Jade. No one knew what had happened in the villages infected with plague. No one wanted to know.

An Ling sighed. Looking around the room, he saw the gray walls and the landlord's heavy rosewood furniture. Old newspapers and movie magazines piled up in one corner. His mother-in-law served him a cup of Oolong tea and sat down across from him, as if waiting to talk. An Ling's mouth felt dry. He sipped the tea carelessly, burning his tongue. Abruptly, he hurled the teacup on the floor, shattering it. His mother-in-law excused herself and disappeared. An Ling closed his eyes, pressing his hands against his temples.

Silver Pearl entered the room, dragging her slippers against the wooden floor. She wore a loose-fitting purple robe. Her large eyes had sunk into their sockets. Silver Pearl looked at the broken teacup on the floor. She said, "You shouldn't smash that teacup in front of my mother." An Ling refused to look at her. He threw an arm over his face. "Don't talk to me," he said.

Silver Pearl saw him sitting before her, covering his face like a child afraid of being hit. She felt a tenderness springing within her. She reached out and touched his hand. An Ling shook off her hand. Silver Pearl stiffened. She sat down on a chair and said, "An Ling, we've been waiting for you and worrying because you took so long. It's dangerous outside the city limits. And the minute you get home you break the tea cup." She paused but could not suppress a sudden rage. She blurted out as her face turned red, "Just like your daughter!"

"Leave me alone, Silver Pearl!" An Ling shouted, holding his head as if in pain.

Startled, Silver Pearl looked at him and said, "Why are you screaming at me? What have I done? We've been worrying. Anything could have happened to you. How come it took you so long to bury...," her voice trailed off and grew silent.

Silver Pearl started to sob. "Our son is dead and all you can do is yell at me. My mother says that Little Jade put the stool where it tripped me. It's her fault." Silver Pearl wiped her eyes with her sleeve. "It's your daughter's fault. She broke that teacup on our wedding day and brought bad luck on me. She deserves to die—just like my son!"

Silver Pearl felt someone grab her hair in one jolt, jerking her head backward. Her face was slapped to one side, then the other. She was dizzy and she could not see.

"When will you stop? What a poisonous tongue you have! How can you curse a little girl like an enemy? Wishing her dead? You are a stupid woman!" An Ling's eyes reddened and he pushed Silver Pearl away.

Silver Pearl's mother ran to her and held her. "Are you mad?" she asked them. "Aiya, what a time to fight! I beg you to stop fighting."

Silver Pearl's cheeks were swollen. A thin stream of blood trickled from the corner of her mouth. She lay on the floor, wailing: "I don't want to live anymore! Go ahead and kill me! My mother didn't raise me to be beaten by you. An Ling, you're a coward. If you care so much about your daughter, why did you leave her at home? You have no heart. You don't care for your daughter, you don't care for anyone. I curse her because she cursed me! Go ahead and kill me! My son is dead and I don't want to live anymore."

An Ling stood up, exhausted, leaning against the wall. He buried his face in his hands, sobbing. His shoulders shook uncontrollably. The mother knelt next to her daughter, muttering, "Stop babbling, Silver Pearl. Let's go inside."

With her hair all over her damp face, Silver Pearl sat on the floor and wept, "You can't shut me up, An Ling. Where is your precious daughter? Where is my son? Haven't you heard that there is a plague? The entire village has died off. You're afraid to go back because you're afraid to die. You know Little Jade is already dead. The paper said no one survived. It's too late, An Ling. Why don't you stab me with a knife? I'm dying anyway, bleeding all the time. All of us will die soon, except for you. You're too selfish to die."

"Silver Pearl, stop talking like this!" the mother pleaded.

"No, Mother!" Her voice bit at An Ling and did not let go. "Are you crying now, An Ling? I hope you are. I didn't see you cry a tear when our son died. Why are you crying now? Why? Yes, I want to talk loud and clear anywhere I go. I'll tell it to the Buddha when I die..." She shook violently, gasping.

"Are you finished?" An Ling said with hatred, tears streaming down his face. "Very well, I'll leave to find Little Jade right now. You think she is dead, but I think she is still alive, waiting for me. You evil woman! How can you curse her life? If Little Jade is dead, what about your father? Do you wish him dead too? I'm going back to find them. If I don't find Little Jade, I will not come back."

***

Alone in the bedroom, Silver Pearl put her favorite gown over her head, slipping into it quickly. Her skinny arms slipped out of the armholes, rising above her head, white against the dimness of the room—like the outstretched arms of someone drowning. Loose black hair shook away from her yellow face as it emerged from the lush colors of the gown. The fabric was woven under the tropical sun of a distant island. It had a bold mix of deep fuchsia, canary yellow and the overlapping bright green of the ferns that paved the belly of a jungle. Gold threads had been woven through the fabric like traces of sun shooting through a dense forest. The stiff mandarin collar scratched her neck and she frowned, smoothing the gown with her hands. Silver Pearl's fingers ran over the decorative bottoms made of sparkling crystals that dotted diagonally from her throat to the side seam under her right arm. The buttons glinted in the dying light of the room like precious stones excavated from the depth of a mine. A sense of loss came over her as her fingers slowly pressed over her chest. With fingers resting over her breasts, she imagined two jets of thin milk spraying out of her nipples penetrating the night, and feeding her son in the world of the dead.

Chapter 11:
The Plague 1943

The bed was dirty with sand and fallen hair. The center of the pillow was smudged with hair grease. Little Jade pushed aside the mosquito netting and put her feet on the ground, searching for slippers. Her pants were rolled up to her knees. The sores on her calves were large and purple like grapes. She walked into the main room, using a turkey feather fan to fend off the flies that buzzed around her legs.

She pressed the sores with her fingers. They were softer after turning from bright red to a deep purple. She showed her step-grandfather her sores, and he ran his fingers over them, nodding approvingly as if testing the ripeness of fruits. The old man went to the backyard came back with a branch of bamboo. He used the knife and cut a slice of inner bamboo shard, thin as a blade. He used it to pierce open the sores on Little Jade's legs. It didn't hurt at a all. Little Jade watched each sore burst open with black blood and yellow pus, and finally oozed with fresh red blood. The smell of rotten fish filled the warm stuffy air. More flies circled around Little Jade and she tried to hit them with the fan. The old man opened a bottle of alcohol and its vapor broke through the thick stench. He washed the wounds on Little Jade's legs with a piece of cloth soaked in alcohol.

It hurt. A sharp cutting pain spread all over Little Jade's legs as she clenched her teeth. She watched the old man graze the dead skin from her legs with the bamboo blade and clean away dirty blood—the way a cook scrapes clean the scales and innards of a fish. The ugly purple lumps turned into coin-sized disks of pink under-skin, each one covered with a thin layer of blood. The old man gave Little Jade a worn towel with one corner soaked in alcohol. She placed it under her nose, breathing in the cool clean vapor.

Tilting his head, the step-grandfather drank from the alcohol bottle. As he swallowed the knot on his throat slid up and down. Little Jade pressed the damp towel on her forehead and her skin tingled.

"Is everyone else dead, grandpa?" Little Jade asked, wiping the towel all over her face, shuddering.

The old man smacked his lips and turned to his granddaughter, "No, they are just staying inside." His dull eyes stared at her like fish eyes.

She didn't believe him. She was convinced that they were the only two alive in the entire village, perhaps in the world. There were no more parades of mourners carrying the dead on the street. The dead were buried, in coffins, in cabinets, and some in rolled straw mats with their feet sticking out at one end. It was lonely being alive. The bones in his knees made a cracking sound as the old man stood up slowly and muttered, "I'll be back soon."

The step-grandfather picked up a bamboo basket from the floor and walked out the front door wearing pajamas that draped loosely over him. The glaring sunlight filtered through the thin fabric and revealed the outline of his bent body. He stopped in the middle of the street and looked around as if confused. Finally, he made up his mind and threaded out of Little Jade's view.

The old man was going out to look for food again. They had finished eating all the food in the house, and all the tofu and soybeans from the old man's shop. The villagers stole most of the soybeans and there was nothing left. Every day the old man went out and returned with something in his basket—a small bunch of wild vegetables, a piece of root. They never mentioned the lack of food to each other. Every day, the old man cooked two meals and they sat solemnly across from each other at the dining table. They looked into their bowls and not at each other, drinking half a bowl of thin soup as if carrying out an ancient ritual.

They had been hungry for a while. In the beginning, it felt like a slow fire burning the inside of Little Jade's guts, a constant and numbing pain. But after a while, the fire inside died and filled her with smoke. What was in her was scarcely heavier than the air surrounding her. She felt so light that she was almost floating when she walked around the house. She got dizzy often and from time to time she flew a little, skipping steps. She somehow traveled without touching the ground.

There was no wind. The putrid air hung heavily over her head. The flies swarmed through the door and tried to land on her legs as she waved the fan feebly, fighting them off. She felt thin stabs of pain all over, on her back, behind her neck, on her arms. She struggled to get up and limped toward her bed, swatting herself with the fan and the towel. She lifted the mosquito netting and ducked under. A few flies trailed her into the netting. She cornered them with the fan and smashed them against the wall. The bodies smeared into the flaking plaster and spots of black blood dotted Little Jade's palms.

Resting her head on her knees, Little Jade was breathing hard. The wounds on her legs felt inflamed. She was sweating under her hair and on her back, and her skin began to itch. She scratched herself with dirty fingernails, reaching behind her back, digging into her hair, and over her shoulders. She finally gave up in exhaustion, lying restlessly under the dusty mosquito netting. Strands of hair stuck to her sweaty neck and forehead. She covered her face with the towel. The alcohol had evaporated, leaving a faint smell that faded as she strained to sniff. She closed her eyes and tried to sleep with the flies whizzing outside the netting, inside her head.

Little Jade was alone in a garden. The flowers were in full bloom, crowding each other with blossoms as big as babies' heads. Their petals spread open, curling back, giving out a strong scent of evil, like a mixture of opium and heavy perfumes. Giant white lilies were ghastly green under the moonlight, and red roses were a deep purple, bleeding in the night. She stood still, surrounded by flowers, looking around slowly and feeling unsure. In the darkness, the flowers were edging toward her, inch by inch, secretive and purposeful. There was a breeze, light as a sigh, and Little Jade felt a cold hand quickly stroke her back. She screamed and ran. The wind grew fierce, grating her face and ears, wailing under the night sky. She ran faster. Her eyes were burning and her throat was dry. Her head suddenly filled with noises: the sound of bubbles rising and bursting when water boils in a pot, the hissing sound of fire licking the damp air. The moon was bright and nearly green like the color of the tip of a flame, slowly burning, brewing a mysterious potion in the bewildering night.

Out of nowhere, a well appeared in front of her. She held onto its moss-covered wall and panted. Behind her, noises and shadows were closing in. Little Jade looked into the well and saw a moon. Someone pushed her.

She was falling. The air was suddenly thin and icy, and it cut the inside of her nose. When she inhaled, her nose bled. Her mouth was open, but words that she could not speak crawled in her throat like ants.

In the house of the step-grandfather, Little Jade woke up. She did not open her eyes. She had been trying to dream of her father, but he must be too far away and did not care to enter her dreams. Father had promised to come for her as soon as he could. He said that he wanted them to spend the New Year together. Yet the New Year was less than a month away, and he was still not back. Little Jade breathed through her nose which felt cold and a little sore. Her head was hurting.

She curled like a shrimp under the stiff blanket around her. She tried to pray, but her mind was blank. Her feet were numb. She reached down to squeeze them, her fingernails digging into the moist skin, but she didn't feel a thing. She opened her eyes and saw a pale light beaming through the door. She sat up slowly, wrapping the blanket around her. In a trance, she walked out of her room barefooted, into a faint green mist. The air felt oddly damp and cold. Outside the open door, a hazy moon glowed like a firefly in the bottomless darkness. "Grandpa, grandpa, where are you?" She whispered, pulling the blanket closer to her. No one answered. She looked around, holding onto the back of a chair and tightened her grip. The wood felt cold and hard. She was not dreaming. She saw a shadowy figure moving outside the door.

She approached the door slowly, trying to see. Someone was sitting in the street gesturing with his arms toward the night sky. "Grandpa!" She called. Her voice was quickly swallowed by the thick darkness.

He ignored her and went on signaling with his arms over his head. She called again, yelling loudly, "Is that you, grandpa?"

She heard her own voice trailing off as the black clouds unveiled the moon. Suddenly, she saw a silvery layer of snow blanketing the ground. The step-grandfather sat half-naked in the snow, throwing handfuls of snow all over himself. His dirty gray hair and beard were covered with snowflakes, and his face was fixed in a wide grin. His mouth hung open, trembling as if in joy, as if in pain. The dust of snow twirled about him, gliding down his bony shoulders and landing on his lap.

Little Jade ran toward the old man, her bare feet sinking into the soft snow. The stiff blanket flapped around her like clumsy wings. She stood in front of the old man and kneeled down. She scooped a handful of snow, and buried her face in it, smelling the scent of heaven and clouds. The icy grains slipped out between her fingers and she looked at her step-grandfather. He looked back wildly at her. She wrapped the dirty red blanket around them both. "Let's go home," she said gently.

He nodded sadly at her as she helped him stand up. They walked slowly back to the house, the red blanket still draped around their shoulders.

She sat the old man down next to the dining table and covered him snugly with the blanket. She went into the kitchen to start a fire. Hitting two flints against each other, she tried to catch the orange sparks with a piece of old scrap paper. Eventually, she built a small fire to heat up the soup, placing her hands close to the fire for warmth. They had been living on this soup of grain, wild vegetables, and bones.

The damp wood gave out a smoke that made Little Jade's eyes water. Steam rose from the pot as the thin gray soup grumbled to a boil. She poured a bowl of soup and carried it to her step-grandfather. He sat quietly, huddled in the red blanket like a statue of Buddha. Little Jade put the bowl in front of him and said, "Have some soup, grandpa."

The old man looked down at the soup for a long time, but did not reach for the spoon. The snowflakes on his eyebrows and beard were melting into droplets of water. Little Jade went back to the kitchen and poured herself a bowl of soup, drinking it slowly, standing next to the stove where the fire was dying.

Everything is going to be all right now, Little Jade thought faintly as she drank up the soup. A warm current traveled down her throat, flowing slowly. She narrowed her eyes and covered her mouth with both hands, breathing into them. Thin strands of white steam escaped between her fingers. A sweet and sturdy feeling rose up in Little Jade, like clearly remembered happiness from long ago. Just like this, one breath after another, she kept on living, living.

"Come, Little Jade. Come here, come." Little Jade looked up and saw her step-grandfather beckoning at her by the kitchen door, whispering loudly. "Come, I want to show you something." She followed him into the main room.

He pointed to a dozen or so snowballs on the dining table and said, "Look here, look at these eggs."

Little Jade looked at him with alarm and said hesitantly, "Grandpa, they are snowballs, not eggs..."

"Sh-h-h-h, not so loud." The step-grandfather smiled conspiratorially and checked to make sure the door was locked. He came close and whispered into Little Jade's ear. "They are phoenix eggs."

Little Jade felt a claw grasp her heart as the old man's wet beard brushed her ear and neck. His breath was short and shallow and he said, "These eggs are treasures and will turn into magnificent phoenixes when spring comes. Only I know the secret of turning them into phoenixes."

He held up a snow egg in front of Little Jade's eyes. It was shining, translucent and beautiful. She reached out, wanting to touch it. But the old man put it back on the table and said, "Don't tell anyone. This is a secret from up there." He pointed skyward. Little Jade watched him turn around and arrange the snow eggs carefully on the table, piling them up into a small mound. She could only think of the chickens he had killed and burned on the evening of the bloody sunset. The black smoke that had rushed toward heaven had carried with it the scattered spirits of the dead birds. Now, she thought, they had been reincarnated into these magical eggs and would be reborn when spring came.

* * *

An Ling slowed down the mule cart as he approached the village in the waning evening light. The village was so quiet that he was sure he would have missed it if he had arrived during the night. He could not see any cooking smoke rising above the snow-covered rooftops. There were no signs of life. The evening light was fading, but the windows of the houses were not lit up into warm patches of yellow and orange glow.

It was too late to turn back. He had come so far. An Ling drove the mule cart forward and entered the village. There was not even a barking dog to welcome him. He was weary from the long journey, and in his weariness he was not sure whether this was the village he was seeking. He had passed through many, and all were desolate like this one. For all he knew, this was the wrong village, and when he would knock on the door the little girl who answered would not be his daughter.

As An Ling drove down the main street, he could see that the shops were closed, abandoned. All that remained of the flag in front of the wine shop was a few shreds of string hanging in the still air. When he looked closer, he realized that the doors of most store-fronts were missing. The wind must have blown the snow and dust into the shops which had accumulated on shelves and counters. There was once a wine shop, a pawnshop, an incense shop, a grain shop and a tea parlor—all were empty. The shops lined the roadside, decaying in the harsh wind and weather, inhabited by insects.

At last, he found his in-laws' house. The door was shut tight. He hesitated for a moment, then knocked on the door and called, "Open up!"

Between the cracks of the wood panels, An Ling saw light inside the house, moving toward the door. "Who is it?" an old man's voice asked.

"It's Little Jade's father," he answered.

The door opened a crack, and An Ling saw his father-in-law holding a candle, squinting and smiling at him. The old man said, "Come in, come in. It's An Ling. Little Jade, it's your father! An Ling, it's so good to see you. We weren't expecting you at all. Have you eaten? We have already eaten. What an old fool I am! You couldn't have eaten. You've been traveling. You must be hungry. Come, sit down. I'll make you some tea."

In a daze, An Ling followed the old man into the house and sat down on a chair. The old man lit a candle on the table and went into the kitchen to make tea. Little Jade hadn't made a sound since his arrival. Her face was a gray shadow moving about in the darkness of the room. Her eyes followed her father like the eyes of a small creature that comes out only during the night.

Finally, Little Jade approached his chair. Her face entered the range of light cast by the single candle in the room, a short stub of red wax burning in a small white china dish. An Ling smiled at his daughter and said gently, "Come here, Little Jade. Let me look at you. I haven't seen you for so long. Don't be afraid. I'm here to take you home."

He heard a few loud rasping sounds from the kitchen, but ignored them. He looked at his daughter as her face became fully visible in the candlelight.

Little Jade's face was skinny and dirty, but her eyes shone at him happily. "When are we leaving?" she asked in a strangely clear voice that sounded, to An Ling, like bells from a faraway temple.

"Soon," An Ling answered enthusiastically, cheered by her smile.

She looked at him deeply again and disappeared into the darkness.

The old man came into view and gave him a steaming teacup from a tray. An Ling looked into the teacup and saw no tealeaves. The old man grinned at him and said, "Have some tea. I'm making dinner for you. You must be hungry after all the traveling. It's good to see you. This is a surprise. This is a pleasant surprise."

An Ling interrupted the old man. "Listen to me!" he said, urgently. "It's not safe to stay here anymore. I'm taking you with me. We're going to join Silver Pearl and her mother in the city. They're safe and living in a rented house. You don't know how dangerous it is to travel." An Ling's voice echoed in the quiet room. "I have been extremely lucky that I wasn't killed by the bandits or the soldiers. We must leave soon. There is no need to cook me dinner. I have dry food in the mule cart. We can eat while we travel. There's no time to lose"

The old man smiled vacantly as he sipped his water carefully and blowing the steam away from his teacup.

"Father," said Little Jade in a small voice, "you said that you have food in the mule cart?"

"Yes." An Ling turned to look at Little Jade, who was carrying a bundle in her arms, ready to leave.

"Can we have some of the food?" Her voice was weaker now. "We haven't eaten for a long time."

An Ling looked at the old man, who was smiling blankly, and realized that the rasping noise he'd heard earlier was the sound of a bowl scraping against the bottom of the urn for storing grain. They must have been hungry for days, or even longer. He was afraid to think any further. He got up in haste and took the candle to get the food from the mule cart.

An Ling took the candle and made his way to the kitchen. In the darkness, he saw a pot slowly boiling on the stove. A few grains of barley and strands of wild vegetable leaves were floating on the surface of a thin soup. The candle flickered, about to die. He pushed the short wick with his fingers, maneuvering the yellow flame, but the melted wax burned his fingers and finally drowned the flame. He stood still in the darkness, feeling his eyes stung with tears, but he was unable to cry. With his eyes closed, he could clearly see a thin blue strand of cooking smoke rising straight upward from this tiny kitchen to the heaven above—a tenuous signal of the fragile and stubborn existence of the lives below.

✳ ✳ ✳

An Ling turned uneasily on the filthy bed. He had not slept on a bed for many days. He was exhausted but could not fall asleep. He had not eaten tonight, but he felt full with something warm and sore, brimming in his eyes, at his throat. He knew that he had to rest so that he could get up early tomorrow morning. That was what he told Little Jade when he sent her to bed.

He had stumbled out of the kitchen and back into the reach of the single candle on the dining table. He had sat down wordlessly next to the dining table to be with his daughter. Little Jade came to An Ling shyly for a piece of bread. She stood in front of him, and he pulled her close to him, lifting her slight figure gently and placing her on his lap. She leaned against his chest weakly. She held a piece of bread with both hands and ate silently. An Ling sat there feeling relieved and ashamed at the same time. He sensed the smallest movements of his daughter, a lift of her elbow and an adjustment of her leg, as he listened to the tiny sound of her chewing and swallowing the bread.

The old man sat across from them and ate slowly, dipping the bread gingerly into the cup of water and then biting off a small piece at a time, as if he wanted the meal to last forever. He looked up at them from time to time. Each time he was surprised to see the two of them sitting across the dinner table. He asked if they had eaten, and offered them his bread. They looked at each other knowingly and said yes, they had eaten, and please grandfather, please go on eating. The old man looked relieved and went on eating his bread.

The candle was burning low when the old man finally finished. He smacked his lips and drank what was left of the water in his teacup. He seemed happy. He nodded at them good-naturedly and went over to open the front door. The moon was already visible in the night sky, a silver sickle hanging from the tree. The sky was blue and clear, the shadows of the world below were mere residue settled at the bottom—impurities to be discarded.

An Ling pulled his daughter tighter into his arms. He had a thousand questions he was afraid to ask. Even simple questions like "How are you, and how have you been?" He didn't want to know the answers to his questions. Suddenly the old man stood up and walked towards the door. They watched as he went outside, walking noiselessly in the snow, dragging the dirty red blanket with his left hand and holding a spoon in his right hand. He wrapped the blanket around his shoulders and squatted on the snowy ground. He started to dig in the snow with the spoon.

Little Jade called out to the old man, "Grandpa, look at me, I am Little Jade. Grandpa, please don't stay out all night digging in the snow. Your feet are covered with frostbite and your toenails are falling off." Little Jade gently helped the old man stand up and cleared away the icicles on his eyebrows and beard.

An Ling turned to look at Little Jade, but before he could ask, she said, "Don't worry, father. Grandpa is only making snowballs that he thinks are eggs. I thought he wouldn't do this tonight because he had food to eat. I thought the food in his stomach would wake him from his dream of phoenixes. But don't worry, he's been like this ever since the snow."

An Ling looked at his daughter desperately under the flickering candlelight, the flame was slowly drowning in its own puddle of wax tears. She looked back at him unblinking, her eyes large in her small pointed face. An Ling looked away. He could not look back at eyes that seemed to be hiding nothing and demanding everything. A gust of wind came through the door and blew out the flame. Blinded by the sudden darkness, he tried to get up but his legs were numb. He mumbled, "It's time to sleep. We have to get up early tomorrow morning." He tried to lift Little Jade off his lap. Even in the darkness, he could feel her eyes staring hotly at him. Clumsily, he got up on his feet, holding the back of a chair, and found his way into the bedroom.

An Ling lay on the bed half-dreaming and half-waking. He imagined that the house was shrinking around him, into a coffin, a tomb. Little Jade and the old man were spirits transformed into shapes to fool him, to trap him. Silver Pearl was right. Little Jade was dead and so was the old man. This was just an illusion, to punish him for his neglect of his daughter. People who died unnaturally turned into vicious ghosts, especially the starved ones. They had no family to burn incense and paper money for them. They were not properly buried and therefore could not reincarnate. They lingered between the world of the living and the world of the dead, forever wandering, looking to avenge their anger. In his half-conscious state, An Ling listened to the house, to the footsteps shuffling in the main room next to the dinner table.

Something warm and sore burst in An Ling's chest, flowing free over the dam that had contained it. He shed tears silently in the darkness, relaxing and clenching his fists in turn.

✳ ✳ ✳

Little Jade had gone to sleep that night singing a song in a tiny voice only she could hear. She was happy and had thought that she would stay awake all night, but she fell asleep listening to her step-grandfather walk about the house. The next morning when An Ling and Little Jade woke, the old man was gone. The only thing he had taken with him was a bamboo basket, and he left the dinner table covered with snow eggs. They looked for him all over the village, calling out for him from house to house. Little Jade called him until her voice became hoarse and she started to cry, stamping her feet in the middle of the empty street. She cried and cried as An Ling led her back to the house. He sat her down and tried to calm her. The old man had simply disappeared.

An Ling told Little Jade they must leave quickly and return to the rented house in Tianjin. There was no point staying in this village of the dead. They must leave even if they could not find the old man. But Little Jade sat on her step-grandfather's chair covering her face, crying, refusing to go. She didn't want to leave the house she had thought she would die in. She didn't want to leave the village that stank of death. She had hated the house, and she had wished ten thousand times for her father to return and take her away from this dusty, narrow house. This house of shattered windows and lives, of the strangling and burning of chickens and souls, the house of prolonged hunger and diminished hopes. But she didn't want to leave without her step-grandfather. The red-paper gods on the walls stared down at her, expressionless and helpless.

She was certain that the old man had just gone out to look for food. When he went to find food, he always carried that bamboo basket. He would come back with his new finds for their soup, the soup that tasted of unbearable sadness. But he did not return. An Ling said they could not wait any longer because they were running out of food. They waited until they could not wait anymore. Finally, they left for the rented house in the city.

They set the front door ajar so the old man wouldn't be locked out of his own house if he returned. Little Jade left him her glass box with the dancing lady. She placed it on top of the mound of snow eggs, now frozen together. She wound up the key before she walked out the door. The sun was bright and the snow was melting on the ground. On the dinner table, the mountain of snow eggs glistened like giant pearls in the early morning sun. The warmth of the sun was causing the snow eggs to melt. Water was dripping down the corner of the table—one drop, another drop, counting time for a world that had been abandoned.

"*Ding ding ding dong, ding dong dong dong...*" The snow-covered ground was so bright that Little Jade had to wince. Sitting on the mule cart she looked back at the open door of the house. "*Ding ding dong dong, ding ding dong dong...*" The melody played on in her mind.

Little Jade was quiet on her way to the city. She had imagined countless times how happy she would be traveling with her father, just the two of them sitting side by side. How she had anticipated his arm brushing accidentally against her shoulder. She wanted to tell him how much she missed him, how she waited for him until she gave up all hope and was ready to die in her bed inside the mosquito netting.

She had looked forward to death, believing that her grandmother would be waiting for her. She had been weary of staying alive, the days and nights following each other in an endless tedium while her hair matted together and her nails grew long like vultures' claws. She hadn't taken a bath in a long time. Her teeth were turning green and she smelled like a stray dog. The step-grandfather had made snow eggs every day piling them up high on the dinner table. She sometimes tried to talk to him, but he only looked back at her blankly.

An Ling never asked his daughter what happened to the village, and a strange pride prevented Little Jade from telling him. Had he asked, she would have told him about the poisonous sun, the dust, and the wind. She would have told him about the plague and the death, the hunger and the fear of being the last one to die. But maybe Little Jade would just tell him how she missed him—how the thought of him encouraged her to want to live so that he could come rescue her in time.

Chapter 12:
The Rented House

They traveled all night to arrive at daybreak in front of a faded red door. A few branches of bamboo from the yard reached beyond the wall extending a welcoming gesture. An Ling stopped the mule cart and climbed off. He knocked on the door with his fist. The mule was heaving, its breath labored. White foam dripped from its mouth. Little Jade sat on the cart, smelling the odor of the mule and listening to the dull, tired knocks. The air was chilly and still like a block of ice, freezing everything into an endless moment. It was New Year's Eve, and no one was expecting them.

The door opened with a moan. Through the crack, an old woman's surprised look turned into an exaggerated smile. She turned and called, "Silver Pearl, Silver Pearl, the master is home! Silver Pearl!" Her voice rose high from the small yard. A few blocks away, roosters were crowing, answering her. Silver Pearl appeared at the front door of the house, wearing a creased black and gold embroidered gown. Her face was blank as her hands reached behind her neck, attempting to hurriedly tie her hair into a knot. She looked at the door and her fingers turned numb, letting go of her hair. Her hands rested on her neck, fingers extending, touching her chin and the one of her earlobes. An Ling walked toward her, raising his right hand as if wanting to embrace her, but instead he merely tapped her shoulder, ever so lightly. She looked for his eyes and saw that he was looking away.

"Come, Little Jade," he said.

The room smelled of mothballs and wet dust. The windows were closed and the curtains were drawn. Unopened newspapers were piled thickly on the coffee table. The old woman said, "We will have to clean up the house. Tomorrow is the New Year, and it will be a new beginning for our family. Aiya, the family is finally together!" She stopped abruptly and asked An Ling, "Where is the old man? Is he still in the mule cart?" She went toward the door and said, "I'll get him."

Little Jade lowered her head and wiped her eyes with the back of her hands as An Ling explained with great difficulty that the old man had disappeared and that they looked everywhere for him and waited for him until they had to leave. The old woman sat on the floor and wept. Silver Pearl was expressionless as she tried to help her mother up. She refused. Finally she rose on her own and went to boil bath water for An Ling.

* * *

The evening light fell over the bamboo trees as Little Jade stepped into the yard. An Ling was squatting next to a copper basin. He was trying to light a cigarette, his back against the wind, his hair blown over his forehead. In the darkening yard, Little Jade watched as a fire lit up next to his face and died, briefly illuminating his profile. After several tries, he finally lit his cigarette. She could see a red dot burning as he inhaled, soon to be lost momentarily in white smoke. Little Jade walked toward her father, stopping beside the bamboo trees. She leaned against one of them. An Ling was untying bundles of paper money that were stacked in the copper basin. He twisted them into smaller bunches, as he readied them to be an offering to his ancestors. He struck a match and started a fire. The edges of the paper money quickly caught fire and burst into flames.

While watching the money burned in the backyard, Little Jade remembered earlier that day how her step-grandmother had stripped her of her clothes in the kitchen and later she burned her dirty clothes outside in the yard. "They were full of fleas and diseases," she had said.

Afterwards, she dressed Little Jade in Silver Pearl's old quilted jackets and pants that she rolled up around her ankles. The clothes constantly gave out Silver Pearl's body odor mixed with a perfume that smelled of jasmine. Little Jade felt oddly grown up in these clothes. She cut off Little Jade's hair, which was infected with lice. To do this, she spread newspapers on the floor and sat Little Jade on a chair in the middle of the kitchen. Sheets of newspapers were also clipped around her shoulders with clothes-pins. With each snipping sound of the large pair of scissors her long hair fell onto the newspapers. Little Jade bent her head, looking at the newspapers on the floor, as her step-grandmother parted her newly short hair and surveyed her scalp. She said, "Aiya, the lice eggs are all over the roots of your hair. The warmth of your scalp will incubate them and they'll grow up living on the blood of your brain. We'll have to kill the eggs and the lice." She went to the kitchen to boil water while Little Jade waited, sitting motionless on the chair.

Little Jade imagined that her hair grew into an infinite forest of lush trees that fed on a rich soil as red as blood. At the root of each growing plant nestled eggs, exquisite and white, like the snow eggs her step-grandfather made. One sunny day, the air would be warm and the forest would itch with expectation. And the eggs would break open letting out thousands of birds that fluttered their wings toward the sky. Then the step-grandmother came back with two buckets of steaming water. She washed Little Jade's hair many times with a strong-smelling soap and a purple medicine that stung her eyes. Dead nits washed out of her hair and floated atop the buckets of dirty water.

In the yard, the fire was dying, as Little Jade watched the light and shadows gliding across her father's face. His cigarette was only a stub, still burning and laden with ash, clenched between his teeth. He blinked at the smoke. The wind lifted the tissue-thin ashes that seemed to turn into black butterflies and disappear over the rooftops. Inside the too-long sleeves of her jacket, Little Jade clenched her fingers into fists as if wanting to squeeze something out of herself. The wind, coming from nowhere, shuddered through the bamboo trees.

The sky blackened and there was no moon—only a basin full of fire glowing in this small yard, its light filtering through the bamboo trees, throwing overlapping shadows on the walls. The spirits were coming. Their voices trembled like the bamboo leaves in the wind, sobbing and sighing. They circled about the fire for warmth, for the world of the dead was cold and damp. They gazed at the solemn face of the man feeding the fire with paper money, and read his silent prayer. *My ancestors, I am among the last of our clan. I don't know where the others are. If they are still alive, I don't know whether they are burning paper money on this New Year's Eve. I am away from our ancestral land, and you have traveled far to receive this modest offering. I am here temporarily. I don't know where I'll be this time next year. Please bless what is left of our family. With your blessing I hope to continue burning paper money year after year in my lifetime and have someone do the same for me after I am gone.*

CHAPTER 13:
HUSBAND AND WIFE, TIANJIN
1945

The early afternoon sunlight came through the frosted window of the darkened kitchen, turning the flames a paler shade of orange and yellow. Silver Pearl's mother stood next to the stove, watching a steaming kettle, and waiting for the water to boil. She rubbed her hands on a blue apron impatiently and bent down to look at the fire. Her face was red and moist from heat and steam. She straightened slowly, wiped her forehead with the back of her hand and said, "It'll be ready soon."

Silver Pearl sat on a chair by the greasy wall, wearing a dark purple robe. Her legs were crossed and a worn red slipper dangled from the toes of her right foot. Her hair was wrapped in a white towel. Under it, her face looked yellow and blank. She fingered a strand of wet hair absently, narrowing her eyes as if the light were too strong.

The mother picked up the kettle from the stove and walked heavily toward a red wooden tub half-filled with cold water. Silver Pearl felt dizzy as she watched her mother pour hot water into it. She listened to the sound of running water and watched the rising white steam. Her mother tested the water with her hand and said, "Come, the water is just right." Silver Pearl took off the robe and stepped into the tub. She slowly sat down in the middle of the steaming water. Her mother squatted behind her and rubbed her back with a sea sponge. Silver Pearl crouched over holding her ankles with her hands. She closed her eyes and wished that the water were hotter so that she could curl up inside the tub and let her skin turn red in the scalding heat. Her husband had not slept with her since he had returned, and she had become desperate and afraid.

Before An Ling came home, Silver Pearl had been sleeping alone in her bed of clammy sheets and damp quilts over which the mosquito netting hung like opium smoke. She withdrew beneath the cold, heavy quilt like a hermit crab seeking shelter under a rock, and she kept the windows closed and the curtains drawn. Refusing to leave her bed, she contemplated her life in the darkness of the room where cobwebs flourished and fallen hair and dust balls gathered under the bed. She ate little of the food her mother brought her. She dwelled on every detail of her short time with her infant son, keeping her wound fresh and bleeding. Still, with time her pain grew dull and her body healed steadily, and her health improved under her mother's care.

While An Ling was away, Silver Pearl had wondered whether he had found Little Jade, and whether he would ever return to her. What if he kept his word and abandoned her? What would she do if he didn't come back? Silver Pearl had not dared to think of it. She never mentioned her fears to her mother out of a vague superstition that expressing her fears might somehow hasten their realization.

In time, their money ran out, and Silver Pearl's mother pawned a few pieces of jewelry. The money would last them through the New Year and not beyond. Because An Ling had returned with Little Jade, but not with Silver Pearl's stepfather, the old woman's eyes were always red and swollen from tears. Since then, An Ling had acted like a stranger, sleeping in the living room. His suitcases lay filled and open on the floor—as if he was only staying a short while and was ready to leave given the slightest provocation.

Silver Pearl was indeed afraid that he might leave her again. It was easy for a man to leave his wife. Her mother had been telling her how lucky she was that An Ling returned. "You have to hold on to your husband," her mother repeated. "He still has money, and he'll take care of you. Don't fight with him. Don't let him leave you again. What would you do if he didn't come back?"

The fire was still burning over the stove, but the flame was smaller now and it wavered gently in the still air. The bath water was already lukewarm and Silver Pearl felt cold. She lowered her arms and pressed down on her knees, trying to immerse herself in the cooling water, drawing from it all the warmth she could. She looked at the wilting fire fading into its own ashes. *How could she keep her husband from leaving?* She wondered. *She was a useless woman who had only herself—her face and her body. Would this be enough to hold on to her husband?*

With her mother's help, Silver Pearl was willing to try. There was no other way. Silver Pearl dropped her head, feeling small and humble. The mother bathed her daughter with great care, the way she had when Silver Pearl was a child. She scrubbed her daughter's skin until it flushed pink. She complained that her daughter was too skinny and that she must eat more so that her bones would not show through her skin. After the bath, the mother rubbed jasmine oil all over her daughter. Then she sat Silver Pearl in front of the big, foggy mirror, and combed her wet hair free of knots.

✳ ✳ ✳

An Ling could not sleep. He closed his eyes and inhaled deeply. Next to him, Silver Pearl was already sleeping. He turned slowly, not wanting to wake her. He wanted to be alone. Silver Pearl shifted in her sleep pulling the quilt up to cover her shoulders. Her movements stirred up a torrent of jasmine scent, bringing back the memory of a warm summer evening of long ago, when he was still a child...

In the summer, the jasmine grew next to the kitchen door. It bloomed at the same time every evening—the hour when the maids cooked the dinner. An Ling could not forget the overwhelming scent of jasmine mixed with the smell of steaming buns along with a whiff of the smoke of burning firewood, the scallions being chopped and the hot oil sizzling in the wok. An Ling had just bathed, and he was wearing a fresh cotton shirt and shorts. His neck was white with talcum powder, and his crew-cut hair was still damp. He poked his head into the kitchen and saw his mother bending over the pot to taste the food with one hand on her waist and one hand holding a pair of chopsticks. Her head was cocked slightly. A cluster of delicate flowers, the color of yellowed pearls, nested beside the loose bun of hair at the nape of her neck. At night, before she blew out the candles, she would remove the flowers from her hair.

His mother always wore blue—powder blue and lake blue during spring and summer, and gray blue and inkwell blue in autumn and winter. The colors of her clothes were like the different shades of the sky. There were no stars and no clouds. An Ling wondered whether her heart was as clear and changeless as the sky her clothes evoked. During the summer nights he slept beside her. The windows were open and the nights were warm. Inside the mosquito netting, An Ling would listen to his mother sleep as he inhaled the scent of jasmine. She slept fitfully. Her bare arms were the color of the moonbeams, faded yellow with a hint of frost. Her soft-looking skin made him want to touch her. But she would turn abruptly, her throat fluttering and grumbling. She dreamt violent lonely dreams, from which she called out in a muffled voice, her hands fighting blindly in front of her face begging to be awakened. An Ling would watch her twisted face and listen to her shortened breath as her mouth opened and closed as if she were calling for help from a distant place. He would grow afraid and pull her arms and shake her. She woke with frightened eyes and sweaty palms and hugged him tight in her arms whispering his name over and over to calm herself.

In her arms, he was overcome with the intimacy of being so close to her while feeling the moist skin of her neck and the softness of her chest. He felt a suffocating happiness in the middle of those dreamy summer nights as his mother's hands held him and stroked his hair.

Was it the beginning of the month? The new moon loomed outside the window, beaming a thin, frosty light. An Ling grasped the cool, slippery, satin quilt and felt an inexpressible emptiness in this rented house. What had surely been his—the people he loved, the family fortune—were not certain to be his any longer. He could no longer plan his future with the casual optimism he used to have. An Ling propped up his head with the pink satin pillow, and he looked at the woman sleeping next to him. Silver Pearl's thick black hair spilled over her pillow. Her face emerged from the dark waves looking fragile under the moonlight. He moved closer and closer to her. Every strand of her hair reeked with the smell of jasmine. His body tightened, and his breath turned heavy as he reached for Silver Pearl's shoulders peeping from beneath the quilt. He turned her toward him. She opened her eyes and looked at him meekly, and then smiled, closing her eyes again.

* * *

The next morning Silver Pearl sat on her bed and looked out the window. It opened to a small back yard covered with snow and a brick wall that separated the house from the rest of the city. She listened to the dogs barking and the cars honking from blocks away. An Ling told her to get away from the window and close the curtains. Tianjin had become far more dangerous since December 7, 1941, the day that the Japanese bombed Pearl Harbor and precipitated war with the United States. The sky buzzed with American airplanes as bombs exploded over Japanese quarters and the Japanese in Tianjin had become warier and perpetually on edge. This disturbed Little Jade. So during the night, when it was quiet, she sought to calm herself by focusing on the predictable ticking of the clock that her step-grandmother kept on the top of her bureau.

Little Jade shared a room with her step-grandmother. The room was decorated with pictures of opera stars that she cut from a calendar. She listened to operas on the radio all day long. The gongs and cymbals lost most of their effect due to the static and the frequent interruptions of the transmission. But the voices came through somehow, singing about a gentleman eavesdropping on his beloved lady who was praying to the moon goddess. Sitting on her bed, Little Jade peered out the window. Outside the window, beyond the brick wall and high up in the bright metallic sky, a black bird was flying. Her eyes followed it until it cried hoarsely and disappeared from her view. The radio was screaming, and a woman's shrill voice was singing, "Peach Blossom River in the springtime, the little sister washing clothes by the river, she is thinking of her lover, Ai ya ya ya, ai ya ya, Peach Blossom River in the springtime..."

Little Jade remained all day in this rented house, waking, eating, sleeping, looking through the windows. She hardly ever went outside. Her hair was still short, not yet reaching the tops of her ears. Whenever she unexpectedly caught her image on the smooth surface of the water urn in the kitchen or the dark reflecting windowpanes at night, she could not recognize herself. She could not be sure that she was this girl with hair wild like a demon and eyes sad like those of ox. She still wore her jade and pearl necklace. An Ling had had it restrung with new red thread. The old thread had become worn and dirty.

Little Jade was still wearing Silver Pearl's old clothes with her stains and dirty collars. She felt ashamed and self-conscious in her step-mother's clothes, especially the cotton jacket with the reddish-purple color of a bruise. Little Jade wore it constantly during the gray, winter days. She hated the jacket and hated Silver Pearl who had new gowns made for herself. Only beggars' children wore other people's discarded clothes. The step-grandmother called Little Jade a "little beggar" when An Ling was not around. Maybe it was because Little Jade was always hungry. At the dinner table, she ate bowl after bowl of rice, shoving it into her mouth with her chopsticks as if she hadn't eaten for months and would not eat for months to come. Silver Pearl frowned when she saw Little Jade eating, chewing loudly and hurriedly, but she didn't dare say anything to Little Jade in front of An Ling.

On August 15, 1945, the Japanese Army surrendered. The city of Tianjin burst into spontaneous celebration. Gunshots and firecrackers were heard for days and nights. Yet the excitement was accompanied by a great deal of confusion as Japanese soldiers and their Chinese collaborators were rounded up and killed by angry Chinese mobs.

In the rented house, sitting together on their bed, An Ling and Silver Pearl conversed in lowered voices. They needed to decide whether to stay in Tianjin or to go south to evade the Communists. Even with the Japanese defeated, the war of the Communists against the Nationalists raged on. An Ling and Silver Pearl worried about money. Silver Pearl felt helpless and fearful, but An Ling could not make up his mind to stay or to go.

An Ling became obsessed with cleaning himself. Every morning and after each meal he brushed his teeth vigorously in the bathroom, rinsing his mouth noisily. Little Jade heard him turn on the bathroom faucet. The sound of running water slapping against the enameled sink drew her out of bed. Little Jade watched her father through the half-opened bathroom door. He stood in front of the mirror, his cheeks bulging and shaking, and then, he bent down to spit out the water, clearing his throat. He straightened and watched himself in the mirror as he combed scented oil into his hair. The gray light of the narrow bathroom made his face look overcast. He opened his mouth to check his teeth again, and then, he left the room.

After An Ling brought Little Jade home, he began to go out alone at night and return late, loudly singing operas as he switched on the light in the living room. Then he would turn on the radio waking the house. He was sleeping in the living room. But one night he moved back into the bedroom with Silver Pearl. Ever since, the two of them went out in the evening leaving Little Jade at home with her step-grandmother. Silver Pearl would spend hours putting on makeup and tweezing her eyebrows into two perfect arches while humming along with the song on the radio. Then they would go to a friend's house for dinner, or attend opera parties, during which An Ling and others performed short skits from well-known operas.

While Silver Pearl and An Ling readied themselves to go out, Little Jade would hide in the bathroom. Her father's presence seemed to linger there. The mirror was speckled with white dots of his toothpaste, and Little Jade smeared the white dots together with her fingers. Some of them were caked on. She turned on the rusted green copper faucet, sending a cold stream of water into the enameled sink. She leaned back against the wall. The white paint was peeling on the ceiling and on the wooden cover of the privy. A faint smell of urine mixed with the scent of yellow detergent soap, An Ling's hair oil, and mint-flavored toothpaste.

Silver Pearl was dressing in the bedroom, putting on earrings before the large, cloudy mirror. Her eyes were glistening as she laughed at something An Ling had just said. The green crystal earrings dangled, sparkling against her powdered face. Her red lips opened a little and she sang along with the radio. An Ling's hands rested heavily on her shoulders, his fingers played with the tear-shaped crystals that resembled drops of seawater from a distant place, salty and bitter. He smiled, watching her brush her hair and count the strokes. His hands slipped down the round curve of her shoulders and cupped over her breasts. Silver Pearl pressed her cold fingers over An Ling's hands, trying to remove them. She muttered weakly, blushing: "Is the door closed?"

An Ling withdrew his hands and put them in the deep pockets of his trousers. He looked around the room for cigarettes and a lighter. He remembered leaving them in the pocket of his tweed jacket. He glanced at Silver Pearl and saw that she was drawing her eyebrows with a pencil, holding her face still, completely absorbed. He left the bedroom.

Little Jade heard his approaching footsteps. She hid behind the bathroom door. The towels hanging from the nails on the back of the door were damp next to her face. The house, full of its own secrets, was darkening around her. The walls turned from ash gray to charcoal gray. Her father switched on the light in the living room. The naked light bulb emitted a dim yellow glow, the color of water in a rusty bucket. He sat on the sofa, lowered his head to light a cigarette, and then he leaned back to blow out a puff of white smoke. He hummed absently to himself as he flipped through the newspapers on the coffee table. Little Jade listened to the rustling of the papers and his off-key humming. She wished that she could sit next to him. She wanted to put her head next to his and see what he was reading. She wanted to lose herself in the fog of his cigarette smoke.

Silver Pearl's high heels made a clicking sound on the living room floor as she entered the room with music from the radio trailing her. The air in the room changed when Silver Pearl appeared. Little Jade bit her lips with envy. Silver Pearl was wearing a beautiful lush green satin gown embroidered with countless pink peach blossoms. Her hair was shining and smooth and her lips and cheeks were red like a bride's. An Ling gazed at her attentively, looking her up and down, as if seeing her for the first time. He pressed his cigarette into the ashtray and got up from the sofa. She stood there waiting, swaying her body to the melody of the music. Something got into Little Jade eyes and she couldn't see clearly. An Ling walked toward Silver Pearl and somehow she was in his arms, his right hand squeezing her hip, creasing the smooth fabric of the gown.

Little Jade's face was burning and her hands and feet felt cold. She waited for an eternity for them to separate. Finally, they put on their coats and left the house. Little Jade emerged from the bathroom, feeling dizzy as she walked across the living room. She sat on the sofa, gazing at the newspaper in front of her, wondering which pages her father had read, smelling his pungent cigarette smoke that filled the still air.

CHAPTER 14:
THE ADDICTS, 1946

How does one tie down the heart of a man? Silver Pearl lay on her side, her fingers deep in the tangle of her hair, holding up her head as she looked out the window. She was lying on top of a platform next to the bedroom window—the opium platform. She spent more time here than anywhere else now. An Ling lay across from her. His eyes closed and his face still in anticipation of the pleasure of opium. A small lamp was burning brightly between them, always burning. *Oh, it must be kept burning in the purple smoke from the opium pipe.*

"You must hold on to your husband," Silver Pearl remembered her mother telling her again and again. Her old eyes would shine fiercely as she spoke like a predator intent on a kill. She would clench her fists in front of Silver Pearl's face as if ready to strike. "During a chaotic time, there are no such things as rules of heaven or rules of men," she would say in a voice that sounded like a rushing stream, as one word tumbled onto the next. "There is only the rule of survival. There is nothing in this world you can depend on but yourself. Never be so foolish as to feel safe, even in your husband's house. He can change his mind, and he can change his heart. Even in peacetime, men change their hearts. In a time like this, they don't need excuses. The future is hard, harder than it has ever been in the past. With the war, everything changes, and nothing stays the same." Silver Pearl understood very well what her mother sought to tell her. She couldn't blame her for being afraid. When An Ling left them to look for Little Jade, her mother had become a desperate, frightened old woman.

But Silver Pearl had a plan. She would get An Ling to smoke opium again. Silver Pearl felt that they were truly husband and wife during the times they smoked opium together. She recalled how they'd had the same flow of pleasure traveling through their brains, a sweet dizzying rush fogging their eyes. They would gaze at each other as if they had always been together. Silver Pearl had never felt so safe. She would get him to smoke again, and then he wouldn't want to leave. He wouldn't want to go anywhere. They would stay in the rented house—or any other house because it didn't really matter—and live off his inheritance until the civil war ended.

She knew that An Ling had never been an addict, but he often smoked opium when he felt pressured or afraid. She knew that he felt the burden of providing for the family. She couldn't imagine how he asked for the rent from the tenant farmers, or how he could look into the faces of people who tilled the land and harvested the crops and asked for a share of their hard work.

Silver Pearl didn't know how much money An Ling had. She thought of money in a vague, narrow way—the cost of a pair of shoes, a new gown, and a month's rent. She didn't know where An Ling's money came from or even where he kept it. She only knew that what held a man was not a woman's scented skin or family obligations to his children and wife, but something less apparent and very simple. It was a need for a safe haven, and opium was nothing less than a haven clouded with sweet, numbing smoke.

With opium, they would wake up in the late- afternoon when dusk was not far off. It would be late enough to look forward to the comfort of night, to anticipate it, to long for its opaque darkness, and its ability to provide a soft, enclosing place to dream.

Dreaming, the two of them shared an opium lamp. Everything else was nothing but darkness, a darkness that was all-consuming. The world beyond had nothing to do with them. It was just an opera playing somewhere far, far away. Then and there, it was just the two of them. She was his woman, his one and only for neither future nor past mattered anymore. There was only the present.

The yellow ring of light from the opium lamp lit their faces. They looked at each other through the curvature of the glass that enclosed the flame. His face looked strange and contorted. Suddenly it became the face of a stranger. But then she glanced again and thought: *Yes, it's him.* He wouldn't leave her again. He was like an insect under a glass jar, and she was there with him, an insect as well—the two of them trapped inside the same glass jar. They could see the world outside, but the turbulence and threatening noises barely reached them. They were here together, gazing at the same flame, breathing the same intoxicating air

It was a suicide pact in a way, but it was not unpleasant. They would go through this together, and they would have each other's company. They wouldn't be lonely. In this unreasonable, unpredictable world—who could come out alive? Who could outlast this madness? Silver Pearl had few choices. Opium was one thing she understood, and with it, she could understand An Ling.

✳ ✳ ✳

Dawn hovered outside the window. A lone rooster was crowing somewhere. The sky was fading and the moon was translucent and spent, hanging exhausted over the horizon. Little Jade lay on the bed and pulled the quilt over her head. Her face was warmed by her own breath under the heavy, musty quilt. She listened to her step-grandmother get up from her bed, coughing loudly. She turned on the radio, keeping the volume low. In the quiet of the morning, the scratchy transmission reached through the quilt and filled Little Jade's ears with news of the civil war reported in a monotone by a solemn-voiced man—news that frightened the twelve year-old child. The Nationalists were coming to rescue the people of the northeast. The Communists must be defeated. The Communists had replaced the Japanese as the enemy. The newscasts were followed by a woman's high-pitched voice urging listeners to buy a palace-formulated pearl cream that would keep skin forever young. Little Jade could hear her step-grandmother making breakfast and boiling water in the kitchen, heating up the leftovers from last night's late snack. There was the sound of the spatula shoveling inside a wok and then the smell of food, oily and heavily seasoned with scallions and garlic. The smell of burned soy sauce made Little Jade hungry.

The noise of the day started to rise from the house in the gray, misty morning air. Little Jade turned in her bed fighting the smell of food and the pangs in her stomach, not wanting to get up. Her throat was sore and her eyes were hurting, as if they had been soaking in vinegar. But she had to go to school. Little Jade sat up slowly and rubbed her eyes with the back of her hands. In the chilly air, she stepped into the shoes next to her bed and dressed quickly. She pulled on the padded jacket and pants and closed the buttons with icy fingers.

Little Jade walked toward the kitchen. She stopped and leaned against the greasy doorframe. Her step-grandmother hunched over the stove. She tucked her hands into her sleeves and walked over to her step-grandmother who was looking at the contents of the wok. Next to the wok, the porridge was bubbling in a pot, and as Little Jade lifted the lid to check it. Her face was momentarily lost in a rush of white steam.

The step-grandmother turned around, and frowned as she looked at Little Jade. "How come your eyes are swollen? They are as big as walnuts."

Little Jade answered hoarsely, "My throat hurts." The old woman walked away, muttering that the girl must have caught a cold and that she should stay in bed. Little Jade looked inside the wok, picked up a greasy steamed bun with her fingers, and bit into it. She chewed slowly. The steam from the kettle condensed into tiny droplets of water all over her face. Little Jade was warm on the outside, but the inside of her chest and stomach felt cold and hard.

The old woman returned with a dark green bottle with a bright pink label. She unscrewed the cap and poured out its thick, black contents into a large spoon. "Take this," she said. Little Jade swallowed the sweet, minty syrup that cooled her tongue and squeezed out a smile at the old woman. The step-grandmother said, "You better stay home today. You shouldn't go to school."

Little Jade touched her forehead with the back of her hand and said, "I don't have a fever. I can go out." The old woman looked at Little Jade suspiciously and pulled at her eyelids, looking inside them for infection. The pulling hurt and brought tears to Little Jade's eyes. She felt nauseous from smelling the old woman's breath.

"You're fine," the step-grandmother said finally.

Little Jade slammed the door shut behind her and headed for school. There was a layer of white winter frost covering the gray tiles on the neighbor's roof. It covered the top of the red brick wall that lined the narrow stone-paved road. Strands of smoke rose from the chimneys in straight lines, into the pale morning sky. There was no wind. The wet gutters along the road were shimmering, reflecting the sunlight that warmed her face. She shoved her hands deeply into her jacket pockets as she walked down the street.

She had been going to school on and off since spring, and had been living in the rented house for nearly a year. During the summer, her father talked about moving the family to the south where there was no war. He said that they would move as soon as he could sell more land and get enough money together. He often went away, sometimes for a few days and sometimes for nearly a month. He would come home haggard and even quieter. He hadn't said anything about moving since the weather turned cool. Little Jade's father and Silver Pearl no longer went out during the evenings. Instead, they stayed in their bedroom smoking opium and listening to the radio. They had a platform built beside the window on which they laid side by side sharing an opium lamp. Sometimes Little Jade heard them moving about in the house, running water and clearing their throats in the bathroom, looking for food in the kitchen, their slipper-clad feet dragging across the squeaking wooden floor, but Little Jade didn't see them much.

Still, there were times when Little Jade's father called her into his room, turned down the radio, and told the girl to recite texts from her school book. Little Jade found herself standing uneasily in front of the opium platform while her father and Silver Pearl watched her with half-opened eyes. The purple haze made Little Jade blink as she recited from the ancient text, "If a man doesn't learn, he is less than an object. He learns when he is young, and he works when he is grown." As Little Jade recite, Silver Pearl cracked salted melon seeds and threw them into her mouth or fed them to her husband.

Silver Pearl was pregnant again. She had cut her hair and had it curled. Her hair spread around her face like a heap of overgrown weeds. She didn't wear much make-up anymore, except for blood-red lipstick, carelessly applied. It stained the food she ate and the rim of her teacup. She didn't look so beautiful anymore. Her face had grown thinner as her waist had thickened. Little Jade's father was looking gaunt as well. His gown lay in deep folds along his lanky body. He glanced at his daughter's textbooks as he listened, nodding his head.

✳ ✳ ✳

Silver Pearl looked at the overcast sky and murmured, "It's going to snow today, look at the sky." Her voice trailed off, heard by no one. She leaned against the window, listening to An Ling flip through the newspaper as he reclined on the sofa. Her mother was sweeping the room. The brittle broom scratched the wooden floor as waves of dust rose up around her giving off a dull shimmer in the sluggish gray light. It was only late morning and Silver Pearl was already tired. The oppressive sky outside the window made breathing harder. Her lungs felt tight as she inhaled the dusty air. She fingered the butterfly knot at the base of her collar, touching the intricate twists of the smooth silken cord, feeling bloated in her gown. Her eyes were filled with the shadows around her—the bookcase with a few books and piles of movie magazines, the tall basket of coal next to the kitchen door, a slender blue vase filled with dry stems of coiling vines and dusty peacock feathers on a tall rosewood stand.

An Ling got up from the sofa and entered the bedroom dragging the heels of his slippers along the creaking floor. Soon she could hear him adjusting the radio dial. A loud voice burst out from the static behind the half-closed door. Her throat felt grainy and dry. She went to the kitchen to get something to drink. There, in the darkness, a kettle of water was steaming on top of the stove about to boil. She looked around for a jar of tea leaves, and heard shuffling footsteps behind her.

She turned and saw Little Jade standing next to the cupboard, holding a red bean cake in each hand. Little Jade looked startled, but she was still chewing with a full mouth. Silver Pearl frowned at her. "Always eating," she said, "you little motherless beggar."

A narrow beam of sunlight filtered through the dirty windowpanes and lit up Silver Pearl's face. Little Jade watched her garish red lips spit out the hateful words. Her eyes burned. She strode up to Silver Pearl and pushed her as hard as she could.

It was the one of the few times she had ever touched Silver Pearl. The fabric of her gown felt cold and slippery. The flesh underneath was soft like dough and gave no resistance to her push. Everything happened in a flash. Silver Pearl let out a short cry and stumbled back, her left elbow knocking over the kettle on the stove as she reached back to steady herself. She fell against the greasy kitchen wall. Boiling water splashed all over the kitchen floor. White steam filled the kitchen and warmed the air. She covered her belly with her hands, groaning as she slid down against the wall. She stared at Little Jade with hatred and fear.

The step-grandmother and the father rushed into the kitchen, pushing Little Jade aside. "What happened?" An Ling asked loudly, shooting accusing looks at his daughter. Little Jade avoided his eyes and hid her hands behind her back. Silver Pearl pointed at the girl with her hand, unable to speak. "Aiya...Aiya..." The step-grandmother shook her head nervously. They carried Silver Pearl into the bedroom leaving Little Jade alone in the kitchen.

Little Jade stood there trembling, blinking hard, and trying to absorb the magnitude of what had just happened. She clenched her teeth and her fists, thinking that the fight was over all too soon. And she had lost. The smoke-blackened portrait of the hearth god looked down at her in silence.

She had crossed a forbidden line, and she did not know what the penalty would be for this violation. She felt her heart tightening. "I'm doomed," she whispered, though there was no one to hear her. Yet hearing her own voice, Little Jade felt strangely assured. In the corner of the kitchen, she found a dry spot and crouched down snuggling next to a bag of rice. She could see water gathering into puddles on the concrete kitchen floor reflecting the weakening beams of sunlight from the window. She hugged her knees and closed her eyes, imagining herself shrinking smaller and smaller, into a bug or a mote of dust, disappearing altogether. Her father was shouting at her step-grandmother to get a doctor quickly. Little Jade knew only too well that Silver Pearl had become a victim, just as surely as she had become a villain. Left with the choice of protecting his errant daughter or his pregnant wife, her father would have to protect Silver Pearl.

* * *

Soon afterwards, An Ling decided to send Little Jade away to an abbey school for girls run by Catholic nuns from France. He explained to his daughter that she needed better schooling, and then he paused and promised that he would come to get her when everything calmed down. Little Jade stared at him as he told her this, feeling her fingers turning cold and her eyes filling with tears. She felt ashamed. She said nothing.

The doctor assured Silver Pearl that her child was unharmed. It was lucky that she did not fall on top of the stove. Just to be on the safe side, she was to stay in bed for the time being. She openly accused Little Jade of placing a curse on her and said that having Little Jade around was dangerous to her unborn child. Little Jade thought that her father believed Silver Pearl.

On the day of departure, Little Jade followed her father out, letting the door with peeling red paint slam behind her with a cruel finality. An Ling lifted his daughter into the waiting wagon and stepped in to sit beside her. As they pulled away from the rented house, Little Jade was overwhelmed by a sense of loneliness so absolute and so without hope that she dropped her face over her knees and began to sob. *I hate her, I hate her, I hate her!* She screamed silently, gasping as tears washed over her face, drenching the coat over her lap. *Silver Pearl was right. I wished for her death. Without Silver Pearl, father and I would not be apart. Now that Silver Pearl has won, and I've lost, Silver Pearl will never let the father come back for me. This is the end. I have no one now, no father, no mother, no grandmother. Where is my mother? My own mother. Will I ever see her in my lifetime?* Little Jade repeated these questions silently over and over again. *Who could answer these questions?*

She refused to look at her father when he reached over to touch her hand. An Ling patted his daughter's head tentatively, and then he withdrew his hands into the pockets of his coat. They rode in silence. Every bounce of the wagon reminded Little Jade that she was alone again.

The sky hung low overhead. Somber gray clouds rolled slowly, moodily, contemplating a storm. The folds of the clouds were tinted a soft green like the patina of rusted ancient weapons. A yellow light was dimming over them. The day was fading fast. A chill set in, and a swarm of blackbirds soared suddenly into the sky like a dense shadow, screaming and scrambling and finally diving into a cluster of evergreen in a nearby cemetery.

CHAPTER 15:
THE ABBEY SCHOOL, 1946

After Little Jade's father left her at the abbey school, she knew he wouldn't come back for her. But she was determined to find a way to return to him and to somehow make Silver Pearl disappear. Maybe she would run away from the school and find her way back to her father like an abandoned dog refusing to be left behind, whether Silver Pearl liked it or not.

Little Jade shared a dormitory room with five other girls. One of them was named Bai Feng, which means White Phoenix. Bai Feng became her friend. During the first few weeks at the school, Little Jade avoided talking to anyone. But as she slowly came to notice the things and people around her, Bai Feng was always there. She followed Little Jade everywhere and sat next to Little Jade whenever she could. Bai Feng was determined to be Little Jade's friend, and Little Jade allowed it.

Bai Feng was at least fourteen, maybe even fifteen. It was not until much later that Little Jade realized that Bai Feng had had no friends before Little Jade arrived. No one else would befriend her because she was overweight and because her face was covered with pockmarks. Little Jade felt an affinity with Bai Feng and her imperfections. She rolled up her trousers to showed Bai Feng the smooth discs of slightly indented skin on the surface of her legs.

Before long, they were going everywhere together. They became inseparable. They sat next to each other in the classrooms and in the dining room. Bai Feng always gave Little Jade choice pieces from her portion of the meal. She was trying to lose weight, she would always say, I shouldn't eat so much.

Every Sunday, it was mandatory to attend mass at the school chapel. The chapel was a rectangular building with a tall ceiling and high windows. It used to be a warehouse and was the only room large enough to accommodate all the students and teachers from the abbey school. At one end of the room, there was a wooden stage decorated with heavy green fabric. The podium was draped with white cloth elaborately embroidered with a golden cross. Behind the stage, there was an altar of white painted wood with touches of gold. A pair of heavy pillar candles were placed stood on either side of the altar and in the center there was a statue of the Madonna holding baby Jesus. The full-cheeked face of the baby Jesus had an impossibly wise expression. The Madonna had golden hair and dull blue eyes. She looked down at the baby resting on her chest and the corners of her lips lifted just a bit in an almost-but-not-quite smile. She wore a long robe of blue and white with gold trim at the edges. Little Jade thought she bore a striking resemblance to the Kwan Yin statue from her grandma's room. When Little Jade was a little baby, her own mother must have looked down at her and smiled, but no matter how hard she tried, Little Jade could not recall her mother's face.

* * *

Usually, the sermon was delivered by a visiting priest from the local church. He was a thin, Chinese priest with hair parted in the middle who wore gold-rimmed glasses and spoke with a heavy southern accent. He told the students to keep their hearts as pure as the heart of the holy Madonna who gave birth to Jesus while still a virgin. Little Jade had heard of similar stories of the Immaculate Conception from Chinese fables: women who were impregnated by forces of nature—a shooting star, a five-colored cloud, or a dragon that emerged from a storm. The resulting child always became the emperor or the empress.

The priest told the girls stories from the Bible puzzling them with tales of the suffering Job and the rivalries between Cain and Abel. No one could ever understand the points of these stories, but nevertheless, the students listened politely. From time to time, an old French nun played a small organ, and the Chinese nuns led the students in singing choir songs.

"Don't think evil thoughts," he warned sternly. The audience was timid and silent. He went on to tell them the story of King David and Bathsheba. This was a tale of adultery that was not entirely suitable for the young girls sitting before him. Fortunately, his delivery was dry and his accent was thick, and the students did not pay much attention.

There was another wood statue that hung high from the ceiling of the chapel. It was of the grown Jesus suffering on the cross. It was placed discreetly behind a pair of dark green curtains. So much nakedness of a grown man would be scandalous in a school for girls. Little Jade caught a glimpse of Jesus' face and was taken by the sadness of his eyes and the blood dripping from his open wounds. It was a disturbing sight. It reminded Little Jade of the tortured scenes on the Buddhist temple walls that portrayed different punishments in hell. The mountains made of knives and the sinners being fried in the depth caldrons of oil, the gossips and liars having their tongues cut out. The adulterers were naked and were half-eaten by wolves. Grandma always told her to close her eyes while she led her by the hand through that stretch of the temple galley. The only difference was that all the sinners in the picture looked horrified while the face of Jesus was filled with a peace and acceptance that belied his suffering. Little Jade could not bear to look at him for long.

The curtains were pulled open only once during a special visit from a French priest. The entire school got into such a stir in preparation for his visit. Even the ever-serious French nuns became giddy with excitement. They fussed over every detail. Everything had to be just right. The furniture and floor were polished to a high sheen and the students were told to press their uniforms for the occasion. On the appointed day, all the nuns dressed in their snow-white habits instead of the usual gray robes while the students wore perfectly pressed white shirts and long, knife-pleated blue skirts. The celebrated guest was a tall man with orange hair, bushy orange eyebrows, and ruddy skin. Little Jade had never seen such coloring on a human being. And his eyes! They were blue as the tip of a flame burning in hell. Little Jade had seen such eyes on the face of a demon in Buddhist paintings on temple walls.

That special Sunday, the chapel was brightly lit with extra candles. Two kerosene lamps hung high to illuminate the figure of Jesus on the cross. After the choir sang a welcome song for the special guest, the foreign priest stood on the altar and said his sermon in a strange accent that was difficult for Little Jade to understand. He wore a flowing white robe with a thick gold sash draped around his neck. He urged the audience to believe in the Holy Trinity: the Father, the Son and the Holy Ghost. He explained that we were all sinners since birth because Adam took a bite from the apple offered by Eve. We should confess our sins and pray for forgiveness.

Little Jade knew that it was Mencius, a student of Confucius, who stated that all human beings are good at the beginning of their lives and that it is what they learn later on that changes human nature for the worse. Grandma had believed that sins and good deeds are carried from lifetime to lifetime through reincarnation. She believed that she suffered because she had done something bad in her previous lifetime. All she could do in this lifetime, she would say, was to perform good deeds and hope for a better life in her next reincarnation. How odd to think that you could be free of your sins by simply confessing them. It would be too easy! The logic of sins, confession, and forgiveness was confusing to Little Jade. The nuns burned sweet smelling incense during the mass. It brought tears to its audience's eyes. The sound of the organ music swelled again and the priest said, "Let's pray."

The priest sipped from a glass of red wine and took a small white wafer from a gold cup. He lifted the cup high in front of the altar and chanted in a foreign language. The students were told to line up to receive communion. The elderly French nun held a golden goblet covered with a piece of neatly folded white linen. The priest picked up thin white wafers, one at a time, and placed one into the mouth of each waiting recipient. Little Jade inched forward watchful of the girls in front of her. Finally, it was her turn. She stood there facing the towering priest. He held the wafer and deftly placed it on her tongue as he said something in a language she did not understand. Little Jade avoided meeting his eyes and was trembling as she walked away.

She knew that the wafer symbolized the body of Jesus who died on behalf of a sinful mankind. Little Jade was afraid to swallow the wafer certain that if she did an unknown force would fester within her and one day take over, but the wafer began to melt. Little Jade held the last trace of the wafer on the tip of her tongue. She wanted to spit it into her handkerchief, but she knew that this would be disrespectful. She did not know what to do and the wafer had melted in her mouth before she could make up her mind.

✳ ✳ ✳

In the classroom they memorized and recited Confucius' words. They recited out loud that "their bodies, hair, and skin were given to them by their parents and they must not damage themselves." They also learned the rules of proper behavior for a woman according to the Book of Etiquette and Conducts for Women: "Do not show your teeth when laughing, do not sway your skirts when walking, always observe the expressions of others and listen carefully before speaking."

In sewing classes, they cut patterns and learned to make simple smock dresses tied with a sash. They learned to put together colors: bright red should never contrast bright purple, scallion green is compatible with peach blossom pink, aqua blue and sky blue are calming to the eyes. They learned to embroider and made flower blossoms on pieces of silk with hair-thin needles. Little Jade often helped Bai Feng, who had poor eyesight, thread the needles and finish a stitch just right, hiding the knot, and the end of the thread under the fold of the fabric. In nursing classes, they learned to make bandages from clean white cloth and to wrap bandages in different ways depending on the nature of the injuries. They learned to make a sling for a broken arm, and to secure a wooden stick along the injured arm or leg to keep it in position. Bai Feng was good at tying neat knots and wrapping bandages nice and tidy—but not so tight that the blood could not circulate. The nuns helped out in the local hospital and the older students were expected to assist them. Bai Feng was one of the students who accompanied the nuns during these visits.

Bai Feng told Little Jade of the things she saw in the hospital. She helped with dressing the wounded soldiers from the Nationalist Army. She overheard the soldiers saying that the Japanese had been defeated and that the Chinese were fighting each other now that battles were being waged by the Nationalists against the Communists.

When the Japanese had surrendered, the hospital was taken over by the Americans. The American doctors and Chinese nurses worked with the French nuns. One of the nurses, Miss Du, was friendly with Bai Feng. They often took breaks together. Miss Du had an American name, Lily. She told Bai Fang that only Nationalists soldiers received treatments at the hospital because the Americans were friends of the Generalissimo Chiang Kai Shek. Without the weapons from the Americans, the Nationalists wouldn't be able to fend off the Communists advances. A captured Communist was a dead Communist. Thus, the Communists have no use for hospitals, Lily said.

✳ ✳ ✳

In the nursing textbooks, there was a chapter on midwifery, a subject that was not taught in the classroom. The students were told that they should read it on their own and that it would not be on the exams. One night, Bai Feng and Little Jade flipped through the pages of the textbook together and read it carefully while looking closely at the crude drawings that illustrated the birth of a child. They tried to decipher the names on the arrows pointing at the different parts of a woman's body. The womb was the "fetus's palace," the ovaries were the "egg nests," and the vagina was the "dark passage."

"That is where the baby comes out," Bai Feng said pointing to one of the pictures.

"Ah-h-h-h...!" Little Jade marveled at the new discovery. She stared at the drawing of a woman's body. "But it's impossible, Feng. The baby is too large to come out of an opening so small," Little Jade whispered, thinking of her own body.

*** *** ***

The eggshell-white schoolhouse stood on a gentle hillside facing Jade Lake. The lake was green and reflected the bamboo forest surrounding it. A mud road led from the side of the school through thickly grown bamboo trees and ended at the cobble stone beach where Bai Feng and Little Jade liked to take walks. Watching the green silk lake wrinkle into delicate fish-scale patterns at each breath of wind, Little Jade would settle on one of the large stones that littered the cobblestone beach. Bai Feng walked bare-footed in the shallow water, her skirt tucked at her waist, and her white slip was showing underneath.

One day, while they were at the lake, Bai Feng told Little Jade that years ago there hadn't been any large stones on the beach. She said that a long time ago the lake had belonged to no one. Women from nearby villages used to go to the bamboo forest in groups to dig for bamboo shoots after a good rain, but young women were warned not to go into the forest alone. People said that there was a dragon king living beneath the surface of the tranquil lake. After a while, rumors circulated about a certain young woman, who seemed to be gaining weight steadily and whose voice drifted easily. She pricked her fingers too often when she did her needlework in the company of other village women.

One day she disappeared. A web of bloody membrane was found floating in the white reeds that grew along the shore of the lake. Some of the membrane covered the cobblestones and made them look like blood-shot eyes that had lost their pupils. The village people said that the dragon king came out of the lake to find young women to be his brides. They said that the dragon transformed himself into human form—except he still had dripping hair that coiled like waterweeds as if he'd just gone swimming, and tiny blue scales behind his ears and under his arms. When he found a young woman alone in the forest, he would pretend to be lost, and he would ask for directions. The unfortunate woman, her hands muddy from digging bamboo shoots, would look up and see his strangely liquid eyes which were of the clearest blue, pouring over her. She would follow him into the lake.

After the dragon king made the young woman pregnant, he let her go knowing that she would return on a moonlit night to the cobblestone beach. There, she would give birth to a stone the size of a newborn infant, and die. And he would watch from the center of the lake, weeping as he witnessed the death of his bride. Then he would cover her face with her long black hair and bury her at the bottom of the lake. The stone would be left on the beach to absorb the essence of the sun and the moon, and it would break open one day when its time had come.

Listening to Bai Feng, Little Jade ran her fingers over the coarse surface of the stone which had been warmed by the sun. She imagined something alive and monstrous inside the stone, something that was moving and turning beneath her. But Bai Feng did not notice how quickly Little Jade stood up from the stone. Bai Feng merely said, "Let's go, it's getting late." The shadow cast on the water by her plump body grew longer and longer as the sun slowly dropped behind the forest.

Little Jade followed Bai Feng through the bamboo forest pushing the thick branches aside and feeling the dry leaves crackle softly underfoot. The rustling of the leaves stirred up memories of another bamboo forest from long ago, her very own forest. An unsettling darkness rose within Little Jade. It was like the secretive tides of the lake which were rising steadily now under the sickle of the new moon hanging just above the forest.

* * *

Little Jade's father was coming to visit. His letter had arrived the other day. Carefully, Little Jade had opened the blue envelope with her name on it. It read "Miss Su Bright Jade," her school name.

Each stroke of the characters was written in a determined, strong hand, denting the envelope. It was a short letter, written in a formal language, as if he expected the nuns to open the students' mail.

Bright Jade my daughter:

How have you been recently? Is everything well at school? I'm fine and so is your second mother. I will come visit you at the end of this month. Study with attention and be well.

Your father

It was the first letter Little Jade had ever received. She read it over and over. It was so short that she soon memorized every word. Her father did not say that he was coming to take her back. This she noted with a needling anxiety. At least he had not forgotten her. She liked the way he had addressed her by her full name. She carried the letter with her everywhere and used it as a bookmark, and refused to show it to anyone, including Bai Feng. At night, Little Jade pressed the letter against her cheek, feeling the smooth paper. She imagined the ink seeping into her skin, leaving blue imprints like tattoos.

✳ ✳ ✳

Little Jade's father arrived during a class one afternoon. As soon as the nun knocked on the classroom door and interrupted the teacher, Little Jade knew that the nun had come for her. She closed her notebook and hurried out of the classroom. She could feel her classmates' eyes on her back like black flies. She followed the billowing gray robe of the nun down the empty concrete hallway. The day was cold and the sky sparkled like a great gem. The air was pure and icy and filled with white sunlight. She balled up her fists and bit her lip, she remembered the first time she had seen her father: *Had it also been a blindingly bright day then?*

Little Jade remembered her grandmother's hand holding firmly onto hers and her grip squeezing tight as she led her to see the returned father. She remembered her heart racing ahead of her. As she walked down the hallway, her heart was already outside the door, anxiously waiting for her grandmother to open it. But here at the school—seeing the door of the guest lounge approaching at the end of the hallway—she wanted to run away.

The door opened without a sound. Little Jade saw her father sitting on the deep green sofa smoking a cigarette. His hand dangled from the armrest which was covered with a crocheted square of yellow and white daisies. Seeing her father, Little Jade's heart took so great a leap that she could imagine it bursting from her chest and landing between the two of them. Without openly staring at him, Little Jade devoured her father with her eyes and inhaled his cigarette smoke deep into her lungs. He was wearing a white shirt. Its starched collar was crisp against his clean-shaven face.

An Ling looked up and smiled at Little Jade. He nodded at the nun as she closed the door and turned to Little Jade. He asked her whether she wanted some tea. He had brought along a box of candy for her, and he pointed at the red velvet box on the coffee table. Little Jade was glad to be treated like a grown-up, and she accepted his offer of tea. An Ling poured the tea from a pot that the nuns had left in the lounge. The thin white teacup with its gold rim felt hot in Little Jade's hands. She put it down and rubbed her hands together stealing glances at her father's half-frowning face waiting for him to speak. But he kept on smoking, drawing deeply at his cigarette and blowing more and more smoke into the space between them. Little Jade looked down, and studied the shadows on the polished wood floor that had been cast by crystalline sunlight streaming through the rippling white lace curtains.

An Ling leaned back, resting on the sofa. He smoothed back his thick hair, shining with hair oil whose sight and scent were so familiar. "Have some candy," he said suddenly. "Here." He pulled at the pink ribbon on the candy box. Ash from his cigarette fell on the red velvet box and he brushed it off clumsily while thrusting the opened box in front of his daughter. Little Jade stared at his hand and at the gold-foil-covered candies. She took one, peeling the foil carefully. *What is he going to say?* Little Jade picked up the teacup with a shaking hand and took a sip. The tea was bitter.

An Ling drew at his cigarette and did not speak a word. His brows were knitted as they always were whenever Little Jade was around and his cheeks were more hollowed than they used to be. There were more angles and lines on his face. Through his open collar, the bony knot at his throat looked bare and helpless.

Little Jade did not know when they started, but she was startled to find tears crawling down the sides of her face. At first An Ling did not notice because Little Jade did not make a sound. She was thinking of her grandmother—the way she looked at her and shook her head, and the way she sighed. Little Jade closed her eyes and felt a curtain of tears streaming down her face and dripping from her chin. "What's the matter, Little Jade?" An Ling went over to his daughter, pulling a large handkerchief out of his pocket trying to wipe her face.

Little Jade blew her nose and said between sobs, "I miss grandma..."

An Ling's face turned pale just as it had the first time Little Jade ever saw him. Little Jade looked hard at him with blurry eyes. *There's no use, no use*, she thought. He stood up. "I've got to go," he said, "I will come see you again in a month's time."

He spoke quickly, airily, each word light as a feather.

"The end of next month?" Little Jade asked.

"Yes," he said, as he put on his black trench coat. "I promise."

There was something in his voice this time, which reassured Little Jade in a small way. But the feeling was fleeting, and it dissipated as soon as she saw him walk out the door of the guest lounge. The door swung open behind him, letting in enormously bright sunlight and a frigid wind. He must be walking quickly down the corridor now, as fast as he could, without breaking into a run.

Instinctively, Little Jade ran after him and called out: "Baba!" She felt her throat tearing. Halfway down the hall, he stopped amidst the sunshine and turned back to look at his daughter, his hair blown back by the incessant wind. "Baba!" She called like a small child. She could hear her own voice, thin, wavering, piercing against the wind.

An Ling stood there, the length of his body blocking the hallway, his trench coat blown open, flapping like wings impatient to take off.

Little Jade ran to him. "Take me home," she pleaded in a small voice as she clutched his sleeve. "Please..."

He looked at his daughter and then down at the concrete floor. A nun walked pass them, and they averted their faces. Little Jade knew that many eyes were peering out of the classroom windows. Chattering students were being hushed by their teachers.

"I can't," he explained softly. "Not today. Silver Pearl is giving birth soon." He stopped, staring over the girl's head, and then looked down at her again. "I promise I'll come back to see you," he repeated. "I will come again soon."

"I'll change," Little Jade said, pulling at his sleeve. "I'll change." She couldn't think of anything else to say. "Please, Baba." Tears still streamed from her eyes. In shame and fear she tried to hide her face with her free hand knowing that she was making a scene.

"Don't do this, Little Jade." An Ling's voice grew impatient. "I'll come back next month to take you home." Hearing this, Little Jade loosened her grip. An Ling looked deep into his daughter's eyes for a moment, then quickly turned and walked away.

CHAPTER 16:
THE DRAGON KING, 1946

It must be true, Little Jade thought. *He will come for me and take me home. He couldn't lie in front of so many people.* She walked back toward the guest lounge in a daze as the sun was glaring above her.

Everyone had seen what happened with Little Jade and her father in the hallway. From then on, everywhere she went, she felt people's knowing eyes glancing quickly past her. They whispered to each other, "It's her…she's the one," and pretended not to notice her.

Later that day, when she was eating lunch in the dining room, Bai Feng came to sit quietly next to her. "Are you going home, Bright Jade?" She asked after some hesitation. She was looking away as she spoke.

"No, I'll stay here and rot," Little Jade replied curtly. Bai Feng looked startled, and stayed silent. Little Jade ignored her. She was fighting not to cry—not here, not again, where everyone could see. She ate slowly and concentrated on her bowl. She did not lift her head to look at the people around her. After a while Bai Feng left without saying a word.

Later, Little Jade told Bai Feng that she was sorry, but she said nothing about her father. She couldn't. What if he didn't come back as he promised? She could not allow herself to believe him this time. If she told everyone he was coming next month and he failed to show up and shamed her, then what would she do? She couldn't bear to think about it.

One day, Little Jade and Bai Feng were leaning against the dormitory window, as was their custom, looking at Jade Lake gleaming like a mirror in the distance, reflecting the early afternoon sun. Summer was in full bloom. The bamboo forest was a luxurious green. That was the day that Bai Feng told Little Jade that her friend Lily had introduced Bai Feng to her brother. They had had tea together during a break from Bai Feng's hospital duty. His name was Kai, and he told Bai Fang that China needed young people like her to build a new future, a future without corruption. Bai Fang went on and told Little Jade that it was a waste of time to learn about Jesus and Confucius; Kai had said so. He said what China needed was modern ideas and the hearts and souls of young people to fight for an ideal future. The old ways are dead and religious superstition and idols were useless symbols that only hold people back. The force of going forward could not be stopped. Communism was the only savior for China.

Bai Fang was excited when she repeated what Kai had said to her. Her eyes were shiny and her cheeks were flushed. Little Jade did not say much. She was preoccupied by thinking of her own trouble with her father. Eventually, Bai Fang also fell into silence looking away with glistening eyes and pressed lips. They stood quietly, next to each other, each was deep in her own thoughts, their shoulders nearly touching while they drifted further and further away from each other.

* * *

The sky had fallen, Little Jade thought, as she lay in bed staring out the window at the moonless night sky. Soon she would be back in her father's house—two weeks and three more days from today. She would be sleeping in her own bed in the same room with her step-grandmother and listening to the sound drifting from the radio in her father's bedroom.

The melody of a song played in Little Jade's head. It had been a popular tune a while ago and the radio had played this song in which a woman sang about roses blooming everywhere all day and all night long. She listened to the music repeating itself in her mind, humming along under her breath. Everywhere and all over, roses were blooming, in her hair, outside the window, under the night sky. Little Jade made herself smaller, tucking her feet together, and curling her toes. Her tongue pushed against the back of her teeth and her mouth tasted sweet and wet.

She woke suddenly with damp cheeks and forehead. She sat up drowsily and saw someone standing next to the window, looking out. It was Bai Feng. Recently, she had been acting strange. Little Jade, deep in her own turmoil, hadn't paid much attention and was only vaguely aware that Bai Feng no longer followed her around.

Those days Bai Feng sat alone in the back of the classrooms and ate by herself in the dining room. She seemed to have stopped talking altogether. She appeared distracted. Little Jade tried to talk to her a few times during meals, but she soon realized that Bai Feng was more interested in the food and had grown even fatter.

Little Jade stared at Bai Feng against the background of the night that was slowly withdrawing, diluting its darkness with an increasingly generous infusion of light. Bai Feng was fully dressed and probably hadn't slept at all last night—or for many nights before. For the first time, Little Jade began to worry about her friend.

✳ ✳ ✳

Little Jade's heart stood still when the nun handed her the blue envelope—the second letter of her life. She turned and walked away, slowly at first, trying to decide where to go to read it. She walked faster and faster away from the school. The envelope was folded twice in her pocket. She held it between her fingers with all her strength while squeezing it so hard that ink seemed to seep out of the blue paper.

Little Jade had to get away from the school. It was almost evening, and the sky was the color of fire and smoke. In front of her, the road was narrow and long. She hurried past the schoolhouse, the dormitory, toward the bamboo forest. "I'm coming," Little Jade called out to the greenness with all her heart. She slowed down as she approached the outskirts of the forest. Lush and thick, it drew Little Jade in with a sense of inevitability. All around her the forest sobbed and sighed. It whispered: "Come...come...here..." Little Jade knew she had better hurry, or it would be dark before she reached Jade Lake. She rushed through the forest, hearing thousands of leaves cooing around her urging her on. Finally she could see the lake, opening itself in front of her, all pale silver and bright under the darkening sky. *Maybe the dragon king would come out tonight*, Little Jade thought as she looked for a large stone to sit on. She pulled the blue envelope out of her pocket. She opened the envelope with numb fingers and struggled to read in the fading light. The wind was turning cold.

Bright Jade My daughter:

I will not come to take you home at the end of this month. Your second mother is quite ill after giving birth to a daughter, your sister. I will come to see you as soon as she is better.

Your father

Little Jade didn't know how long she sat there. The sun was setting over the lake. *Where is the dragon king?* She would like to meet him. She could hear the wind whipping the forest around her. "Why?" Little Jade asked aloud in the windy darkness.

"Why, father?" She asked again, this time as loud as she could, clenching her fists. Heaven was silent, the moon gazed down. Little Jade imagined her father emerging from the lake, his black trench coat dripping, his hair slicked back in a wet sheen, his forehead white and forlorn. "Say something!" She shouted at the apparition of her father, "Say something! How come you never say anything to me?"

Standing up, she found that the cobblestone beach was flooded with water from the lake. She stood ankle deep in water beneath the moonlit sky. Heaven was silent, but she would not let up.

"What do I have to do, father?" Little Jade asked, quietly this time, as if asking herself, and then she knew the answer right away. It was so clear, as if he had told her himself. Jade Lake! Jade Lake was where she belonged. She started walking into the lake, her legs cutting through the cold, throbbing water.

"I'm coming father," Little Jade whispered, trying to steady herself as she stepped blindly over the slippery cobblestones.

"Little Jade!" She thought she heard someone calling her name, but she was not sure. "Little Jade!" She turned around and saw Bai Feng emerging from the bamboo forest. Bai Feng grabbed her wrists and pulled her toward the bamboo forest. Bai Feng's thick arm held onto her shoulders as Little Jade leaned against the soft shoulder of her only friend.

Bai Feng brought Little Jade to the edge of the forest where it met the school. She gestured toward the dormitory and nudged her forward a few steps. Bai Feng whispered, "Goodbye, Little Jade." and headed into the forest, disappearing into the encompassing darkness.

Little Jade was alone again. She stood there shivering and confused. Soon she heard someone calling "Su Bright Jade! Su Bright Jade!" Dots of a flashlight moved in a distance. It was a search party. She fell into the arms of a man and was carried back to the dormitory. The dormitory mistress settled Little Jade into her bed. Bai Feng never returned.

The next day Little Jade was called to the headmistress's office. Two uniformed men sat in the office. Mother Superior told her that they were from the sheriff's office and asked her to tell them what happened to her. They listened to her patiently. They asked her if she was a close friend of Bai Feng. Little Jade said that they had hardly spoken to each other recently. They interrupted and asked her whether she knew if Bai Feng had a boyfriend. Did Bai Feng ever talk about any man? Was she ever seen with any man—the gardener, the errand boy, anyone?

Little Jade wanted to mention Lily and her brother Kai from the hospital, but she swallowed her thought and said: "No, Bai Feng never mentioned any man to me, no one." Her voice was shaky. Mother

Superior told her to go to Bai Feng's room with the uniformed men. They wanted to go through her belongings. Little Jade might be able to help them discover whether any of Bai Feng's clothes were missing. Perhaps she simply ran away.

Little Jade followed the two men out of the office. It was another bright, clear morning, and the sun was warm. The schoolyard was quiet because classes were in session. The two men were tall and took long strides. They talked casually to each other in low voices as they walked toward the dormitory. The wind was blowing toward Little Jade as she trailed behind them. Along with a whiff of their dizzily strong body scent, she caught snatches of their conversation. "Another student missing…every year there's always one or two…young girls blossoming too early…some men…in the forest…"

Even though she couldn't tell whether any of Bai Feng's clothes were missing, they decided that Bai Feng had run away. After the men left, Little Jade sat on Bai Feng's bed and wondered what happened to her friend. *Did she run away with Kai to join the Communists? If she did, was she meeting other idealistic young men and women in secret places and safe houses? What would her fate be? Would she become pregnant – a young woman barely out of childhood carrying her own child? Would she one day be captured by the Nationalists and sing patriotic songs while facing a firing squad?* Little Jade never knew the answers. She never saw Bai Feng again.

* * *

Little Jade returned to the thick bamboo forest several days later. She walked down the muddy path to the cobblestone beach. She looked at the lake beyond the cobblestones and felt a rush of chill wind from its center sweeping over her blowing her hair away from her face. The sun was setting and half the sky was molten gold. The cobblestones were the color of brown eggs with gentle shadows on one side. The lake was shimmering as if dusted with gold. As the light faded and the wind grew stronger she listened to the sound of the bamboo forest washing over her again and again. She lay on the cobblestone beach feeling the hard, uneven surface of the stones beneath her. She looked up at the rising half moon and the sky full of fierce, beating stars. She folded her hands over her chest and felt the intimate warmth and the pounding of her heart.

Her thoughts drifted to flowers for no apparent reason. Then she realized why: She was thinking of what the two men said about young girls blossoming in the forest. She didn't understand what they meant, but as she lay there on the cobblestones, she imagined herself turning into a beautiful flower. The dragon king was emerging from the lake, brushing the wet hair from his forehead, and walking toward her. He knelt down next to her, and the blue water of his eyes filling her heart. The petals started to open, a forest of flowers, blooming, blooming, blooming at night.

CHAPTER 17:
A TURNING POINT, 1946

The Communists peasant soldiers were moving rapidly into northeast China as they competed against the Nationalists for the weapons left behind by the defeated Japanese Army. The abbey school that Little Jade attended had sent out letters to all the parents.

"The chaos of the war is closing in and the school can no longer be responsible for the safety of its students," these letters read, in large words surrounded by a deep red border. "Please come fetch your child as soon as you can."

The students were leaving in droves. The nuns requested that all students pack up their belongings. Every day, parents came for their daughters. There were tearful embraces and hurried farewells among the students and teachers. Time was running out.

As the student body thinned, the school cut back on the curriculum. Classes were combined. Most of the school buildings were shut down, except for one administrative building that also doubled as the dormitory for the school's last inhabitants. Toward the end, three Chinese nuns were left, along with two servants, a cook and a cleaning woman. The Chinese nuns wore gray habits and fluttered around like ghosts.

Finally, there were half a dozen students left, the unclaimed and presumed discarded ones –Little Jade among them. They were taught one class a day, a Bible study class. It was a ritual for the last few students. On Sundays, an elderly nun led the six girls into the chapel through the side door. She opened the door with an ancient key tied with a thick black string to her waist. Inside the chapel, she lit a single candle with trembling fingers. There were no more masses and visiting priests.

Another nun with a deeply creased face led the students in and knelt in front of the statue of the Madonna. Little Jade was at the edge of the half-circle of praying nuns and students. The nuns began the singsong chant of the Madonna. The chant glorified the beauty and kindness of Mary the Madonna who had given birth to baby Jesus.

In the chapel's semi-darkness, Little Jade closed her eyes, barely touched by the faint glow of a precariously flickering candle. She prayed hard to the white-robed deity above. She stood silently reciting bits and pieces of Lotus Kwan Yin Sutra that her grandmother had taught her.

Little Jade stared up at the statue of the Madonna who was gazing at her infant son. *What was she thinking? Was she contemplating the unknown future of her child? Did she know that his soft fingers and toes would one day be stained with blood?* The curtains at the back of chapel rippled ominously. Behind the curtains lurked the statue of the suffering Jesus nailed to the cross.

How terrible! Little Jade closed her eyes to block out the image in front of her. *This Jesus, this Madonna, had nothing to do with me.* Little Jade shifted uneasily in the kneeling position. She did not belong to the lighted part of the altar. She wanted to shrink into the darkened part of the chapel. She closed her eyes and remembered her grandmother who had been the sky above and the earth below—someone who would never change and would always be there. Yet she was gone. In Little Jade's life, her father was like a long-anticipated guest who finally came to visit, sometimes for a day, sometimes for months, but he was never expected to stay forever. And her mother—where could she be? Little Jade couldn't form any image of her. She remained a mystical figure like a goddess who existed long ago and about whom stories were woven into fables. Whether they would be told as an example of good deeds or a warning against a bad deed, Little Jade did not know. And then there was her step-grandfather who cared for her during a nightmare that stretched into months and had not yet ended. Step-Grandfather's sad eyes still haunted Little Jade. She missed him terribly. Bai Feng was gone too, probably forever.

Little Jade lowered her head, resting her forehead over her interlaced fingers. Her thoughts returned to her grandmother and to how the old woman's hands had touched all over her face. She could almost smell her scents of jasmine and sadness.

"Don't worry. Kwan Yin will protect us." Little Jade could hear her grandmother chanting:

"When traveling in a dangerous land, where bandits come with knives and swords, say the name of Kwan Yin aloud and the bandits will throw down their weapons. When crossing the ocean with treasures of pearls and corals, and when the waves of the sea threaten to turn over the ship, say the name of Kwan Yin aloud and the waves will calm. When the executioner is ready to befall his ax, say the name of Kwan Yin aloud and the ax will fall apart. When traveling in the forest, tigers and wolves will hunger for prey, but say the name of Kwan Yin and the beast will walk away. A thousand people pray to Kwan Yin, and she has appeared to them in a thousand different places. She always hears your prayer and she always protects you."

Little Jade felt as if she was in her grandmother's bedroom again. She could hear the chanting of the Lotus Sutra rising and falling, sounding clear for one moment and fading away the next. She was curling up inside the mosquito netting under the heavy quilt of blue silk. She wanted to stay there forever. Inhaling deeply, she could smell the sandalwood incense. Each strand of incense smoke carried to heaven an urgent request, a desperate plea, a fervent wish. The scent lingered in Little Jade's memory, a promise deferred indefinitely into the future.

Little Jade thought she heard the sound of bells ringing. With her eyes closed, she felt something brushing past her forehead. Maybe it was the tip of the trailing blue sash from Kwan Yin's robe. In an instant, an unfamiliar stillness overtook her. With it, a cool, clear feeling rose steadily within her. All the noises and burdens of life, the sharp words and painful edges, all that she had endured, and all the thought she could never be free of, never able to overcome were dissipating.

The future that was yet to come, yet to emerge in shapes that she could not, dared not imagine, no longer seemed so foreboding. Her cup had been empty and wanting for such a long time, but now it was brimming with a perfect stillness. It was as if a voice was telling her, "Don't worry, Little Jade. Don't worry."

* * *

As rumors abounded that the Americans were preparing to pull out of Tianjin, the school was nearly empty of students. Only four were left. Two older students had become nuns. They changed into the gray nuns' habits and wore kerchiefs over their hair. They explained to the younger students that they had decided to become God's brides and would serve God for the rest of their lives.

Little Jade was lying on her bed. She had become quieter after Bai Feng disappeared. She was turning into a mute. She prayed a great deal, partly because the praying comforted her and also because there was not much else to do.

The nuns prayed incessantly. There was a sense of impending doom, but no one mentioned this for fear of hastening its arrival. Little Jade and other three students were assigned chores around what was left of the school. They were glad to perform these small tasks because it kept their minds off the future. They helped the cook in the kitchen, washing and cutting vegetables, scrubbing pots and pans. They helped the cleaning lady with laundry, taking turns washing bed linens and the nuns' habits, which were heavy when wet.

It was getting cold and the late afternoon sunshine was waning. Everything was still and quiet in Little Jade's room. Someone was laughing far away and someone else was talking loudly about something she could not make out. Dust motes floated in the rays of the sun. She knew that she should be doing something—collecting firewood, washing dishes, sweeping the hallway, anything to keep busy, but for now she just wanted to be by herself in this desolate room. It would be evening soon, then the night, and then morning again. How many evenings, nights and mornings did she have left here at the abbey school?

A nun knocked on the door.

"Someone has come to see you," the nun said. "It's a woman, a young woman." Little Jade looked at the nun not understanding. She got up slowly and followed her quietly down the hall. She could not think of anyone who would visit her. A woman that Little Jade had never seen before was standing by the window in the guest lounge. She looked to be in her early twenties. She was wearing a camel-colored trench coat and a matching hat. She carried a black purse and held a pair of black leather gloves. She wore a pink lipstick and an eager expression. She walked toward Little Jade and nodded at the nun, dismissing her.

She took Little Jade's hand and sat her down on the sofa. She asked her, "What is your name? Do you have a nickname?"

"My name is Su Bright Jade. They call me Little Jade."

"How old are you? Where are you from?" The young woman leaned forward and smiled and encouraged the girl to say more. Little Jade could smell a faint scent of rose in her hair.

"I am twelve. I am from the Su Village." Little Jade answered without thinking.

"What is the name of your father? Your mother?" The stranger asked more questions.

"My father is Su An Ling. My mother…" Little Jade hesitated, "her name is Chang Wei Jen, my father told me." The questions were getting harder. Little Jade was glad that she knew all the answers. She dreaded being asked a question that she could not answer, but it never came.

She had told the young woman the facts that she knew about herself. The facts that she had held onto tightly. It had been strange to say her mother's name out loud, yet as she did, she saw the young woman's smile deepen. She reached over to squeeze Little Jade's hand and said, "I am so glad that I found you."

Then the young woman told her some things that were amazing. She said that she was Little Jade's fourth aunt, which meant that she was Chang Wei Jen's cousin. She told Little Jade that her mother had married again. She said that Wei Jen had been searching for Little Jade these past few months. She had learned that Little Jade was at the abbey school and had been waiting for the right time to get in touch with her.

Little Jade watched this stranger talking and talking. She tried to absorb what was being said. Someone had been looking for her and that someone was her mother. Carefully, in a whisper, she asked, "Are you taking me to see my mother?"

The Fourth Aunt paused for a moment and then explained that she could not take Little Jade with her, nor could Wei Jen come for Little Jade. The Fourth Aunt opened her purse and took out a piece of folded paper on which an address had been written. She also gave her a thick, heavy envelope made of coarse, sturdy paper. The only way for Little Jade to see her mother, said the Fourth Aunt, was for Little Jade to travel to the city of Peking. Little Jade could not go to her mother directly. First, she must go to a house where Wei Jen's extended family was staying. Wei Jen did not want to be accused of kidnapping. The Su family still knew a lot of people. The young woman urged Little Jade to act fast. Peking was two day's journey by horse wagon. The Communists were coming soon.

"Do you understand me?" The young woman asked. She looked into Little Jade's face, searching for a reply. Little Jade averted her face, and her eyes filled with tears.

"Don't cry, Little Jade. You will see your mother soon. You *will* go to her, won't you? She said that it is your choice. It is up to you. Why don't you take some time to think it over?"

Little Jade nodded, biting her lower lip. Her shoulders were shaking. The young woman sighed and said, "I am sorry I can't take you with me today. Your mother asked me to give you this message. If you go to your mother, you won't be able to return to your father. You must understand this. Your father cannot know about your mother." She squeezed Little Jade's hand, got up, and put her gloves on.

"Don't wait too long to decide, Little Jade. I hope to see you soon." The young woman took another look at Little Jade and walked out of the guest lounge.

Little Jade watched the door swung open letting in a splash of waning daylight. The door swung shut and the room darkened again. Over and over, she read the address on the piece of paper through teary eyes. Were these words written by her mother's hand? Perhaps her mother hands had touched the same paper that she was touching now.

She was careful to not stain the piece of paper with her tears. Her trembling fingers opened the thick envelope. Inside was a thick stack of ten thousand Yuan bills tied together with a rubber band. It was a large sum of money, even with the rampant inflation. As she tried to count out the bills, she paused to wipe the tears from her streaming eyes. Then she would lose count and start all over again, blinking the tears away as she tried to concentrate. The bills rustled between her fingers: red, green, and purple bills that scattered across her lap and drifted onto the floor. She lost count again and stopped. She sat there, letting tears wash down her face as a single thought rang through her mind: *mother, mother, mother! My mother wants me, has been looking for me, and is waiting for me. She sent for me, gave me money so that I can go to her in Peking. It doesn't matter anymore if father doesn't come for me. It doesn't matter because, at last, mother has found me.* Little Jade sat sobbing quietly in the room among the fallen bills scattered around her. After a while, she wiped her face dry and carefully gathered up the bills, one by one, and placed them back in the envelope.

She got up and pushed opened the door. Outside, a brand new world awaited her. Everything looked different somehow. The world now had a pink glow. Over the horizon, the setting sun dyed half the sky a festive flaming orange and purple, as if even the heavens were celebrating the news of her mother. Little Jade's shadow followed her as she headed for her dormitory room. She wanted to start packing right away. She walked quickly, almost running, ignoring someone who called out to her. It was getting dark. It was too bad she could not leave today, right now. But no matter, she would see her mother soon enough. It did not take long for her to pack her meager belongs into a simple bundle. At dinner, she ate little and did not say a word. She had to keep quiet in order to contain herself. The nuns were used to her silence by now. Everything would have to wait until tomorrow. She would savor this feeling tonight. Her mother wanted her.

Little Jade was too excited to sleep. She felt swept by a torrent of alternating sensations of hot and cold as if a fever were about to break. Her head was spinning with make-believe images of her mother, whose touch she could not fathom, whose face she could not recognize if she walked up to her on the street.

Two days of journey to Peking: there was only that short a distance between them. She wrapped herself into the quilt and held herself tight, squeezing hard. Her mother would embrace her just like this, only much better as she had long ago when Little Jade was a baby. As an infant she must had looked up to see a familiar face, smiling and cooing, looming over her like a sun, a moon, a universe. Little Jade drifted off to sleep, dreaming shapeless dreams of the impending future.

CHAPTER 18:
WEI JEN

Chang Wei Jen was born in 1911, the year of the birth of the Republic of China and the end of the Qing Dynasty. In that sense, her birth heralded the modern age of China. She was the third child of a wealthy silk merchant in the city of Shen Yang. She had two older brothers. The Chinese culture did not esteem the merchant class because they were a class of people who profited from the labor of others. The ranking of classes from high to low were soldiers who protect the nation against invaders, farmers who produce food for all, laborers who trade their strength and skills for a living, and lastly, the merchants. Scholars ranked above all and China had a traditional civil examination to recruit the talents of the Middle Kingdom to work for the emperor. The best scholar and the best poet had the potential to rise and become the first advisor to the Emperor—a position that would situate him below one person and above all others.

The family of the scholar was deemed The Family of the Fragrance of Books. Wei Jen's father hired a private tutor to school his two sons and his daughter. It was not long before the tutor reported to his patron that Wei Jen was a far better student than her elder brothers. Wei Jen was a diligent learner and a talented calligrapher. Wei Jen's father was pleased that one of his children had a mind for the books—but a daughter?

Wei Jen's mother was alarmed. She was concerned that she would have difficulty marrying off a daughter who aspired to be a scholar. "Who would want a scholar for a wife?" she asked.

The mother did not want Wei Jen to continue her studies beyond the second year and offered to bribe her daughter with gold bracelets. For each month the daughter did not study, she would be rewarded with a heavy, elaborately carved gold bracelet for a bridal dowry. Wei Jen chose to continue with her studies.

Wei Jen's calligraphy portrayed her personal strength and decisive nature. The strokes were fluent without hesitations and without uncertainties. She went on to study in a school opened by missionaries from America. She studied English from the Catholic nuns. She also studied western history and philosophy. She had a voracious appetite for learning and informed her parents that she would like to attend Peking University, which was the most prestigious university in China.

Her parents refused to give their permission. After Wei Jen graduated from the missionary school, she stayed as a teacher. She also wanted to improve her English by practicing with the nuns. Wei Jen was eighteen and her mother was eager to marry her off. Many matchmakers came and went from the Chang household. As Wei Jen turned twenty, the matchmakers made fewer visits.

The older students from Wei Jen's class had married at age sixteen and gotten pregnant soon afterwards. Wei Jen was practically an old maid at the age of twenty-two. She secretly applied to Peking University and was accepted. Her parents were not impressed. Wei Jen was not permitted to go anywhere unless she got married first.

But how to marry? There were no more visits from matchmakers. She had had many marriage proposals in the past and turned them all down. It appeared that she was fated to teach at the missionary school alongside the nuns. She was known in the village as the lady scholar. Prospective mothers-in-law were leery of young women like her.

It did not help that Wei Jen was not considered a beauty. Her face was unpainted and her gaze direct. She had a well-defined chin, prominent cheekbones, and full lips. She wore her shoulder length hair tied at the nape of her neck with dark red strings. She dressed simply in a white man-tailored shirt with a gently fitted navy blue skirt that nearly reached her ankles. A wide leather belt cinched her small waist, her only physical asset. She wore sensible low- heeled leather shoes.

Then, one day, a matchmaker knocked on the door of the house of Chang. The Su matriarch had heard about the lady scholar in the family. She was interested in making a match with her son, the young master Su. The Su family was from the north, where it was customary to marry older girls to younger boys. The young master Su was eighteen and Wei Jen was only four years older—a small difference according to the northern custom. Sometimes the difference of age between the older bride and the young groom could be as much as ten years. The young master Su was applying to Peking University. The Su family would agree to let the new bride attend the university with her husband so that she could take care of him.

Wei Jen's prayers were answered. She had secretly converted to Catholicism under the encouragement of the nuns. She had been praying every night for a chance to attend the university—to get away from her home and from the circle of people she had known all her life. When her mother discussed the marriage offer with Wei Jen, she agreed at once and her parents were overjoyed and very much relieved. It was such a simple solution to a long drawn-out impasse. Wei Jen was sure that the Virgin Mary had heard her prayers. Wei Jen's mother was sure that Buddha had finally heard *her* prayers and granted her only wish. She thanked Buddha for finding a home for her daughter. No longer did she need to fear that Wei Jen would become a ghost nun, a nun of the Catholic order.

During their first meeting, arranged by the families at a restaurant, Wei Jen had studied An Ling from across the crowded, round dinner table. He was a tall youth with searching eyes and a shy smile. Wei Jen did not exchange one word with An Ling, but at least they knew what the other looked like. It was better to marry someone not much younger than someone very much older. Both families were agreeable and a date for the wedding was set.

Unlike other educated young women of that era, Wei Jen did not enjoy reading romantic novels—not even the famous classic, *The Dream of the Red Chamber.* She did not harbor any illusion about romantic love. She observed her parents' marriage and the marriages of her older brothers. She was familiar with the petty bickering, the moments of affection, and the big fights over money and children. She was aware of the grinding, incremental existence of a man and a woman in close quarters, sharing meals, sharing a bed, and sharing their intimate selves.

An Ling had been an overly sheltered youth. He had grown up without a father. His mother hovered over him taking care of his every need. Wei Jen found An Ling immature and indecisive. It was his mother's idea for him to leave home to attend the university. An Ling's mother felt that her son needed to get out into society to gain some experience and harden his gentle ways. An Ling's mother had bargained for Wei Jen to help him with his schoolwork and with everything that he might need. She never thought that one day she would be out-smarted by the lady scholar daughter-in-law.

At her wedding, Wei Jen sat in the satin chair and was carried into the Su household with great ceremony. At nearly twenty-three, she felt much older than the young man who blushed when she looked his way. When they were alone together, he was like an eager child, and she was a compliant, indulgent wife. Wei Jen was much more excited about the prospect of traveling to Peking and enrolling in the university than she was about sharing intimacy with An Ling. Her new life was about to begin.

After the wedding, they went to the university and settled into an apartment next to the campus. He studied literature while she studied economics. Wei Jen soaked up the wide-open world of Peking University. She especially enjoyed participating in student discussions in classrooms. She pored over economic textbooks in English. An Ling and Wei Jen both made many friends. Wei Jen was one of the few female students on campus. She excelled in her classes and attracted much attention. She was happier than she had ever been until she found out that she was pregnant during the second semester. An Ling and Wei Jen went home to the Su family estate during the semester break in spring of 1934. It was there that Wei Jen gave birth to Little Jade. As soon as she was well enough, she wanted to return to the university. She had had a taste of university life, and there were no turning back for her. The red- faced infant sleeping quietly in her arms would not deter her from her goal—the goal she had set her sights on for as long as she could remember. Once she knew what it was like, she could choose no other life. She was addicted to the debates in the classroom, and the endless discussions over tea on the future of China. Everything was changing around her. She recognized that a great transformation was on the verge of taking place, though no one knew precisely what would happen. Wei Jen knew only that she had to return to her studies in Peking no matter what. She would not let the world move on without her. She would not be left behind in the countryside where women's roles had been codified for centuries, and where nothing ever changed. The following fall, she left Little Jade with her mother-in-law and returned to the university with her husband.

Because Wei Jen did not want to get pregnant again she encouraged An Ling to study in Japan, a nation that was occupying Manchuria and determined to present a friendly front to the Chinese public.

In the spring of 1935, An Ling went to Tokyo University for a year-long program in modern literature. Wei Jen's in-laws pressed her to return to the Su household to care for her daughter. But Wei Jen insisted on finishing the semester. Her mothering consisted of knitting sweaters in gradually increasing sizes and sending them home to Little Jade.

An Ling visited Wei Jen in Peking during summer break in 1936. Soon afterward, Wei Jen became pregnant again. She did not tell An Ling or her in-laws. She knew that if the Su clan found out, they would demand that she give up her studies. She wanted to continue with her degree. She kept her pregnancy a secret from her own family as well. Wei Jen gave birth to another daughter in the summer of 1937. An Ling didn't know about the second child until much later when he was told of the birth by a mutual friend at Peking University. While Wei Jen was recovering from the birth, the Japanese invaded deep into China. With that, she never saw An Ling again.

Wei Jen found herself alone with an infant. She was quickly running out of money. Transportation and communication with home were cut off. She moved to a friend's apartment and pawned a few pieces of wedding jewelry to get by. In desperate need of funds, Wei Jen started submitting articles to local newspapers and magazines which earned her a meager living. She used one of the characters of her name as her pen name, Jen, which means truth. It was both mysterious and modern to use one character as her identity. It gave Wei Jen a new persona. She wrote about her life as a female student at the university. As Jen, she began to build a name for herself and soon had a small following of readers. Her fees were doubled, and she was given a regular column in a local newspaper.

Jen named her new daughter Mary, the name of the American nun who had taught her English in the missionary school. She paid her landlady a small fee to care for her daughter. She still knew many classmates and professors in the university, but she was no longer a registered student. With her reputation as a writer, she was invited to many gatherings at the university.

Inevitably, some of these gatherings were political. Communist elements were infiltrating into the university even as the Nationalist government sought to gain student loyalty. Jen's notoriety attracted the attention of the Nationalist government. She was contacted by a certain General Tung, who, asked her to write favorable articles about the Nationalist Army.

Jen was a great find for the Nationalists, for she represented the new generation of China. One day, the writer Jen was invited to a government-sponsored event. It was a dinner party for representatives from the academies, industries, and government to get to know each other. Madam Chiang, who had started the New Life Movement in the 1930s, was going to be the keynote speaker. The government was trying to promote a renewed morality and a healthy attitude toward life among the young people of China.

Out of curiosity, Jen decided to attend. She arrived at the great hall in her usual white shirt and long navy skirt. Her chin length hair was smoothed behind her ears and fastened with simple clips. It was a warm, late spring day. Her sleeves were rolled passed her elbows, and she dabbed her forehead with a handkerchief as an attendant soldier looked for her name on a list. Women in sleeveless mandarin gowns and glittering jewelry walked past her on the arms of men in starched uniforms. The sound of high heels clicking on the marble floor mingled with the people's greetings.

Jen smiled at the young soldier who checked her name off the list and handed her a pink ribbon with her name on it attached to a safety pin. She was ushered into the great hall. She glanced about her. She shouldn't have come. She didn't know anyone here. Jen was already looking for ways to leave as she was led to a round table covered with a white tablecloth and laden with arrangements of place settings. There were about twenty tables in the hall, each with an ice sculpture depicting plum blossoms as a centerpiece.

She sat down on the plush red velvet chair and took a deep breath. She was thinking about her infant daughter. She wondered whether the landlady had fed Mary her bottle. Nodding at her politely, people started to sit down around her. Then a tall man introduced himself. He was General Tung who had organized the evening's event and was the leader of the Nationalist Army's northern unit. He extended his hand, Western-style, to shake Jen's hand. Her slender fingers were gently squeezed in General Tung's warm, firm grip. He leaned over to listen to her attentively in the noisy hall as they exchanged polite conversation. He continued holding her hand as he sat down beside her.

General Tung was an exceedingly handsome man in his late thirties. He had deeply set eyes and a bright smile that showed off his even, white teeth—a rarity among the heavy-smoking military ranks. He told Jen that he was a faithful reader of her column. They talked mostly about the student movement and current worldviews. He lavished attention on her throughout the evening. He excused himself a few times to shake hands with various important-looking people, but always returned to her side. At the end of the evening he accompanied her home in his black, private sedan.

She bid the general farewell in front of her apartment and returned to her room and to her crying, infant daughter. There, thinking about the evening, she did not remember much about Madam Chiang's speech. All of her thoughts swirled around the charismatic general. The next day a soldier delivered a case of powdered milk and a box of American chocolate to her apartment.

She couldn't quite discern what the general might want from her beyond writing a few articles praising the New Life Movement. The general's supply of women must be long. What could she offer to such a man of power? She took stock of herself. She was just beginning to have a taste of independence and freedom. Her writing was providing a modest, but steady, stream of income. She no longer felt on the verge of losing everything. Yet, she could not dare to be complacent about her circumstances. The world around her was changing fast, and she knew that she must keep pace with it.

The Nationalist government, already well known for cronyism and rampant corruption, had appointed the youthful, charismatic General Tung to take charge of the anti-Communist propaganda campaign. It was a significant undertaking, for The Nationalists were battling the Communists for the critical allegiance of the students.

General Tung's refined manner distinguished him from his peers. He found himself attracted to this quietly confident, woman writer who was, unbeknownst to her, the rare embodiment of an ideal modern Chinese woman. Jen was outspoken, confident, and fearless, and she had the audacity to think of herself as an equal to any man, should he be a general or a husband. On the evening that she and the general met, she stood out from the crowd of women with powdered faces and red lips in their colorful silk gowns. The general was accustomed to beguiling socialites and coy dancing hostesses. At nearly forty, he had had his share of temperamental opera singers and clinging concubines. Jen's plain style and direct ways were irresistible to him. He was impressed by her fluency in English just as he was fascinated by her intellect. He could not help but pursue her. Cases of powdered milk and boxes of chocolate continued to arrive at Jen's apartment along with bolts of fabric and boxes of canned goods.

During the 1930s, Chinese society was just beginning to adapt to the modern notion of marriage between one man and one woman. For thousands of years, it had been customary for a respectable man to have three wives and four concubines. A man with only one wife was to be pitied. The purpose of marriage was to produce sons—the more wives, the more chances of having male heirs. In the early years of the Republic, it was common for married men to propose to single women with offers of becoming a second wife or a third wife. The founding father of China, Sun Yat-Sen, had three wives. Generalissimo Chiang had had two wives and two concubines before he met the final Madam Chiang.

General Tung was a powerful man. He grew up near the northern border of Russia and was of Manchurian stock. He was from a family that valued learning and was well-versed in the classics. He had chosen to attend Bao Ding Military School during the late Qing Dynasty. He worked his way up to becoming a three-star general under the northern warlord Chang Tso Ling. When the Nationalist Army took over Chang's force, he came under Chiang Kei Shek's command.

Although he was twelve years older than Jen and had a wife and grown children back home, he pursued her for a year. But she was not about to become a fling for him, nor a kept concubine set up in her own apartment whose job was to entertain his ego and satisfy his lust. She intended to be his wife, not another wife, but the only wife. Jen did not consider herself a poor match for the general just because she was married already and had a child in tow. After all, it was he who had pursued her. She was not entirely unmoved by the ardent pursuit of the handsome general. But she had no illusion about the constancy of a man's declaration of undying love, especially from someone with as much experience in handling women as General Tung. She returned his blazing gaze and caressing touches with a request that he declare to the world that she would be his legal wife by having a formal Catholic wedding and inviting all of his superiors and the officers of the Nationalist government. This way, there would be no turning back for him. Once again, her keen instinct to weigh risk against reward served her well. The general decided to forsake his first wife and children. He adopted Mary, who was two when he married Jen in 1939 in the presence of the most important members of the Nationalist military and government. Jen was never sure whether she actually loved General Tung. At times she convinced herself that she was in love with him. What could not be denied was that marrying the general had been a good move. She soon joined the ranks of Soong Mei Ling, also known as Madam Chiang Kai Shek. Jen's Catholic faith was fashionable in military circles. General Tung converted to Catholicism. Both Jen and the general had their previous marriages annulled by the Church. It was a new beginning for both of them.

There was a photograph of Jen from this period. She wore a khaki military uniform with a narrow straight skirt past her knees, her waist cinched with a wide leather belt. She stood erect and was looking far away, smiling proudly and defiantly. She was beginning to sense the vast possibilities of her life ahead. She had struck another bargain with fate and moved ahead with her life.

✳ ✳ ✳

The Nationalist government lost Nanking during the fall of 1937 and hastily withdrew to the land-locked western province of Sichuan. The university moved with the Nationalist government and settled into a monastery compound in Mount Lu. It took eight years of fighting and the dropping of atomic bombs on the Japanese cities of Hiroshima and Nagasaki which forced the Japanese surrender to Allied forces and end the Sino-Japanese War.

After the victory over Japan on August 15, 1945, Chiang Kai-Shek ordered General Tung to hurry up north to take over the military equipment from the surrendering Japanese Imperial army. The Russian army was crossing the border to reap the spoils of war in the northern territories. The Chinese Communists were mobilizing their troops up north.

Jen followed her husband north to reunite with her family. She was thirty-four and was pregnant again. She had been married to the general for nine years. She yearned for a son. In addition to the two daughters, Little Jade and Mary, from her marriage with An Ling, she now had three daughters with the general—ages six, three and two. A fortuneteller once told her that only after five phoenixes would she bear dragons. She hoped that the fortuneteller was right.

As the Japanese were surrendering across the northern provinces, General Tung had to beat out the Communists and reach the Japanese supplies of guns and military vehicles first. The forces of the Nationalist government intended to fill the power vacuum left by the imperial Japanese army, but things were not working out as planned. The Communists were gaining strength and had successfully infiltrated at the grass-root levels. It would be difficult for the Nationalists to secure the nine provinces after such a long absence.

As the fighting went on, Jen was making her own plans. Being a good daughter, Jen made sure that her extended family was well protected. She had settled them into a compound near her own residence. Distant relatives were dropping in almost daily—aunts and uncles, cousins, nieces and nephews. She did not turn anyone away. As she rushed to get ready to move her entire clan, she felt an empty space within her. She had not seen Little Jade since leaving her behind with her mother-in-law years ago. Little Jade should be twelve by now. Jen remembered her only as a soft, newborn infant. She could not envision her first child's face.

CHAPTER 19:
REUNION

The day after the visit from the Fourth Aunt in abbey school, Little Jade rose early and put on a padded jacket and pants. The time had come for her to go and to begin the journey to her mother. She tied a kerchief to cover her hair. She picked up her small bundle of clothes and the precious letters from her father. She informed the nuns that she wished to go home on her own. A young nun gave her a brief embrace and wished her well.

Little Jade stepped away from the front gate of the school. She knew that, with each step, she was walking away from her father, possibly forever. She did not look back. Feeling suddenly adventurous, she walked toward a busy spot of the town and inquired about hiring a wagon to take her to Peking. She decided to share a wagon with a group of travelers.

Little Jade was short for her age and very skinny. With her padded cotton jacket and trousers, and her braids hidden, she tried to pass for a boy. Her clothes were not refined, but anyone could tell that she was not a peasant because of her cultured accent and the paleness and smoothness of her skin.

They stayed overnight at a roadside inn. The four men settled down with their bundles in a communal room. It was then that Little Jade told the innkeeper that she was a girl and therefore could not sleep in the same room with the men. The innkeeper frowned and called for his daughter. The travelers did not pay attention. They were tired from traveling all day on the bumpy road and were looking forward to the luxury of being able to stretch out on a bedroll. The innkeeper let Little Jade share a room with his daughter. Little Jade leaned against the windowed wall that looked out to the stable. She stayed awake most of the night and was thrilled by the prospect of meeting her mother and worried that the wagon driver might leave her behind.

The next day, at the outskirts of Peking, the wagon driver discharged the passengers and collected the payments. Little Jade gave the driver a few bills and got some coins back. She hired a pedicab and showed him the address on the neatly folded paper. The pedicab brought her to the front door of an old-style house at the end of a narrow street. Little Jade paid the driver with all the coins in her pocket. She took a deep breath, smoothed her hair and her jacket with her hands. She knocked on the wooden door of peeling red paint—one of many identical doors that lined the street. The number written on the door matched the number on the slip of paper. It was dinnertime, and she hoped that someone was home. She was tired from her two days of journeying. She had been sustained by a shining warm feeling of hope.

The door was opened by a sickly-looking middle-aged man wearing pajamas. His face was the color of yellow wax. Little Jade knew right away that he was an opium addict. She picked up the scent of the opium as soon as the door opened. She wished she hadn't made the trip. But now it was too late.

"I am the daughter of Chang Wei Jen," Little Jade told the man. "She sent for me." She uttered the words without thinking. The name of her mother rang in her ears, familiar and foreign at once. She must have sounded convincing because the sickly looking man gestured to let her in and quickly closed the door.

"Wei Jen's daughter is here," he announced as he let her into the hallway.

Little Jade felt faint when she heard the man referred her as her mother's daughter. She was weak from hunger and followed the sickly man into the dining room where a table full of people looked up from their bowls. Little Jade scanned the faces one by one, but she did not see the Fourth Aunt. There were men, women, and children. The sickly man returned to an empty chair, sat down and started eating. Little Jade felt like a stray. An old man with a long white goatee put down his chopsticks and frowned. He called to the maid, "Amah, take her to the back and clean her up. Feed her something from the kitchen."

Little Jade followed the maid into the back room. She sat by the kitchen stove and dug into a large bowl of rice topped with a soy chicken leg and some stir- fried vegetables. The maid knew she was the daughter of Wei Jen—the general's wife who paid for the house, the food and the clothes on the backs of everyone living in it.

That night, Little Jade wore clothes borrowed from a cousin. Her name was Lan and she was three years younger. They shared the same bed in a small room. Little Jade wondered when she would see her mother. Too tired to think about it for long, she fell into a deep sleep.

The next day a tailor arrived with Fourth Aunt. Little Jade was happy to see a familiar face. The tailor was a skinny man with a hunched back. He looped a soft measure tape around Little Jade and scribbled numbers into a worn notebook held together by a rubber band. Fourth Aunt explained that she ran errands for Wei Jen. As soon as the new clothes were ready, Little Jade would meet her mother.

It is almost like getting ready to meet the emperor in the old days, Little Jade thought. Her head was checked for lice. A doctor came to give her a thorough check-up, listening to her heart and asking her to breathe deeply. A cobbler came by with five pairs of shoes for her to try on. Fourth Aunt decided on two pairs—a pair for everyday use and a pair of patent leather Mary Jane's for special occasions. Little Jade could not imagine what kind of special occasion would warrant such beautiful shoes.

✳ ✳ ✳

Three families and a few stragglers lived in the compound. They were nice to Little Jade, but no one tried to get to know her. She was an oddity from the countryside. Little Jade was most comfortable around the Fourth Aunt who wasn't around much. Lan was friendly enough though she eyed Little Jade suspiciously. People whispered things about the newly arrived child.

On the fifth day, the Fourth Aunt arrived, excited. She carried a new leather suitcase and put it on the bed Little Jade shared with Lan, who lingered in the room wanting to see its contents. Fourth Aunt opened the suitcase triumphantly and pulled out one piece of clothing after another. The suitcase was filled with everything from fine cotton knit underwear to western-style coats with Peter Pan collars and turned up cuffs in a fine soft wool fabric of deep blue. Little Jade had never seen such a coat for a child. Everything fitted her perfectly.

Fourth Aunt pulled out a few choice pieces. There was a long-sleeve cotton shirt with ruffled collars and a pair of pants made of darkly shining blue Shantung silk. She also pulled out a sweater vest of mixed red, pink, royal blue and sky blue yarns. "Your mother knitted this vest for you, Little Jade, Fourth Aunt said as she helped Little Jade into the vest, "She didn't have enough time to knit the sleeves." The vest hugged her gently. "Your mother used to knit sweaters for you when you were a baby. She knitted sweaters in graduating sizes. It was when she was in the university and you were a baby at the old house with your grandmother."

Little Jade sat at the edge of the bed, her arms crossed over her chest with her fingers feeling the softness of the wool. She was anxious at the prospect of meeting her mother. She couldn't understand why she had to wait for days. She secretly feared that her mother had changed her mind about wanting her back. She pictured what it would be like to meet her mother. She could see herself racing into her mother's waiting arms. Her mother would embrace her and tell her how much she missed her.

✳ ✳ ✳

It was a cold autumn day. The wind from Siberia swept over the humble rooftops of the northern city. The entire city hunkered down under the oppressive sky. People walked quickly with their heads down, their mouths covered by surgical masks or scarves. Fourth Aunt hired a pedicab and told the driver to take them to the athletic stadium on the outskirts of the city. Little Jade peeked out from behind the drapes of the pedicab. She could hardly contain herself. She was shaking from excitement and from the cold. Her eyes searched the road ahead. She felt tiny dots of sand dust bounce off her cheeks.

At last, the pedicab slowed down and passed through an opening in a tall metal fence. The Fourth Aunt directed the driver inside the fence and told him to wait there. She got off the pedicab and extended her hands to Little Jade. Little Jade climbed out of the pedicab and looked up at the fortress-like wall of the stadium. The concrete wall stood impossibly tall in front of her. She could see the cracks in the wall and the green moss along the base of it. Fourth Aunt's gloved hand held onto Little Jade's. She searched the number on top of the gate: "Number nine," she mumbled to herself.

They walked together through the wooden door with peeling blue paint into a tunnel. Coming out the other side, Little Jade's eyes adjusted to the gray glare of the low clouds as she looked around the empty stadium. A scattering of crows flew across the sky and disappeared beyond the edge of the stadium wall. Fourth Aunt motioned Little Jade to sit on the bench next to the aisle.

They waited in silence. They wind was getting stronger and Little Jade was visibly shivering. Her hands were deep in her coat pockets, her fingers digging into her palms.

Suddenly, Fourth Aunt stood up and pulled Little Jade up next to her. Little Jade saw a woman emerge from the same tunnel and walk toward them. Little Jade knew at once that it was her mother. The woman stopped about three steps away. She was wearing a long wool coat trimmed with black mink at the collar and hem and a pair of black leather riding boots. Her hands disappeared into a matching black mink hand muff. The fur-lined collar was pulled up and framed her face. She wore no rouge or powder. Her short straight hair was parted on the side and clipped back with a simple silver ornament. Her eyes were steady and unblinking. Her brows wore a trace of a frown. Her lips pressed tightly. She betrayed no visible emotion. Little Jade looked at her- studying the face she had not remembered. Now, she was sure that she had seen her before, but could not place her. Somewhere between the eyes and definitely the lips, there was a distinct resemblance. Now she realized, with a start, that she had seen traces of her mother in her own reflection. Wei Jen looked at Little Jade. Then she said to no one in particular, "Oh, so this is she." She sounded almost disappointed. Little Jade waited for her mother to embrace her, but she did not.

"She is short for her age," the Fourth Aunt said apologetically, "and a little skinny."

"Nevertheless…" Wei Jen studied Little Jade for what felt to the girl to be an unbearably long time. Finally, she addressed her daughter. "It is your decision now," she told her, "Do you regret coming?"

Little Jade shook her head. She couldn't speak. She openly stared at the woman in front of her. Tears were pouring down her face. She tried to wipe her eyes with the sleeve of her beautiful coat.

"Have you decided to stay with me? If you stay, you can never return to your father again. Is this understood?" The woman looked intently into Little Jade's eyes.

Little Jade nodded emphatically. She was trying very hard not to cry out loud. She wanted badly to give her mother a good impression. She wanted desperately to say something, something clever maybe. But it was impossible. She was silently crying with her mouth open, sucking in frigid air. She wanted so much to hug her mother. But the elegant woman's restrained manner held her back. Little Jade sensed an invisible chasm between herself and the woman standing in front of her who was coolly planning the logistics of adding another girl to her complex household.

"From now on, you will take my surname Chang. Do you understand?" Little Jade kept on nodding. She couldn't take her eyes off her mother.

"This is important. You will call me Gugu (Auntie) from now on." Little Jade nodded again. The elegant woman was leaning over to talk to her now. Little Jade could almost touch her, but didn't dare.

"Your given name will be 'Lee'—the 'Lee' that means independent, not the one that means beauty. You must be independent now. You will have to stand on your own. Do you understand?" Little Jade nodded and watched her mother straighten up to speak to Fourth Aunt.

"I hope she hasn't been too much trouble."

"No, no trouble at all. She is quiet mostly," Fourth Aunt replied eagerly.

Little Jade wiped her eyes with the backs of her hands, trying hard not to sob too loudly. She would be a good child. She would stay quiet, out of the way, and be no trouble at all.

The elegant woman nodded at Fourth Aunt and took another look at Little Jade. "I have to go now." She turned and walked away, down the aisle, and into the tunnel to exit the stadium.

After her mother disappeared from her sight, Little Jade was able to cry out loud. She cried and cried as Fourth Aunt pulled her along toward the exit. The wind was picking up, getting stronger, whistling through the empty benches of the stadium and whipping at Little Jade's tear-stained face. She had never felt so cold or so small in her life.

CHAPTER 20:
LEE AND JEN, NIECE AND GUGU
(AUNT)

Little Jade was still sobbing as she was led away from the stadium and back to the waiting pedicab. Fourth Aunt was quiet as she kept one arm around the girl's shoulder. She patted the Little Jade's shoulder, looking at her with a frowning, worried face. Little Jade slumped into her aunt's arm. She was comforted by the warmth of Fourth Aunt's slender body wrapped in a soft wool coat. Fourth Aunt's hair smelled of citrus scented shampoo. Little Jade strained to remember the last time someone had embraced her. It was when her father had rescued her from the ghost village so long ago. She had sat on his lap in that cold dark room lit by a dying candle. She closed her eyes and tried to recall the touches of her father, but she could remember nothing. Her heart was like a dying candle, a tiny flicker of flame cupped by both hands, the stub of wick curled up and drowning in its own tears. The love she had had for her father was worn down by the endless waiting, day after day, night after night, hour after hour. The cruelty of hope raised then crumbled into grains of sand that slipped between her fingers and were lost forever. Maybe her father was capable of just the one heroic act of saving her. Perhaps there would be no follow up. She would probably never see him again.

Little Jade trembled as she thought of her mother's pale, frowning face framed by lush black mink collars. She thought of her mother's words which were so carefully measured and without warmth as if she was negotiating a contract. Her mother had looked disappointed when she saw her and did not touch her once.

Little Jade knew that she had to stop crying. No one likes a crying child. A crying girl draws too much attention to herself, unwanted attention. What would strangers think or say? A girl kidnapped? The pedicab turned a corner. They were approaching the Chang house. She could not be seen sobbing by the people in that house. Little Jade quieted down and wiped her face dry. What was the use of crying? She had to accept that everything had changed. Her grandmother was dead and buried. Her step-grandfather was lost in the ghost village which had now turned to dust. The bamboo forest was lost to her. Little Jade was no longer six years old. She was no longer a child. She was twelve, and there was no one to blame. She felt very tired. In silence, she entered the Chang house where she would be known as Chang Lee. She did not speak a word for the rest of the day.

✱ ✱ ✱

Lee knew that everyone in the house talked about her because they stopped talking as soon as she entered a room. The patriarch of the house, the old man with the long white goatee, Lee's maternal grandfather, always frowned when he saw her as if she gave him a headache. The two uncles were opium smokers, skinny sickly men who walked around in pajamas all day long dragging their slippers against the wooden floor. The familiar sweet smell of opium permeated the house. The house, its inhabitants and the drifting smoke made her perpetually listless and drowsy. She had not come all this way for this. If her life was to be subsumed by opium and hopelessness, she might as well have stayed with her father. Lee wished she could be nearer to her mother, even if she had to accept the pretense that she was merely her niece. After living at the Chang house for one month, Chang Lee told Fourth Aunt that she wanted to move to her mother's house. No matter what her mother felt about her, nothing could change the fact that they were mother and daughter. If only they could get to know each other better, all they needed were chances to be near to one another. Living under the same roof there were bound to be more opportunities. She longed to feel loved again. She had not felt loved since her grandmother died.

* * *

Lee gradually became accustomed to her new name. She wrote the new name down on a piece of paper next to her old name: Chang Lee and Su Ming-Yu (Bright Jade). Lee liked that she was sharing her mother's last name. The character Chang consists of two words, the word "bow" for a bow and arrow, and the word for "long" as in distance or size. "Long-bow Chang," someone would say, identifying oneself and at the same time distinguishing this "Chang" from other words that were pronounced the same way. Her new given name, "Lee", was a lonely word. The character is a solitary, standing figure, tall and erect, ready to face the world. Now that her name was changed from Bright Jade to Lee, she knew that she was no longer a treasure. She did not mind. In this chaotic time of running from one disaster after another, it was useless to be a piece of jade, no matter how precious, for gold and jade could not always be exchanged for rice and bread. Better to be someone who could stand alone with a long bow squinting hard into a distance to shoot for a future. Any future.

Chapter 21:
General Tung

In the study of General Tung's estate, Jen sat in a soft cushioned chair that was covered in heavy burgundy brocade and situated beside an open window. Her legs rested on the matching ottoman. A glass of chrysanthemum tea was steaming on the desk beside her. One side of the desk was piled high with opened letters, telegrams and documents with the red seal of "top secret" stamped on them. There was a stand from which hung calligraphy brushes in different sizes. Jen had not practiced for a long time. She glanced at the faces of her royal blue satin slippers with their embroideries of yellow chrysanthemum flowers. The thin petals curved gracefully inward overlapping each other like golden scales on ancient armor; deep green leaves with scalloped edges balanced the oversized flowers. Autumn was her favorite season. In autumn, the blooms of chrysanthemum in elegant white, yellow and deep purple contrasted against the background of bamboo stalks outside her window. Of the four gentlemen plants–bamboo, chrysanthemum, orchid and plum blossoms, Jen preferred bamboo and chrysanthemums. She liked the latter flower because it bloomed in the chill of autumn when other flowers had long gone limp and soggy and brown. She favored bamboo because it is both strong and flexible which was the two qualities she most admired. Jen picked up her knitting needles and began to make an infant size cardigan, pulling yarn from a large ball of multicolored yarn resting in a willow basket beside her chair.

The study was paneled in dark wood and lined with bookcases. There was a great variety in the many volumes: Chinese classics, *The Book of*

History, Poetry from Tang and Sung Dynasties, The Art of War, Luen Yu, a collection of Confucius's anecdotes, economics textbooks on capitalism and Marxism, and most prominently, a leather-bound Bible. A portion of lower shelves was dedicated to magazines and newspapers. Recent issues of Time magazine were arranged into the shape of a fan. Above an ornamental fireplace mantel of carved milky white marble, shot through with gray veins was a large painting by Chang Da Chien whose famous splash-colors style of bright blue and green paints bought out the majestic scenery of Mount Huang. In front of the fireplace, two large, tufted burgundy leather sofas trimmed with brass nail heads faced each other. They were divided by a long dark wood coffee table with an artful arrangement of chrysanthemums in the center. Next to the sofas, was a pair of reading lamps with China blue Shantung silk lamp shades. This was the room in which Jen received guests and fired servants, and where she did her thinking and made her decisions.

Jen was in the sixth month of her pregnancy. Her body was weighted down by the growing fetus within. Her breasts ached and softened like bruised peaches, and her feet and ankles were swollen and red like sausages. Her breathing had become shallower and her movements sluggish. Today, she wanted to spend time by herself. She looped the yarn over the tip of the needle and knitted as she looked out the window. She wondered whether the child she carried would be a boy. She had never forgotten the fortuneteller who had told her that after five phoenixes that there would be dragons.

She did not mind being pregnant again for the sixth time. This way, General Tung would go to other women, as he did during her previous pregnancies. He needed to be with a woman every night. It was a sickness of his. *Men are weak that way,* Jen thought. In truth, she would rather be pregnant than putting up with his nightly demands. She wondered whether he was patronizing the dancing hall with his lieutenants again. Dancing hall girls were popular these days. In the old days, it was the operas singers who seduced men from prominent families. At least the general was not going with the singsong girls, the "flowers" from the red light district who did not bother to disguise how they made their livings. At age forty-five, General Tung was both charming and predatory. He always had a taste for young women, but Jen knew that he would never bring these girls home. Let him have his fun, as long as it was out of her sight and out of her earshot. Jen was not jealous of the other women. She accepted that as the wife of General Tung that she must fulfill her duty of pleasing him when requested and obeying him when demanded. She accepted that when she was not available, someone must—and would—take her place.

She had come to believe that he had married her primarily because she was college educated, spoke English, and was a Christian. She had married him because she needed a protector. With his connections to the military and her connections to the banking industry through her college classmates, they had forged new ties that afforded them prominent positions. She became a part of the Economic Advisory panel for the Nationalist government, and he was appointed to lead the mission to recover the northern territory after the defeat of Japanese. It had proved a good bargain for them both.

Jen's father had been a successful merchant. She had inherited his talent for calculating an abacus, for weighing risks against rewards, and for negotiating through life. She had already converted most of their financial holdings into gold bars and stored them in safes in several secured locations. She had done this even before the Nationalist government decided to print money in large denominations in order to create a super-inflation that would devalue the war debts they owed to foreign powers. Jen was the only woman on the committee that made the decision. It was supposed to be top secret.

Jen always prided herself for her ability to view things with a clear head. Even as a young girl, she had disdained the notion of romantic love and anything that had to do with passion. She had never been impulsive. Every decision she made had been a necessary trade to get her to the next place she wanted to be. Like a patient chess player making moves at the beginning of the game, she did not waste opportunities or make mistakes. She understood early on that one's life is the cumulative result of one's decisions. As Jen paused to count the loops of yarn on her knitting needle, she was planning as far into the future as she possibly could. She estimated the due date of the baby. The general had told her that they must be ready to move at a moment's notice. The fighting was growing fiercer. He was not sure how long the Nationalist army could hold off the Communist's advances.

Jen was still smarting from what had occurred the other night, after they had retired to their bedchamber. Jen had emerged from her bath, her face flushed from the hot steam and her chin length hair still wet and dripping with water. She blotted her hair with a towel, and rested on a chaise beside windows obscured by floor length copper colored velvet curtains. The Tiffany styled torch lamps cast blue and purple patches of light on the ceiling and walls. General Tung was seated on his saddle brown leather armchair nursing a brandy. He was waiting for her.

"Anything happen in the field today?" Jen asked without curiosity. This was the way she always began conversation with him. Whatever he answered, she would nod, not really listening. "I had to interrogate a few Communists. They were young and very stubborn. It took a long time," said the general.

Jen did not want to know what had happened to the captured young Communists. She flipped through the day's newspaper. The headlines touted victories for the Nationalist army. "China must be united!" "The Communists must be defeated!" She knew that these headlines were lies. The government controlled the press and would only report victories. The general changed the subject, "Jen, I got a letter from home."

"From her?" Jen looked up at him. They both understood that "her" meant his first wife. The general looked away. Bracing himself, he gulped down half the yellow liquor in his shallow cut crystal glass.

"From my mother," he said finally, "She wants me to take care of my boys. You know, to find something for them to do here." General Tung continued, "They are coming over to see me. They will be here soon, maybe within a week, if not sooner."

"That's not what we agreed on. Do you remember what you promised me?" Jen said calmly. She kept flipping through the newspaper, as she waited for the general's reaction.

"But that was back then. I didn't think the war would last this long. I have not seen them for ten years." The general said. Of course, he remembered his promise. He had promised Jen that they would start anew. Both of them had annulled their previous marriages, in front of the western god and the western priest. Jen thought back to the day of their wedding. She pictured, with no particular sentiment, the Northern Church in Peking, a gleaming white gothic structure with four tall spires surrounded by deep green pines and cypress trees. The sunlight had poured through the arching stained glass windows of the church. The general had been waiting for her at the end of the red carpet. He was handsome in his well-pressed military uniform with the bronze stars glinting on his shoulders under the lit candles from the altar while Jen had stood beside him, slender and tall. She held a small bouquet of gardenias and wore a close-fitting suit jacket and pencil skirt of ivory satin with matching heels. Her hair, set in soft waves and cut to chin length, was combed back and held behind her ears with an ornament shaped like a flower and made of seed pearls. The pearl choker she wore with a clasp of an emerald-cut deep blue sapphire surrounded by tiny diamonds was a wedding present from the general. Her face had been lightly powdered, and there was a trace of red on her lips.

Just behind her, seated in the front row, a nanny had held their two-years-old daughter Mary, who was dressed in a white lace dress made by nuns. When Jen and the general exchanged vows they had an understanding between them. They had trusted each other.

That was nine years ago. "Your sons are grown men, not boys." Jen said now. "What are they going to do here? Are they going to follow you around? What are you going to have them do? Fight in the front line? Interrogate Communists? Visit whores?"

"It is my mother's wish," the general repeated, ignoring the sharpness of her words. "I want to see them too. It has been ten years. They were ten and twelve when I last saw them"

"What does your mother know?" Jen said. "She is an ignorant old woman living in the same house for the last fifty years. If the general wants to have his grown sons in this house, you may as well bring your first wife and your mother here as well. If that is the case, I better move out of the way with my children. Is this what you want?"

General Tung looked at the woman sitting across from him. Her plain face was framed by wet hair carelessly combed with her fingers. She was thirty-four years old. Early touches of time were traced lightly across her forehead and between her brows. Her simple navy blue cotton robe was wrapped loosely around her swollen body. Her hands leisurely turned the page of the newspaper. Her nails were unvarnished. Her fingers were slender and thin, like freshly washed scallions, the mark of a gentle woman who had never known housework and barely knew how to cook. General Tung looked at his own hands, calloused from military training. His hands were capable of hand-to-hand combat. They were strong enough to strangle a man. But he was no match for his wife. Her hands held the financial key to the household. She was the one who opened accounts in American dollars at Chase Manhattan Bank and wired money to Swiss accounts. She knew where the gold bars were stored and had arranged access with extreme discretion. Her college friends were now in charge of major financial institutions in Peking and Shanghai. He had entrusted all his money to her and she had managed it well.

The general looked up at his wife and saw that she was reading an article in the newspaper and was no longer paying attention to him. It was for this woman that he had turned away from his parents, his wife and his sons. The general was accustomed to having his way, from commanding tens of thousands of men to fight to ordering the swift execution of captured enemies. Yet he was not able to persuade Jen to accept his sons. He had been with many women and thought he knew how to manage them, but Jen was not just any woman. She was stronger than most men, maybe stronger than he was. She was calling him out, reminding him of promises he had made years ago and regretted making. The general took another sip of his brandy.

Jen looked up from her paper. In her quiet way she had made up her mind. "If they come, I will move out," she said, "It is your decision" It was a canny challenge. Everyone in China knew that Chiang Kai-Shek had left his old country wife to marry Soong Mei-Ling, who was much younger, America-educated, and Christian. General Tung knew that if Jen walked out on him, he would suffer serious damage to his career in Chiang Kai-Shek's Nationalist government.

Jen softened her tone. "You couldn't take sons away from their mother," she said. "Who would look after their mother when she gets old? You should leave the boys to take care of the Tung family."

The general hesitated, not quite willing to give in. "How about Lee?" he said. "You are keeping her, aren't you?"

"You can't compare a twelve year old girl to two grown men," Jen retorted forcefully, her face frozen as a stone.

* * *

The two young men sent by General Tung's first wife arrived in the middle of the next afternoon. The general was out, paying an extended visit to one of his consorts, an actress of modern plays, who lived just a few blocks away. Jen received the general's sons in the study. She wanted to see them and find out what they had to say.

The servant announced them and let them in. They entered, the older one in front, the younger one following behind. They were younger versions of General Tung, though not as tall or as stocky, but just as broad-shouldered and thick-necked. They wore ill-fitting western style dark blue suits with starched white shirts, as if they had come for job interviews. Jen did not rise to greet them. She smiled and gestured to them, indicating that they should sit down across from her. She asked if they would like something to drink or eat. They declined politely, clearly uncomfortable to be speaking with her, holding their hats in their hands. She ordered the maid to bring tea and a tray of pastries and cut fruits. As the mistress of the house, she had to show authority and hospitality. They regarded her with caution and did not respond to her pleasant manner. She drank her tea leisurely, making them wait in silence after they inquired the whereabouts of their father. Rather than reply, she asked them, in her most gentle voice, about their mother's health, their grandparents' health, and the general condition of the crops back at home, and whether there had been enough rainfall.

Jen could tell that they had not expected to be conversing with her. She observed that one looked down at his hands while the other's eyes darted about the room. Both avoided looking at her. They were not worthy opponents. Jen pressed on, telling them that the general was very busy fighting the Communists and that it was a very bad time to visit and that even she was not sure where the general was from day to day. She explained that he didn't always return home at the end of day and she was not always sure where he would spend the night, hinting that there were other women. She asked the young men where they were staying and learned that they were staying at the Palace Hotel. She offered to put them up for the night in the event that the general did not return today. They could stay longer if they wanted. Jen told them that they should feel at home here at the Tung estate. It was a meaningless invitation. She knew that as the sons of the proper first wife, the young men could never accept such an offer from a second wife, a mere concubine in their eyes. Jen said that she was sorry when they declined her invitation stiffly and firmly and asked them to reconsider, smiling the entire time.

Jen was determined to assert her position as the mistress of the house. She was not a young concubine who could be easily dismissed by the first wife. She knew that the young men were sent by their mother to remind General Tung of his home and his obligations as a son, a husband, and a father of sons. Jen wanted to take this opportunity to send a message back to the young men's mother. She wanted to show them that her position with the general was unshakable and that they were wasting their time. As the hour wore on, the two young men ran out of things to say. Not once did they ask about her children. They must have known that she had only daughters and daughters didn't count for much. Nevertheless, they soon realized that it was not going to be easy to gain an audience with their own father. They saw a pregnant woman devoid of makeup, wearing a loose fitting white shirt over a pair of black trousers and plain black leather flats. It was not the bejeweled satin clad woman with a waft of perfume that they had imagined. The mistress of the house spoke with surprisingly concise sentences and a direct manner. The young men got up and bid her farewell and never returned.

She later told the general that his sons had visited and were staying at the Palace Hotel. She told the general that she offered to put them up but they declined. "Maybe they had to rush back to their mother to report on me." She smiled when she told him this. Sure enough, when the general went to the hotel he found that his sons had already left to return home.

Jen knew that the only thing she was lacking for the general were sons. She was hoping to give birth to a boy this time. This pregnancy felt different from the previous ones. Jen was sure that the child within her was a boy, a very active boy. She was certain that once she gave birth to a boy for the general, he would soon forget about his other sons. She would not have to wait long. This, too, was part of her calculation.

Yet the timing couldn't have been worse. Danger loomed large, and there was little room for mistakes. Time was running out. She did not know where she would be in a few months when the baby arrived. She planned ahead and took care of the finances. They could move with very short notice, and it was just a matter of who would be coming with her to Taiwan and who would be left behind. Jen pulled more yarn from the ball. She was almost done with the body of the sweater and was getting ready to knit the little sleeves. She made a mental list of her extended family: her parents, two brothers, their wives and children, her uncles and aunts and their children. There were more distant cousins from both her parents' sides of the family. She needed to pare the list down. She would not take the addicts, even though they were her own brothers. They would have to stay. It had been draining to support them. She knew that they stole to satisfy their habits for opium and even heroin, but she was willing to take their wives and children if they wanted to come with her. She had to make decisions for all of them, for all the Changs. She was the one in charge.

At last, all her children were within her reach. Jen was glad that her first-born was finally coming to live under the same roof as rest of her children. Jen shook her head as she recalled how skinny and awkward Lee was as she stood there crying and shivering in that empty stadium with her shoulders hunched over. Her new clothes could not disguise her frail constitution. It was clear that the Su family had not taken proper care of her. Lee's skin was sallow and her voice was small and halting, barely audible, but her eyes were strong. There was no fear in her eyes. They burned with hope and a consuming hunger. Jen could not look into Lee's eyes for long. She dared not ask what her first born hoped for or for what she was hungering. Jen thought that both Mary and Lee resembled her. Both had her trademark too-thick lips. The ideal Chinese beauty has a small mouth. Full lips were perceived as inelegant because they denoted traces of lineage from the countryside, from the people who must work hard for a living in rice paddies, kitchens, or over washbasins. *It was too bad*, Jen thought, that both girls had inherited this unfortunate trait. People might guess that they were sisters when they stood next to each other. Of all her children, she had spent the most time with Mary, raising her with the help of her landlady, during Mary's first two years of life. Mary had received much attention from the general when he was courting Jen. Although Mary's birth father was An Ling, the general had been the only father Mary had ever known. Lee and Mary would never know that they were sisters. This was a key part of the bargain that Jen had struck with the general.

Jen put down her knitting needles and got slowly to her feet. She had a sudden urge to see her children, to touch their hair, and to gather them into her arms. With all the nursemaids and amahs (older household maids) the general employed, she had few opportunities to care for them. Jen clapped her hands twice. A maid appeared at the study door. "Where are the little ladies?" Jen asked, meaning the younger girls. The maid replied that they were taking afternoon naps with their nursemaids.

"Where is the young lady?" Jen asked.

"She is with her English teacher," the maid replied. "Today is Wednesday."

Jen did not want to interrupt the afternoon naps or the English lesson. She waved off the maid and sat alone, thinking of her three younger girls one by one. On the desk, there was a photograph of Jen, Mary and the general that had been taken right after Jen and the general were married. It was a perfect family portrait. General Tung's arm was around was Jen's shoulder, and Mary was positioned on Jen's lap. But when it came to the three younger girls, there was no such photograph. Maybe if she gave birth to a boy, another family portrait could be taken.

All three young girls were faithful copies of their father. They had his deep-set eyes and high cheekbones, his long eyelashes, and thickly grown eyebrows in the shapes of willow leaves. The variations among the three girls were small. One had the pointed chin that denoted a "peach blossom colored life." Jen knew that she would be a beauty. The other had a square jaw, which meant that she would forge boldly into her future, but for the time being, she was the loudest, and crying constantly for attention. The third one had an unassuming round face with a well-defined widow's peak. She would be the clever one, though Jen could not quite tell what sort of cleverness. Would it be the kind that would do some good in the world, or the kind of petty cleverness that amounts to nothing?

She pulled a thick wool shawl over her shoulders and walked out the study into the courtyard. A maid followed a few steps behind holding a heavy wool cape in her arms. Jen felt good as the autumn air hit her face like a splash of cold water. With the child growing within her, she was always warm. She sometimes felt imprisoned in her own body like an animal in a too-small cage. She wanted to go for a walk. She ignored the wind which was getting stronger and carried with it a shrilling sound as it passed through the treetops. She walked past the blooming yellow and purple chrysanthemums and down the stone path that slowly wound past a series of giant, oddly shaped stones that resembled little mountains and had been pulled from the depths of Lake Tai. Along the path, stalks of bamboo created a green curtain against the rocks. Jen sat on a stone bench to rest a moment.

There was never love, she thought with a mixture of bitterness and self-mocking, *only goals and strategic moves.*

Had she missed something important along the way to arrive at this point? In truth, she would never know. *Now*, she thought, *all that's left are duties and obligations.* There was no one to blame because she was the one who had made all the decisions. Her thoughts turned to An Ling. She never wanted to see him again. She blamed the war for breaking them apart, but she never attempted to get in touch with him. She had heard that he, too, eventually got married again. His wife, it was said, was a much younger woman.

Still, she could not face An Ling in this life. He reminded her of everything she no longer was and never wanted to be: the compliant wife and daughter-in-law locked deep within the estate of a once prominent family whose time had come and gone. After Little Jade was born, she was almost trapped within that big house where she was no more than a chess piece waiting to be moved by larger forces. Now she was the one holding the pieces, and the one who plots the next moves against the formidable opponent of fate.

She would not look back. She could only keep going forward. Her duty was to protect this child within her, and all her daughters, and her entire family. For them, she would move ahead and somehow they would end up somewhere with a measure of stability and peace.

CHAPTER 22:
UNDER THE SAME ROOF

Within a few days, Fourth Aunt came to help Lee pack her new clothes into the same leather suitcase. She was taking her to General Tung's residence. A shiny black car waited in front of the house. A young soldier in a khaki uniform and polished black boots was brushing the car with a feather duster. Lee slid into the back seat next to the Fourth Aunt, bumping into her slender frame. The young woman put an arm around the girl and squeezed her shoulder. Lee smiled at her aunt gratefully, and Fourth Aunt returned her smile. There was a trace of cigarette smoke inside the car, reminding Lee once again of her father. She looked out the window as the car pulled away and hoped to never return to this spot. The car drove through the crowded city. It was a rare sunny day during a Peking winter. The blurred faces of pedestrians and street vendors flashed by, and their chatter and noises muffled by the car's windows.

The car glided into a smooth stop in front of the gate of a walled compound guarded by soldiers with machine guns hoisted on their shoulders. Two stone lions guarded the front entry, like the stone lions at the gate of the Su family cemetery. Fourth Aunt nodded at the soldiers and took the girl by the hand. The grand estate was once the residence of an imperial prince from the Qing Dynasty. Both the master and the mistress of the house were away in order to make it less conspicuous for Lee to join the household.

Chang Lee and Fourth Aunt entered the outer gates. Just inside the inner gate they checked in with another soldier who was seated behind a redwood desk. He looked up at them from behind his wire-rimmed glasses. "She is Chang Lee," Fourth Aunt said to him. "The 'Lee' that means 'standing up.'"

"They are expecting you," said the soldier as he checked off a line in the notebook. A middle age amah appeared and took over the suitcase from Fourth Aunt.

"Follow me," the amah said as she walked briskly ahead of them. Fourth Aunt took Lee's arm and guided her through winding corridors and led her into the inner courtyards of the estate. Lee saw soldiers performing household duties throughout the grounds, sweeping stone courtyards, and trimming plants in the garden. She passed through a courtyard paved with a carpet-like lawn and festooned with large topiary trimmed into the shapes of rabbits and bears. They passed a seesaw and a swing which Lee assumed to be part of a playground for the youngest inhabitants of the house. She caught glimpses of a nursemaid holding a toddler and singing to her. Fourth Aunt nodded and smiled at everyone as she walked by. Further down, after passing through a fan shaped gate, Lee stepped onto a paved stone path lined by tall stalks of bamboo on both sides. As Lee proceeded down the path, she heard the familiar rustling of bamboo leaves stirring in a light breeze. The thin blades of the leaves, pointed on both ends, trembled against one another. It was as if they were greeting her, as if they were softly saying her previous name, *Little Jade...* Lee wanted to linger, but she had to keep following the amah.

At last they found themselves in a suite of a bedroom and sitting area where there were shelves and writing desks and chairs. Lee liked the rooms right away. The sitting room's windows were covered by curtains made of blue silk tied with matching sashes. Lee looked out the window and saw more bamboo stalks growing just along a tall brick wall as if they had followed her from the courtyard garden. She pushed opened the window and let in the cool autumn air. "Miss, keep the window closed," the amah said, "or you will catch a cold."

"Do you want to have a cup of hot tea?" Fourth Aunt asked as she went to a tray that held a large thermos bottle and four cups. The tray rested on a round table surrounded by four marbled inlaid red-wood stools. Lee shook her head and walked over to the bookshelf. She selected a book, an illustrated fairy tale about the moon goddess. There were more illustrated storybooks on the shelf. Beside them was a pot planted with paper whites that gave out a rich, sweet scent. Lee breathed in deeply. She felt strangely happy. She had not felt this way for a long time. She wanted to believe that whatever great chaos was occurring in the greater world, she would always be safe inside this room.

The bedroom was a rectangular shape divided in half by moving wood panels. Each half of the room had a window and an identical twin bed. The panels could be shut to form a dividing wall. Fourth Aunt explained that Lee was to share this bedroom with her cousin, the oldest daughter of her Gugu. Her cousin's name was Mary. She was eleven years old, two years younger than Lee.

Lee understood right away that Mary was her flesh and blood sister. Her father had told her that she had a sister whom he never saw because he had been in Japan when she was born. Lee looked at the two beds. Hers had brand new bedding of fine cotton faced with a large piece of rectangular blue silk in an ocean wave pattern. It was cool and slippery to the touch. Lee was glad that there was a window on her side of the room. The sunlight filtered through the bamboo stalks beyond the window, casting slanting shards of light on the room's wooden floor.

Fourth Aunt directed the amah to put Lee's clothes into the drawers of a small bureau next to her bed. After the amah had put away the clothes and left the room, Fourth Aunt and Lee sat next to each other on the bed. Fourth Aunt explained that Gugu had three more daughters in addition to Mary: Little Du, Little Fang and Little Ai, aged six, four and two, respectively. Each daughter had a dedicated nursemaid to look after her. The younger children lived on the other side of the house.

"Lee," Fourth Aunt called the girl's new name, smiling a little force-fully, "I am also getting used to calling you Lee." She reached over to hold her hands. "Remember everything your Gugu said to you. This is a new beginning. She will protect you, but you must keep your promise."

Lee did not say anything. She felt her aunt's warm fingers encircle her hand. She could not wait to see Mary. She had not seen her Gugu since that day at the stadium, but she would see Mary soon, quite soon. They would share a bedroom, and in such close quarters, would surely to get to know each other and become friends.

Lee looked over at Mary's side of the room. Mary's silk bedding was the exact same design as hers but colored coral pink with a curling cloud pattern. The quilt on her bed bumped up near the edge and there was something on her pillow. Lee walked over to take a closer look and found a western style doll on Mary's bed. It was quite a large girl doll, the size of an infant. Its hair was tied in two long golden braids and secured with blue ribbons in bows which rested over the edge of the quilt. The doll seemed to be sleeping. It had a round face with a pointed chin, and long eyelashes sheltering its closed eyes. The lashes were golden and thick against the doll's smooth porcelain face. Lee wanted so much to open the closed eyes of the doll and find out what color they were.

"Don't touch my doll!" a girl's voice came from behind. Startled, Lee turned and saw the girl by the door, looking her up and down. Lee thought her face looked familiar, though she had never seen her before.

That day Mary wore her long hair just like the hair of her doll: tied in braids bound with blue ribbons. She wore opaque white stockings with round-toed leather Mary Jane's and a checkered powder blue dress that came to her knees and had a ruffled collar and cuffs.

It was not until much later that Lee realized that this outfit was the same as the one that Dorothy wore in "The Wizard of Oz."

"Mary, come meet your cousin Lee," Fourth Aunt said. "Your mother must have told you about her."

"Mother told me that I have to share my room with a cousin from the country," Mary said coolly. " But she did not say that she could play with my doll."

"I am sorry. I don't mean to..." Lee stopped, feeling her face turn hot.

"No use saying sorry. Just don't do it again," Mary said.

Lee sighed. It was not an auspicious start.

Mary picked up the doll and showed it to Lee. The doll was magical. As Mary bought it to an upright position, its eyes opened to reveal bright blue glass eyes. It was clad in the same dress that Mary wore. The same seamstress, Lee would discover, had made the dresses for Mary and for the doll.

Lee stared at the doll in silence. Mary held the doll in her arms. Sitting on the edge of her bed, she pulled the ribbons off the doll's braids. Lee watched Mary's slender fingers loosen the braids. Then Mary produced a mother of pearl inlaid wooden box from beneath her pillow and opened it. It was a jewelry box with a mirror beneath the lid. She took out a small doll-sized brush and ran it through the doll's long, golden, wavy hair.

"Look, this is how you fix her hair." She brushed the hair of the doll and finally tied it into a high ponytail with a pink ribbon. She arranged the doll into a sitting position on her pillow. Even the arms and legs were movable. The doll enthralled Lee. She could not take her eyes off of it.

Lee suddenly remembered the music box her father gave her as a gift when he returned from Japan. The beautiful ballet dancer had turned round and round on one leg to a string of chiming notes. She wanted to tell Mary about the music box, but said nothing.

"Looks like that the two of you are getting along," Fourth Aunt said as she rose from the bed. "I better get going." She walked toward Lee and put both hands on her skinny shoulders.

"Lee, remember everything I said," she cautioned. "Be well." She looked deeply into her eyes as she spoke, seeking assurance.

Lee returned her stare and nodded solemnly. "Don't worry. I will remember everything," she whispered.

She understood how important it was to the grown ups that she keep her identity secret. Lee also understood, in that moment, that it was especially important to keep the secret from Mary.

Lee did not see Gugu or meet the general that day. The children ate dinner together with the servants. The cook brought many dishes to the dining table. There were two kinds of dumplings, some with a filling of pork and chives and others filled with beef and pickled cabbage. There was a whole duck cooked in a clay pot until tender with slivers of bamboo shoots and scallions floating in broth. No one except for Lee ate the stirred fried mustard greens that were bitter and crunchy. A simple dish of tofu with minced pork was welcomed by the younger children. Lee did not want to eat too fast. She chewed slowly, and she drank a full bowl of duck broth. The food was better than the Changs where she had always felt that someone was looking at her disapprovingly when her chopsticks reached out to pick up food from the dishes.

The nursemaids made sure the little ones ate their meal. The young girls regarded Lee with curiosity.

"Who are you?" one of them asked.

Mary replied, "She is our cousin from the north. Her name is Lee."

The nursemaids nodded at Lee. "Call her 'big sister', Little Du." one of the nursemaids cajoled her charge.

"No, she is not my sister. Mary is my sister. She is my cousin." Little Du replied.

Lee was embarrassed, "It's fine. They can just call me Lee."

Silence fell on the dinner table for a moment. Then Little Ai began fussing over her food. She only wanted to eat the dumpling skin, not the filling. Her nursemaid told her, "You have to eat the filling. You can't grow strong and pretty if you don't eat the..."

Then Mary cut in, saying firmly, "Little Ai, if you don't eat the dumpling filling, I am going to tell father."

Little Ai burst out crying upon hearing Mary's stern words, but she ate the filling.

Lee ate quietly savoring the food. She was glad that no one was paying attention to her anymore. She could tell that Mary behaved like a surrogate parent and regarded herself as the young mistress of the house when her parents were not around. She told her younger sisters to stop fighting, and to stop throwing food. These admonishments were necessary: Lee was surprised to see how little discipline there was in the Tung household.

Lee went to bed that night feeling warm and full. The bedding smelled like sunshine, perhaps because after being washed, it had been hung from a smooth bamboo stick in the backyard, under the bright autumn sun and a clear blue sky. The pillowcase was crisp against her cheek like the newly ironed dress shirt her father used to wear when he was taking Silver Pearl out in the evening. Ensconced in her soft flannel pajamas and fresh bedding, her jade pendant next to her heart, Lee fell asleep comforted by the sound of the bamboo leaves outside her window. The divider between two sides of the room was drawn, and she could see that the light from Mary's side was still on. Slits of yellow light spilled onto Lee's side of the floor. Mary was still listening to her radio which she had set at the lowest volume. Lee drifted off to sleep carried by the undercurrent of the music from the other side of the room. Her last thought, greeted with a sigh, was that her father would never find her again not even if he wanted to, not even in the next life, because her name had been changed.

✳ ✳ ✳

As if a hand had tapped her on the shoulder, Lee woke from a muddled sleep with a start. She could hear the driving rain against the window, the bamboo leaves scratching the window panes from the outside, as if they were saying, *let me in, let me in, why don't you let me in.*

Lee turned her face into the pillow. She wanted to fall back into the dark sweetness of sleep. Her hands were folded next to her heart as if praying. Unclasping them, she reached one hand into her flannel nightgown to touch her jade pendant. The scratching noises would not let up, *let me in, let me in.*

Was it daybreak already? She wondered. The quilt was heavy and warm on top of her, pressing her down, securing her as if in an embrace. Yes, she was in her mother's house, her Gugu's house. She turned on her side and opened her eyes. The air around her was cold and gray. A veil through which she struggled to see. She could make out the shapes of the furniture in the room. On the other side of the room, Mary slept.

Thinking of Mary, Lee felt tentative again. Mary was not exactly friendly, but she was not unfriendly either. She remembered watching Mary's small hands with their cleanly cut nails busily brushing the hair of her doll as she explained to Lee how it should be done. She had been showing off, of course and Lee had been duly impressed.

Mary herself was dressed like a doll. Lee wanted to loosen up her braids and comb through her hair slowly, a handful of strands at a time, feeling them silky between her fingers, the way her grandma had when combing Little Jade's hair a long time ago. The smooth porcelain face of Mary's golden-haired doll reminded Lee of the impassive, beautiful faces she had seen on statues of Guan Yin and the Madonna. But dolls are merely dolls. *Playing with a friend, a sister,* Lee thought, *would be better than playing with dolls.*

Lee got out of bed. She wrapped the quilt over herself clumsily and walked barefoot to the other side of the room. The floor felt smooth and icy under foot as she walked over to Mary's bed. Mary was still sleeping soundly with one of her arms flung over the top of the quilt. Her doll slept against the wall next to her.

Lee stood next to her sister's bed, looking down at her face. Mary's hair was still in braids. She should not sleep with her hair bounded, Lee mused. It would cause the hair to break more easily. Lee studied the shape of her sister's ears and she looked at her lips which protruded as if she were pouting. To better see Mary's face, Lee bent over until she was only inches away from her sister's face. She could feel Mary's breathe warming the air between them. Lee held her own breath and was afraid to make a sound. Mary shifted her head toward the wall, her brows furrowed. Lee straightened up slowly, gathered the quilt about her, and crept back to her side of the room. Her cheeks felt warm all of the sudden, as if she had stolen something. She let out a sigh and climbed back into her bed.

✳ ✳ ✳

That day Fourth Aunt showed up again. She introduced Lee to Mary's tutors. They were to have private lessons together and be each other's studying companions. There were two teachers, one old fashioned Chinese scholar for traditional Chinese literature lessons and a Western Catholic nun, Sister Anne, who would give them English lessons and teach Bible study. The Chinese tutor, Mr. Fu, was a skinny middle-aged man in a traditional blue gown and thick round glasses with a habitual frown. He always looked as he was about to endure something unbearable and painful. He was polite and not very demanding. After all, he was teaching the general's daughters. Sister Anne wore a black habit and long black skirt all the way to her ankles with heavy leather shoes. She had brown hair shot through with gray, kind, light brown eyes, and a soft pink face. She spoke Chinese with a strong Western accent and taught the girls about the Virgin Mary, and the trinity of the Father, Son and the Holy Ghost. Lee was familiar with this cast of Biblical characters from her stay at the boarding school. She thought Sister Anne approved of her answers when she quizzed the two girls. Mary and Lee were competitive during the lessons. It soon became apparent that Lee was the more diligent student.

However, Mary knew many things that Lee knew nothing about. Lee had never been to a movie. Mary had seen many Western movies such as "Gone with the Wind" and "The Wizard of Oz." She told Lee that she had liked watching "The Wizard of Oz" so much that she saw it at least three times. She had also attended modern, patriotic plays that were popular at the time. Mary also knew many popular songs and liked to sing along when she knew the lyrics. The radio was always playing on Mary's side of the bedroom after lessons were done for the day. Mary liked to turn the volume up. She sat on her bed and sang to her doll. *"The spring wind is soft and the peach blossoms are red, why don't you come outside, Little Sister?"* Lee kept quiet on her side of the room. Although Mary would often close the dividers that separated their respective spaces, Lee could hear everything. She could hear Mary talking to her doll and inviting her other toys to have a tea party. The other toys were a stuffed bear named Bao Bao and a wooden toy soldier named Private Jia. For the first two weeks that Lee lived in her Gugu's house, Mary would play this way until the amah called them to dinner. Lee never once saw her Gugu or the general. She did not ask anyone where they were, not even Mary.

Often, Lee woke up in the early morning hours. Sometimes she would just stay in bed and look at the ceiling. Sometimes, she turned the lamp on and studied what she learned the day before. Most frequently, she went over to Mary's side of the room to watch her sleep. It was the only time that she could study her sister closely. She knew better than to openly stare at Mary during the day. That wouldn't be right especially since Lee knew that Mary had not taken a liking toward her. Once, Lee went as far as giving Mary a quick kiss while she was sleeping, lightly brushing her lips against Mary's cheek. Lee loved her sister, but dared not, could not, show it.

✳ ✳ ✳

One day the amah led Lee and Mary to the study. Gugu and the general were seated side by side on the leather sofa. Lee was surprised to see that General Tung was a handsome man with chiseled cheekbones and the square jaw of a movie star. He was in uniform. Three bronze stars shone on each of his shoulders. Next to him, Gugu looked plain in her white shirt and simple khaki pants. On top of the coffee table there were two gift-wrapped boxes.

Mary noticed the boxes right away. She ran to her parents and plopped herself between them. She pulled at the general's arm and asked him whether the gifts were for her.

Gugu shot Mary a glance that silenced her, and said "Lee, come to meet your Gufu (uncle)."

Lee bowed her head and said, "Gufu, how are you?"

The general smiled generously at Lee, his eyes and his white teeth gleaming, and said "Good to meet you, Lee. I hope you have settled comfortably. Why don't you sit down?" He gestured toward the sofa across from him, "Has Mary been showing you around?"

Lee sat down as instructed on the edge of the leather sofa across from them. She was looking at Gugu and Mary and noting the resemblance between them, around the eyes and nose, and especially the lips. Mary, facing the general, was becoming annoyed that he seemed to be paying more attention to Lee. Mary looked at Lee with sudden anger. She turned to her father. "I caught her playing with my doll," she said.

"Is that so?" said the general. "Well, maybe she won't need to do that anymore." The general handed Lee the larger box across the coffee table.

"Go ahead, open it." Gugu said, nodding at Lee to give her permission.

Lee hesitated for a moment, then tore open the wrapping paper and saw a doll looking at her from behind the glass paper box. She burst into a wide grin and looked up at the general and Gugu, who were watching her the entire time. It was such a surprise. Lee had never even dreamt of having such a precious present. The doll looked almost exactly like Mary's except that she had chestnut brown hair and light brown eyes. She wore a dark green velvet dress with matching ribbons in her hair. Lee hugged the doll tight in her arms and could not stop smiling. She got up on her feet and bowed at the general and Gugu. "Thank you, Gugu," she said shyly. "Thank you, Gufu."

The general also handed Mary a box. Mary quickly opened it and found a white stuffed rabbit wearing a pink dress inside. She leaned over and kissed the general on the cheek. General Tung put an arm around Mary. "You are the hostess here," he said, "You should show

Lee around to make her feel at home. She came from far away. The two of you are close in age and should be like sisters to one another."

He turned to look at his wife as he said this. Gugu gave a slight approving nod and leaned back into the sofa. She looked tired. Just then, Lee realized that she was visibly pregnant, and her belly was protruding like half a melon as she lifted her feet to rest on the ottoman.

"Why don't you two go and play dolls together?" said the general. "Your dolls can be best friends."

Mary squeezed her plush rabbit against her cheek. "Is this all?" she asked the general. "Don't you have anything else for me?"

The general reached into his pockets and took out two silver dollars. He gave one to Mary and one to Lee. It was another extravagant gesture. Lee knew, though Mary didn't, that a silver dollar could feed a family for an entire week. Lee did not know what to do. She cupped the small disc of heavy silver coin in her hands. It was still warm from the general's pocket.

Gugu looked at Mary and frowned. Mary stopped pulling at the general's arm immediately. "Why don't the two of you run along?" said Gugu. It was time to leave.

After she returned to her room, Lee sat on her bed and played with her doll. The doll looked at her with wide-open trusting eyes. To Lee, it was as if the doll was saying, "I am happy to be here with you."

Her eyelashes were soft, her eyelids opened and closed, opened and closed, as Lee sat her up then lay her down on her bed repeatedly. Lee removed the green velvet ribbon from the doll's head. The doll's luscious brown curls fell through her fingers. Carefully, she combed the doll's shining hair. On the other side of the room, Mary was having a grand tea party with her new plush rabbit, the brown bear BaoBao, Private Jia, and her doll. The radio was on at full volume. Mary sang and danced on her side of the room. *"We're off to see the*

Wizard, the wonderful Wizard of Oz." Mary did not invite Lee and her doll to join their party.

Lee needed a name for her doll. She decided to call her Little Princess Jade, Little Jade for short. If Lee couldn't be Little Jade, then her doll could take the name. It was such a beautiful doll! *Had Fourth Aunt told Gugu that Mary wouldn't let Lee touch her doll?* She wondered. Lee mulled over that very question as she took the doll in her arms and opened the door that led outside, and slipped through the door quietly. She stepped outside. It was just beginning to get dark. Dinner should be served anytime now, but Lee needed to get away from Mary's tea party. *Come with me, Little Jade.* Lee said to the doll silently, *come run away with me, just the two of us.*

Lee followed the open corridor outside her room, tracing her steps back to the courtyard of the rock garden and bamboo lined path. The sky was high and empty. The air felt heavy and was tinted a deep blue. The wind was picking up and felt grainy when it hit Lee's face. She walked against the wind with downcast eyes and hugged her doll with both arms under her padded jacket. As she walked she avoided people whenever she could: the nursemaid carrying a toddler in her arms, the soldier gardener lighting a cigarette, the amah carrying a kettle of hot water as she headed down the winding stone paths with their fan-shaped gates. No one seemed to notice her. She could be a ghost walking among them. Gradually, the sound of people faded further and further away. Lee had successfully evaded everyone. She stopped beside a flaming maple tree. Standing alone in an open space in a courtyard, she tried to determine the proper direction back to her room.

The courtyard was flanked by a wall of rooms topped with a roof covered with gray tiles. The rooms had windows and doors, but all of them were shut and dark. The dark windows looked foreboding. The final remnants of daylight were fading fast. The miniature stone mountains and tall maple trees had been clearly visible minutes ago but now were merely dark outlines against the sky. The leaves fell from the maple tree, spurred by the wind. One leaf, then two, then a hundred leaves rained down on her.

Lee hurried to a door at one end of the corridor. She tried to open the door but it was locked. She knocked on the door. "Open up, open up!" She called. No one answered. She ran back to where she had entered the courtyard and found it was also locked from the other side. Someone must have locked it after she entered. Clutching her precious doll in one arm, she pounded on the heavy wooden door with her free hand. "Open up! Open up! Please open up!" She shouted until she was hoarse. The wind was growing stronger, filling her lungs and chilling her from the inside.

She hugged her doll tight against her narrow chest with both arms and whispered. *Don't be afraid, Little Jade. I am right here with you. I will always be with you.*

She wanted to return to the courtyard through the maze of stone paths but she feared that if she were to get lost in the maze, she would not be found for a long time. She knocked on the dark windows and locked doors but no one answered. She leaned against a huge door that faced the courtyard and slowly slid to the ground. She looked up beyond the ornately carved eaves and saw that the moon had risen, glazing bare branches, and the leaves that remained on the maple tree with a silvery glow. The wind had finally quieted down and the courtyard was now perfectly still. Lee kept looking at the moon. She couldn't take her eyes away from it. Her head was growing heavier while her body was feeling lighter. Lee held tightly onto her doll. A doll will not die, will not leave, as long as she held on tight to her, just like now, like this, forever.

✳ ✳ ✳

It was not until near bedtime that an amah noticed that Lee had not been seen for a while and could not be found. The maid and the amah asked each other, "Did you not see her at the dinner?" They asked Mary, who thought that Lee had gone to sleep after she played with the doll. Jen was about to go to sleep when she was informed that Lee had disappeared. She knew that Lee could not possibly leave the estate. She would have to pass two layers of guarded gates.

The girl must be somewhere in the compound. Servants went around each courtyard with hand-held lanterns calling her name. It was near mid-night when a maid found Lee lying next to the door under the roof of an open corridor. Her hands and feet were cold and her lips were almost colorless. She was hugging her doll under her jacket. Lee was quickly moved to her bed where a maid covered her with warm blankets and massaged her arms and legs. Her forehead was burning hot. A doctor was called. A maid put the doll on top of the bureau in a sitting position. It looked down at Lee, whose face was red and whose mouth was dry. A maid dabbed Lee's cracked lips with a corner of a handkerchief soaked in honeyed water from time to time.

✳ ✳ ✳

With muffled, broken sounds in her ears, and pulsing light behind her eyes, Lee felt as if she was being awakened from having almost drowned. She struggled to rise to the surface of a deep dream. Her throat was dust dry and her lungs felt tight and she coughed weakly. Each cough shook her hard. A maid tried to steady her as she massaged her back, kneading it gently from time to time. Her eyes were blurry, as if glazed over by a film of water. As soon as her eyes opened, an amah turned and sent a maid running to tell the Mistress.

Someone asked Lee whether she wanted something to drink. Gasping with her mouth open, she nodded. Her mouth tasted sour and bitter. She took a sip of a lukewarm tea and closed her eyes again. She wanted to fall back into her dream where she had been lingering at the edge of the bamboo forest. She did not want to leave. It had been nice to be there.

"Young Miss, wake up. Wake up! Do you want to drink some ginseng chicken soup? You must be hungry. You have been sleeping for a long time." The amah massaged Lee's arm. The doctor told her that if the young lady wakes up, to be sure to keep her awake and feed her something nutritious. Hearing this, Lee opened her eyes again and nodded. Her hair was damp with sweat, but her fever was subsiding.

Her weakened body felt as if it had been made of cotton batting. Lee was slowly drinking chicken soup from a bowl held to her lips by an amah when Jen entered the room. A maid pulled a chair for Jen to sit next to Lee's bed. She watched her daughter swallow the soup thirstily. *Lee was so thin. So frail. Look how thin she was: the maid could not get anything into her.* Jen shook her head and felt heaviness in her heart.

"Gugu," Lee struggled to sit up.

"Don't move too much, you are very weak." Jen said. She turned to a maid, "Go get the doctor," she said.

Lee leaned back, looking at her mother. She was enormous, much larger than Lee remembered. The baby should arrive any day now. Her face looked puffy and she looked tired. Yet Lee could see concern in her face.

"Gugu, thank you for coming." Lee was too weak to move her gaze, and she kept on staring at the woman in front of her. She felt her presence looming over her, like a giant shadow that comes toward the end of the day.

"No need to say 'thank you' between us," Jen said quietly.

Jen had an envelope with her. Sitting in a chair beside Lee's bed, she opened the envelope and pulled out a handful of photographs. Jen selected one photograph and handed it to Lee. It was a photograph of a young woman holding a newborn. Lee recognized that the young woman was Jen. "The baby is you." Jen said. "Your father took the photograph when you were born." Lee picked up the photograph with trembling fingers. It was a small photograph, but the image was clear. The mother was smiling, sitting in the hospital bed, and the baby was crying.

"You cried a lot as a baby." Jen said gently, as Lee's eyes blurred with tears. Jen handed Lee two more photographs. In them, the infant Little Jade was swaddled in a bundle and propped up against a pillow.

"I took this one." Jen pointed at one of them. "You were smiling and I took the camera from your father and snapped the picture." Jen's face softened as she looked at the picture, remembering the birth of her first child.

Lee looked at her mother looking at the photographs. *I am right here*, she thought, *look at me!* As if hearing her thought, Jen moved her gaze from the photograph in her hand to look at Lee directly, as if searching for the infant she remembered in the sickly half-grown girl in front of her.

"Here is one more. This is the only photograph I have of the three of us." Jen handed the last photograph to Lee. It was a family portrait of An Ling, Wei Jen, and Little Jade from long, long ago, when the three of them were an intact family. Lee could tell that the picture had been taken in a photographer's studio. The photograph was printed on a fine textured paper with ornate scalloped edges. Wei Jen's hair was styled in soft waves like a movie star from the thirties. She was wearing a Qipao of bamboo-patterned silk with dark contrasting piping, and An Ling's thick hair was combed back and shiny. He wore a starched white shirt and a dark tie. Little Jade was a baby with a perfectly round face and squinting, smiling eyes, She wore a light colored knitted outfit, complete with a bonnet trimmed with ruffles, all of it Wei Jen's handiwork. The young couple was smiling dreamily into the camera as if envisioning a bright future in front of them. *Yes*, Lee thought, *I have a mother and a father, just like everyone else.*

"Thank you for showing me this." Lee spoke in a tiny voice as she kept looking at the photographs, holding them with one hand and wiping her eyes with the back of her other hand. Everything had changed so much that she couldn't fathom the fairly tale of an intact family, of herself, her father and her mother all being in the same place at the same time.

"I told you that you don't need to say 'thank you' to me," Jen said as she reached over to hold Lee's hand. Her voice was a whisper. This was her first child, a child she had nearly lost and was not sure how to love. During the years that she had been absent from her daughter's life, things had happened and had shaped her baby into this quiet, watchful girl.

Lee felt her mother's fingers interlacing with her own. They both had long, slender, fingers. She pulled her mother's hand closer, pressing it against her face with both of her hands. The warmth of Jen's palm touched Lee's cheek. "Mama," tears streamed out Lee's eyes. "Mama…" She was sobbing, not able to say a word.

"You still like to cry." Jen tried to smile as she pulled her daughter into her ample bosom. Their arms were entangled. Lee felt her head cradled by her mother's arms. She could hear her mother's heartbeat, strong and rhythmic. This was where she belonged.

The End